Relax, Mack Bo

Forget about an old frie...
concentrate on picking off the enemy. And if the
final sacrifice is necessary, take as many of the
bastards with you.

It was the only way to wage a war, and Bolan knew
enough about living on the edge to realize that
death was never far away. If this was all the time
left tonight, he'd use it to score heavily against the
opposition before they took him down.

Bolan wondered if Hal Brognola had the slightest
chance of showing up before the roof fell in. For
once, the Executioner hoped that Hal would be late.

The man should not be forced to watch his family
die. There would be ample opportunity for him to
witness death before the sun rose over Washington
again. This one time, though, if there was any
mercy in the universe, Bolan was praying that
Brognola might be spared.

But it was not a night for mercy.

It was a night for blood.

MACK BOLAN

The Executioner

DON PENDLETON's EXECUTIONER
MACK BOLAN
BLOOD
TESTAMENT

A GOLD EAGLE BOOK FROM
WORLDWIDE

TORONTO · NEW YORK · LONDON · PARIS
AMSTERDAM · STOCKHOLM · HAMBURG
ATHENS · MILAN · TOKYO · SYDNEY

First edition April 1987

ISBN 0-373-61100-5

Special thanks and acknowledgment to
Mike Newton for his contribution to this work.

Printed in Canada

No real friendship is ever made without an initial clashing, which discloses the metal of each to each.

—David Grayson

Between friends there is no need for justice.

—Aristotle

Justice matters, sure. But this time out it's one for friendship's sake.

—Mack Bolan

To all the Bolan allies
who fought beside him
and died beside him.
Live large and stay hard!

PROLOGUE

The public park was deserted at this hour, and still the tall man's eyes kept roving, following the occasional passing car intently until it disappeared from sight. Uncertain that he and his companion couldn't be seen where they stood in the shadow of a huge oak, his gaze continued to probe the darkened areas of the park for possible signs of unwanted human presence.

Although his vigilance was a trait born of years of conditioning, he berated himself for this sudden case of nerves. After all, it was he who had chosen the site for the midnight rendezvous.

The tall man's nervousness did not seem to faze the stocky figure standing before him. Nick, his companion had asked to be called during the phone conversation. The tall man wondered briefly if Nick was enjoying his discomfiture, and that, coupled with the apparent lack of concern over what they were about to do, made the tall man angry.

"It's set," Nick said, the first to speak.

"Are you sure?"

"Of course, I'm sure."

The cockiness in Nick's voice grated on the tall man's overwrought nerves and it would have pleased him to reach out and lock his fingers around that greasy throat, cut off the bastard's breath, but he couldn't afford to do that. Yet.

"You better get it right."

"Hey! Cam, wasn't it? Don't threaten me, see? Or you can fucking well do the job yourself."

Anger intensified inside the tall man until he stifled it with sheer force of will. "Okay, okay, don't get uptight, Nick."

"That's better. We'll handle our end just fine. Trust me."

Trust me, Cam mimicked in his mind. "I really shouldn't be involved in this at all."

"You've been involved from the beginning, hotshot, and don't forget it." The other's voice was insolent, before it turned to stone. "*We* go down, you're coming with us, you and all your buddies."

Angry silence hung between them for a moment, stretching paper-thin before Nick's voice sliced through it, softer now, and filled with counterfeit concern. "You're worried someone's going to make you on this thing, huh?"

"It's possible."

"What kind of ship you running over there, Cam? I thought you guys keep it strictly need-to-know."

"There's no such thing as absolute security."

"You better hope there is. One slip on this, we all go up in smoke."

Cam had been acutely conscious of the risks from the beginning, which was not to say that he had been presented with a choice. It was a question of survival, plain and simple, with the choices narrowed down to do or die. He had been forced to take a stand, and once committed, there could be no turning back.

"I'm holding up my end."

"I know you are. We're counting on you, Cam."

The phony confidence and camaraderie were sickening. "How are you handling the disposal?"

His companion tried for a smile, and in the gloom it resembled a grimace that reminded him of hungry crocodiles.

"We've got our ways. They worked before."

"You've never bagged this kind of game before."

The tall man felt the old familiar tightness in his stomach, acid fingers worming upward through his chest to lock around his heart. The ulcers had been gnawing at him for a month, but he would have to live with it until the job had been carried through to its conclusion, one way or the other. He stopped himself. It had to be only one way if he intended to survive the coming storm. They would succeed, or they would die. The world would not be large enough to hide them if they failed.

"Let me worry about that," Nick said. Then, in a twinkling, the voice was dripping ice. "But you better not be fucking me."

"You're not my type."

"I'll tell you what type I am, in case your memory's been fogging over lately. Let's say that someone was to try and jerk me on a deal that I've been working on for better than a year. Let's say someone didn't hold his end up in a crunch."

"Let's say."

"I can't imagine anywhere on earth this bastard would be safe, *capisce?* It's like little Bobby used to say: I don't get mad, I just get even. You remember Bobby, don't you, Cam?"

The tall man nodded. He remembered Bobby, sure. And Jack, as well. The years had been unable to erase their memory.

"Good. I wouldn't want you coming up with any second thoughts along the way."

"No second thoughts," he echoed, feeling like a straw man with his guts on fire.

"So, I'll be hearing from you, then?"

"This weekend."

"Beautiful. I'm looking forward to it, Cam. It's been a long time coming."

Like a lifetime, the tall man thought, shuddering involuntarily, and glad for the darkness. He only hoped that there would be a lifetime *after*, that he would be able to find a place among the living. The alternative was nonexistence, and he wasn't up for that. Not yet. He had too much to lose.

And he was risking all of it.

The tall man took in the surroundings once more, amazed at the serenity of the manicured suburbs. A storm was brewing while West Virginia slept, and when it broke he would be in its eye.

1

"Enjoy your weekend."

Hal Brognola glanced up from his open briefcase and returned his secretary's smile. "Still here?"

"I'm playing catch-up with the files."

"Forget it. You can get it done on Monday." Putting on a phony scowl, he told her gruffly, "Anyway, we can't afford the overtime."

"You talked me into it. Good night."

He spun the combination lock on his valise and double-checked his watch against the ugly, standard-issue wall clock opposite his desk. It was approaching six o'clock, and he was running late. As usual.

Without a backward glance he put the place behind him, fighting an urge to click his heels. The three-day weekend beckoned irresistibly, but Hal had more than simple rest and relaxation on his mind. The kids and Helen would be on the road by now, perhaps already at their destination, waiting for him. Anxious to be with them, he signed out, leaving the number where he could be reached in case of an emergency.

It had been too damned long since he and his family had any time together, free from work, school and the countless other things that separate a man, unwillingly, from those he loves. Despite the fact that he had been with Helen almost every day and night for twenty-seven years, he never saw enough of her. As for the kids...

Brognola stopped himself and grinned unconsciously. The "kids" were both in college now, adults with lives and secrets of their own. The man from Justice was intensely proud of them, secure in their maturity and sense of purpose, but experience had taught him that the world was dangerous, full of predators relentlessly in search of prey. Their mother worried openly—it was a woman's inalienable right—but gender and his temperament prevented Hal from expressing his concerns aloud. He had no doubt that Helen was aware of his private fears—she could see through him, always had—but she was generous enough to keep the knowledge locked away. When Jeff went out for football, when Eileen wrote home about the great new guy that she was dating, Helen clucked and frowned and voiced her hope that they would each proceed with caution. Hal, for his part, grumbled that the kids were old enough to take care of themselves and hid his concern behind the pages of the *Post* or *New York Times*—hid his concern from everyone except Helen, who missed nothing.

Christmas break and spring vacation were the only times they came together now with any regularity. The crush of classes, part-time jobs and social obligations monopolized their time, as work had eaten up so many hours of Brognola's life while they were growing up. Instead of looking back on other seasons with regret, Brognola cherished every infrequent moment that they had together these days.

The three-day weekend was their private time before Jeff caught the southbound flight for Lauderdale, before Eileen and friends departed for a week in Provincetown. Brognola had avoided asking any questions, loathe to pry, and equally afraid, perhaps, of what their honest answers might reveal. The big Fed hadn't spent his youth in a monastery, and he understood the modern trend toward free-and-easy sexuality, but it wouldn't do to know too much about his children's private lives. A man with few illusions left, he clung to the mirage of their eternal innocence. He chuckled to himself, imagining that when Eileen was thirty-five with children of her own, he would be cherishing the myth of virgin birth.

The parking lot was nearly empty, bureaucrats decamping early on a Friday afternoon, deserting desks and filing cabinets for the beach, the mountains, anywhere away from claustrophobic cubicles and jangling telephones. Brognola aimed his Buick toward the exit, spent another moment checking out with gate security then merged with weekend traffic, outbound, leaving Wonderland on the Potomac behind. He traveled west on Constitution Avenue, across the Theodore Roosevelt Memorial Bridge into Arlington, on past the endless graves of heroes, catching Highway 211 west toward Rappahannock County and the Blue Ridge Mountains.

They had owned the cabin for a dozen years, and had increasingly relied upon it as a refuge from the grind in Washington as Hal gradually moved up the ladder toward the pinnacle of Justice and a supervisory position with the Phoenix project. He could never really leave the job behind, but in the mountains, with the smell of evergreens supplanting the monoxide haze of civilization, Hal recaptured something of the gentler times. He was on call, of course, no more than ninety minutes from the office, but it seemed a world away.

And Helen made the difference. Helen and the kids.

Another forty minutes south along the Appalachian Trail, the hard core of his Phoenix team was standing ever-ready for another confrontation with the faceless enemy. Extensive renovations had been undertaken since the near-disaster that had claimed the life of April Rose, erstwhile mission controller and overseer of Stony Man Farm. These days the Farm, the U.S. government's ultrasecret command center—originally set up to support the Phoenix Project, and headed up by Colonel John Phoenix, as Mack Bolan was then known—was fully operational again, secure against intruders from without . . . and enemies within.

Brognola thought that this time he would make the drive to Rappahannock County on his own, without the company of ghosts and bitter memories. But there was no escape. Inevitably, as he drove, his mind was drawn to thoughts of April, memories of Aaron Kurtzman, Stony Man Farm's computer wizard who was crippled in the attack on the Farm, and Andrjez Konzaki, weaponsmith extraordinaire, who was mortally wounded in the same assault.

Memories of Mack Bolan.

But the weekend was his own to spend with loved ones far behind the battle lines. He found a music station on the radio and turned it up to blot out the distant memories.

His suitcase would be waiting for him at the cabin. Helen saw to that, along with all the other details of planning a weekend in the mountains that could drive a man to drink. She seemed to thrive on preparing for their rare reunions, lingering on points of trivia that Hal could never seem to keep in mind. He never ceased to marvel at her energy and her efficiency.

For no apparent reason a bleak thought crossed his mind and Hal wondered if he could get along without her....

No.

It would be simpler by far to get along without his legs, his hands, his eyes.

Without his heart.

Two hours out of D.C., he stopped for gas in Cresthill, searching out the tiny local liquor store and startling the owner with his order for a magnum of champagne. The locals were inclined to beer and Cutty Sark, but once the man recovered, he allowed that there should be a bottle somewhere out back. There was, and Hal was beaming as he pushed a pair of twenties toward the register, retreating with his prize before the owner had a chance to calculate his change. It was already dark, and he was in a hurry now.

Another two-and-a-half miles, and he took the cutoff on an unpaved washboard road that wound between the looming trunks of conifers, ascending toward a tiny clutch of cabins overlooking Cresthill and the northern Blue Ridge slopes. The cabins, five in all, were spaced around a sort of cul-de-sac, but trees and natural topography preserved a sense of isolation. Rarely were the cabins simultaneously occupied, and even with a group or families in residence, they might pass days without encountering a neighbor.

Brognola dropped the Buick into low and made the final fifty yards, past cabins standing empty, dark against the trees. His headlights probed around a curve and picked out Helen's station wagon, parked in the carport of the four-room structure. Hal nosed in behind the other vehicle, already marking lights that glowed through the curtained windows. He shut down the Buick's engine and climbed out with his bottle of champagne and his briefcase.

They must have heard him coming, but they would be busy preparing dinner now, perhaps already grilling the steaks that Helen had gone shopping for on Wednesday. Stiff from the drive and looking forward to a drink, Brognola clomped across the wooden porch and gave the knob a twist.

The door was locked.

He frowned, remembering that Helen would require some time to dust away the city's grime and finally relax. When visiting, they rarely locked the cabin door until they went to bed...and then secured it primarily against the possibility of roving bears or overcurious raccoons, instead of human enemies. The urban jungle was behind them for the moment. They were safe.

He found the key among his others, smiling as he anticipated the surprise on Helen's face, Jeff's handshake, Eileen's rush into his arms. Anticipation made him fumble twice before he found the keyhole, but he was already working on his entry line.

"It's pretty sorry when a man's own family locks him out."

The empty living room-kitchen greeted him with ringing silence. Startled by the absence of activity, Brognola raised his voice.

"Hello?"

No answer from the bedrooms, and a little chill of apprehension raised the short hairs at the back of his neck.

Relax, he told himself. They must be here. The car's parked right outside.

He left the champagne and briefcase on the kitchen counter, calling out once more, his voice subdued as he proceeded through the rooms. In Jeff's room a duffel bag rested on the bed. Two matching bags, emblazoned with decals Eileen had picked up on a summer tour of Europe two years earlier, sat on the floor of his daughter's room. In the final bedroom, he recognized one suitcase as his own, the other as his wife's. She had already stowed some clothing in the closet; it was standing open, and he scanned the line of blouses, slacks, the jacket she habitually brought along in case the nights turned cold.

Outside, then.

There was a shed out back, for tools and whatnot. It was likely they had gone outside for something, and had hidden as a joke when he drove up. It might be possible to turn the joke around and take them by surprise if he was quick enough in doubling back.

But they were not outside.

With the lighted cabin at his back, he stood in darkness and called their names. The night was cool, but the external temperature had little impact on Brognola. A deeper chill had crept into his bones, his vitals.

He took a breath and held it, swallowing the surge of panic, willing rationality to take control and suppress the primal terror he felt inside. There were alternatives, distinct and separate from any danger situation. All he had to do was keep his wits about him, think it through, until he solved the mystery.

No. There *was* no mystery.

His family was *out*, but he could not infer from that alone that they were *missing*. Worlds of difference separated one fact from the other, worlds of hurt that made the difference between a pleasant evening and an endless night of madness.

Neighbors. That had to be it.

He had seen no lights in either of the cabins that he passed, but that left two more at the far side of the cul-de-sac, invisible from where he stood. It was entirely possible that Helen and the kids had tired of waiting for him, or had simply sought to stretch their legs by visiting their neighbors down the road. Maybe they had simply gone out walking, but the darkness and the chill reminded him that they would certainly have turned toward home by now.

It would be neighbors, or it would be nothing, and he doubled back to close the cabin door before he set off down the unpaved drive on foot. He might have driven, covering the distance in a shorter time, but he was anxious for the Buick to be waiting when his family returned. It would alert them to his presence, let them know that he was waiting, looking for them.

Brognola reached the nearest cabin in a brisk ten-minute hike. At first he almost missed it, darkened as it was, deserted in the shadow of the forest. Aware that he was wasting time, but loathe to overlook the smallest chance of gaining information on his family's whereabouts, he crossed the porch and hammered on the door. He was rewarded with only the echo of his pounding through the empty rooms inside.

Three down, and one remaining. Fifteen minutes farther on, Brognola felt hope swelling in his chest as he beheld the lighted windows of the final cabin. Parked outside, a Blazer four-by-four with gun racks in the window advertised the presence of a hunter. Hal had met the cabin owner several seasons before, but he could not recall the face or name. Already certain that his family was not there, he felt compelled to ask in any case.

The face that finally responded to his knock was not familiar in the least. The cabin had undoubtedly changed hands, but still he forged ahead, inquiring if the long-haired youth in residence had seen his family, anyone at all? And at the risk of being rude, precisely when had he arrived?

The young man recognized Brognola's tension, and helped as best he could. He had arrived that evening, about the time when Hal was pushing west on Constitution Avenue, and he had marked a station wagon at the second cabin down. Since his arrival there had been no sign of hikers, male or female, on the trail outside... but, then again, he wasn't really watching for them, either.

Feeling drained, Brognola thanked him for his help and trudged back through the darkness toward the cabin, praying silently that Helen and the kids would be there when he stepped across the threshold. They would not be there, of course; he knew that now with desperate certainty. They were not visiting the neighbors, and they had not opted for a hike through darkness.

They were simply gone.

In the yard Hal Brognola stopped to look at the cabin once more, as if his stare could will some message, a clue, of his family's whereabouts. He discerned on an outside wall of the lodge a sailboat, now disused, that he had fashioned out of driftwood for his son in earlier years. Hal's mind raced to the rooms inside, silent witnesses to adolescent dreams of sparkling water and buccaneers; rooms that kept secret tender endearments and the sounds of frenetic love-making on soft summer nights.

But what his eyes perceived instead made him take an involuntary step backward. The orange glow from lighted windows seemed to him a feral glare, the cabin's grim facade now mocking, taunting, slavering for blood. This refuge from the concrete jungle, Hal thought, this haven of love and happy times had betrayed him, surrendered his family to unspeakable and insidious evil.

Suddenly Hal Brognola felt a loathing for the place.

Shivering, although it was still warm, he stepped inside the cabin and called their names. Then he checked each empty room. But only silence greeted him, grating on his nerves like salt ground into an open wound.

Alternatives.

He had already wasted what—an hour?—tracking down the several low-risk possibilities. For peace of mind, if nothing else, the futile exercise had been an absolute necessity. That done, he recognized the need to search for answers on the darker side.

The cabin showed no evidence of any struggle. Clearly they had been here long enough to stow their luggage, and for Helen to begin unpacking. Food was waiting in the fridge, but they had not progressed as far as starting dinner. There, between the everyday parameters of settling in and sitting down to eat, must lie the extraordinary answer to the riddle of a lifetime. And Brognola realized with perfect certainty that everything depended on his own ability to solve that riddle quickly.

If there had been an accident, an injury to any of them, they would certainly have headed back to town. And if the station wagon had perhaps refused to start, they would have called an ambulance.

Brognola knew there would have been a note, as well, but he could not afford to let the notion pass without considering it. He carried keys to Helen's car, as she had keys for the Buick, and a moment later he was in the driver's seat, breathing ragged as he prepared to test the wagon's engine.

It started first time, sparking sudden anger in Brognola, causing him to slam a fist against the steering wheel before he turned off the ignition and stalked back toward the empty cabin.

And on to other possibilities.

If they had been surprised by an intruder, Jeff would certainly resist. As tall as Hal, athletic, muscular, he would be capable of handling any normal situation that arose. But there was nothing normal in the present circumstances, nothing to reveal what might have happened to his family.

The absence of a struggle mystified Brognola, and he scanned the several explanations. Several intruders. Weapons. The advantage of surprise.

There were no bloodstains at the scene, and that was good... unless their captor was a lunatic, one of the transient monsters lately targeted by federal research projects. He had seen those maniacs' work and memories of twisted, lacerated flesh on undertakers' tables brought a sudden rush of nausea that left him dizzy, gasping.

He forced it down as he realized he had no evidence that they had come to any harm. He was well aware that roving maniacs were loners, for the most part, timid when confronted by potential victims in a group. A psycho bold enough to forcibly invade the cabin would have killed them there, for sure. It was a thought that Hal could cling to, and if not precisely comforting, at least it gave him room for hope.

There were other enemies, of course, with motives of revenge that were completely rational, but wouldn't they have waited for him here, to finish off what they had started? There would be no reason to abduct his family, not when they could have as easily positioned gunners in the trees, or inside the cabin, to eliminate him when he left his car.

And yet...

The sudden shrilling of the telephone made Hal jump. He checked his watch, surprised to find that it was one minute short of midnight. Time had slipped away from him, and he was still no closer to an answer than he had been hours earlier.

He grabbed it on the second ring and fairly shouted down the wire.

"Hello?"

"I'll bet it's lonely where you are."

A man's voice, gloating, evil. "Who the hell is this?"

"Just shut your face and listen, huh? That's better. We'll be calling back. You be there."

And the link was broken, the mindless dial tone buzzing in his ear like some demented insect. Brognola gripped the receiver in a stranglehold, white-knuckled, trembling with fear and rage. As he returned it to the cradle, he restrained himself from ripping loose the cord and flinging the telephone across the room.

It was his only lifeline now, his only means of finding out precisely what had happened to his family.

"I'll bet it's lonely where you are."

The message had been crystal clear, and there was no escaping its significance. The bastards had his wife, his children, and Brognola had no way of knowing where—or even who—they were. As for the motive, he would have to wait until they called again, and pray that they would not decide to pass on him, to simply slaughter Helen, Jeff, Eileen.

The bastards wanted him, and he would make himself available, but only at a price. The safety of his family, guaranteed, for openers. Whatever happened after they were safe was secondary, less than insignificant. His own life scarcely mattered in comparison.

But if the bastards didn't call again...

The man from Justice laid his head on cradled arms and wept. For Helen. For their children. He let the moment carry him away, and when it passed, Brognola knew that there was nothing he could do but wait for yet another call, another fleeting linkup with the men who meant to tear his world apart.

He stretched out on the sofa, one hand clutched around the snub-nosed .38 that he had worn from work, unconsciously. He wore it everywhere these days, but he had not expected to be needing it this weekend. They would not be coming for him now, Brognola knew; they would not have aroused him with a call if they intended to attack in force.

His mind was wrestling with fatigue, and losing. In spite of pain, fear and tense anxiety, the man from Wonderland could feel exhaustion gaining on him, reaching out with leaden hands to pull him down. And somewhere in the endless quarter hour after he received the first communication from his enemies, Brognola slept.

And was awakened by the telephone.

He struggled up from sleep, the squat revolver searching for a target, lowering as full consciousness returned with stunning swiftness. Glancing at the mantel clock through blurry eyes, he saw that it was 4:00 a.m.

"Hello?"

"Hang on."

A man's voice, different from the first, replaced immediately by the ringing silence of an open line. He didn't need an introduction to the second caller, but he got one anyway.

"Hal?" Her voice seemed distant, almost ghostly. "This is Helen..."

2

"Helen? Are you all right? Are the kids all right?"

Before Helen Brognola had a chance to answer, one of her abductors slipped a hand across the mouthpiece and twisted the receiver from her grasp, smothering her words. She briefly thought about resisting, then dismissed the scheme as suicidal.

Hal would save them. He would know what to do.

"Awright, so listen up," the blond man in the Army-surplus jacket was demanding of her husband. "We're in charge from here on out, and you will do exactly as you're told."

He seemed to be the leader, separated by his stature and his almost military bearing from the others. She had only seen the three of them so far, but it had been enough. Their handguns and their automatic weapons compensated for the small size of the team. And, then again, how many men were necessary to secure a woman and her children? Helen knew that it would not require a SWAT team, after all.

The blonde had been the first to show himself, all smiles as she responded to the gentle knocking on the cabin door. There was no reason to suspect him, or to doubt his story of a minor pileup on the access road below. She knew the cabins to the east were empty; she had seen them standing dark and cold that very afternoon, and it confirmed the young man's story of his inability to find a telephone. The Blue Ridge Mountains were not Washington, so there was no need to guard against a smiling stranger's secret motives here.

He hadn't shown the gun till he was inside, the door shut tightly behind him. Helen recognized it as a compact submachine gun—Hal would know the make and model number if he saw it—but she didn't have to know the weapon's nomenclature to be thoroughly acquainted with its lethal capabilities. One burst would be all it would take to rip herself, her children to shreds. She had offered no resistance when the blond man ordered her to sit, when he had hailed the rest of his team, their pastel leisure suits incongruous in such a rustic setting.

If it had not been for her concern about the children...

Helen stopped herself and nearly smiled. Eileen would have a fit if she should hear herself referred to as a child. She was a woman now, in every sense, but at the same time she would always be her mother's little girl.

Provided that they all survived this night, the day to come.

But Hal would have the answers at his fingertips. She trusted him implicitly, had placed her faith in him for more than twenty-five years without a single major disappointment. He would see them through, or...

Helen dared not follow where the thought was leading her, but her unconscious mind had grasped the message loud and clear.

He would see them safely through, or die in the attempt.

The gunmen had been swift and sure in their evacuation of the cabin. The gorillas patted down Jeff and Helen for weapons, taking longer with Eileen and snickering between themselves until the blonde had snapped at them to be about their business. A panel truck, its back-door windows painted over, was waiting for them in the driveway. The three Brognolas were forced inside, and a curtain was drawn behind the driver's seat to block their view of any landmarks through the windshield. Under guard, they rode in silence for an hour and a half before the two apes fitted them with blindfolds, led them single file across a sloping, grassy lawn and then inside some kind of house. The drapes had not been opened since their blindfolds were removed, and butcher's paper had been taped across the tiny, frosted window of the bathroom they were grudgingly allowed to use.

Allowing for the stops and starts occasioned by their passage through assorted tiny mountain towns, she estimated that they could have traveled seventy or eighty miles in ninety minutes. Far enough to place them back in Washington, in Maryland, perhaps across the Pennsylvania line. They had not traveled west, across the mountains; she was reasonably sure of that. As for the rest, there had not been a single clue—no airport sounds or ferry whistles, railroad crossings or calliopes—to help her sketch a mental road map. Helen could not have informed her husband where they were if she had been allowed to try.

"Your weekend's over, guy," the blond leader was saying, grinning at his two companions as he spoke. "I want you back in Washington and at your desk by noon today. You got that? Good. You play it straight, we all come out of this laughing. Just save the hero bullshit for the movies, okay?"

He cradled the receiver without waiting for Brognola to reply.

"We're on," he told his two companions. "Noon it is."

The pair of anthropoids exchanged lopsided smiles and settled back in matching arm chairs, weapons in their laps. If they had pooled their IQs, Helen thought, they might have come up with intelligence enough to read a comic strip, but she never doubted their ability to kill without remorse. What worried her the most right now was their apparent interest in Eileen. They had been ogling her, whispering between themselves and winking at her since the man in charge had beckoned them inside the cabin. There had been no overt moves so far, but Helen worried that they might grow restive with the passing time, decide to seek some quick diversion with her daughter. If it came to that, she wondered whether the blonde would hold his men in check, or whether he would even care to try.

She pushed the lurid images away and thought of Hal, alone and doubtless distraught in their empty cabin. Helen knew that underneath the gruff exterior, her husband was a man of feeling and emotion. Any danger to his family would torment Hal; his inability to move at once, to strike against the perpetrators would grate on his nerves. He would obey the blonde's command, she knew, because he had no immediate alternative. As long as there was any chance at all of a negotiation, Hal would hold himself in check. But if the talks broke down, if he perceived that she or either of the children had been harmed . . .

What would he do?

What *could* he do?

They were alone, and each of them would have to watch for opportunities as they arose. A chance to summon help, alert the outside world to their predicament. An opportunity to seize a weapon and . . . And what?

When Hal was working with the Marshal's Service years before, he had instructed Helen in the use of simple firearms, and the automatic weapons of their captors could not be so very different. The problem, then, would not be capability; it would be opportunity, together with the risks involved. If she was able to secure a weapon, train it on her captors, would she have the nerve to kill? And would the very effort doom her children?

No matter.

For the moment, they were waiting on a call to Washington, eight hours down the road. They would be safe until that time, she told herself, because their captors would need evidence that they were still alive. Hal wouldn't buy the bland assurances of faceless men; he would demand to speak with one or all of them before he made another move.

Eight hours, then. And after that?

She couldn't see that far, and speculation was a waste of time. She would be needing all her energy, her wits, to watch and wait for the slightest opportunity that might present itself. Secure that she would recognize the moment when it came, she settled back to wait. And thought of Hal.

THE VOICE ON THE PHONE came back to haunt Brognola.

"I want you back in Washington and at your desk at noon today."

No problem there. It was an easy drive, and while most offices were closed on Saturday, there was a weekend crew at Justice, handling the calls that never seemed to stop at five o'clock on Friday afternoon. His presence might occasion some surprise, but it was not unheard of for the boss to work on Saturday.

"Just save the hero bullshit for the movies, okay?"

The warning was unnecessary. Ignorant of their identity, their numbers and their whereabouts, Brognola had no way of striking at his enemies. Two men, at least. There had been different voices on the phone each time, but he was in the dark regarding any other substantial clues. Incoming calls, if dialed direct, would prove impossible to trace, and he could not conceive of the abductors asking for assistance from an operator. Worse, the futile effort would require assistance from the Bureau, with its agents and computers. He was not prepared to make his problem public yet, not with the three lives dearest to him riding on the line. Perhaps after he had been in touch with the abductors again, determined what they wanted from him, he would take the chance.

And, then again, perhaps he wouldn't.

He would not do anything to risk his wife and children, certainly, but if an opportunity arose once they were free— or if he should suspect that they had been disposed of by the bastards who had carried them away—there might be something he could do to even up the score. It had been years since he had dropped the hammer on a human target, but you never really lost the touch. It was like swimming, pedaling a bike, or reaching for your woman in the middle of the night. A reflex, backed by years of practical experience, indelibly imprinted upon the brain.

And he would kill with relish if the members of his family were harmed. He would pursue the bastards tirelessly, relentlessly, until he had an opportunity to watch the spark of life wink out behind their eyes, extinguished by his hand.

If it should come to that.

But first he had to sleep.

It was incongruous, but Hal would need his strength, his faculties at noon when the abductors called him back in Washington. Four hours to go, five at the outside, before he had to leave again. Enough time to replenish his fading energy reserve, provided he could sleep at all.

The empty rooms around him seemed to whisper Helen's name, to ring with laughter from the children in their younger days. Aware that he might never see his family alive again, Brognola welcomed lighter memories, of birthdays, high school proms and graduations, weekends at the lakeshore.

Weekends...

Somewhere in the midst of a dream of courting Helen, he was suddenly awakened by the shrilling telephone. Immediately terrified that he had somehow overslept, had missed the noontime rendezvous, Brognola checked his watch and found that it was barely 6:00 a.m. Outside, the pearly light of dawn was filtering through ground fog that had twined itself around the trees.

He fumbled for the receiver, brought it to his ear.

"Brognola."

"Chatsworth, here."

He recognized the voice of his direct liaison with the Oval Office, puzzled by the hour and the call itself. No one had ever phoned him at the cabin, and Chatsworth rarely called at all these days, since the debacle with the CIA at Stony Man.

"What is it?"

"Sorry for the wake-up call." But Chatsworth's tone informed Brognola that he wasn't sorry in the least. "The Man desires your presence. Ten o'clock all right with you?"

It hadn't really been a question, and Brognola didn't bother with an answer.

"What's the flap?" he asked.

"I couldn't say."

Or wouldn't. Either one might be the truth. Brognola never really knew how much the President confided in his aide.

"Okay. I'll see you then."

He replaced the receiver swiftly, beating Chatsworth to the punch by maybe half a second, satisfied with the petty victory. The two of them would scarcely pass for friends, Brognola viewing Chatsworth as a combination hatchet man and gopher, Chatsworth doubtless viewing him as something of a bureaucratic drone. But they were not required to love each other. Chatsworth was a fact of life at least until the next election, and Brognola frankly didn't give a damn about the guy this morning.

He had other things in mind.

The summons back to Wonderland eliminated any thought of sleep. In any case, his nerves were strung too tightly now for relaxation to become reality. The drive would do him good, providing him with time to think, uninterrupted, and devise a course of action for the retrieval of his family.

For now the presidential summons was an inconvenience, threatening to blow his schedule and prevent him from receiving what could be the most important phone call of his life. Brognola was determined to be at his desk by noon, no matter if he had to fake a coronary and leave the Oval Office on a stretcher. He doubted it would come to that. The President was busy seven days a week, and he could scarcely spare two hours for a confab with the man from Justice.

Still, the summons on a Saturday was strange. He wondered if the President had somehow learned of his predicament, then decided that it was impossible and instantly vowed to preserve the secret. Theoretically possessed of sweeping powers, there was nothing that America's Chief Executive could do to help him at the present time. If federal officers were mobilized before he knew what the abductors had in mind, Brognola ran the risk of losing everything. A hasty move against the enemy would doom his family, and he was not about to waste their lives in pursuit of reckless vengeance.

There would be enough time to even up the score when they were safe.

With that in mind, he set about securing the cabin, locking up and making ready for the drive back home. They could come back for Helen's car another time, when she was safe and sound. If something happened to it in the meantime, he was perfectly prepared to write the damned thing off. Brognola's first priority was the recovery of three people who meant the world to him, and nothing less would put his tortured mind at ease.

The President could not assist him now, but that did not preclude obtaining help from other quarters. Once he spoke to the abductors, once he learned precisely what they wanted, there was still a chance of rescuing his family, of bringing down the predators without conceding anything of substance. It was chancy, but there just might be a way to pull it off.

With luck.

And with a little help from friends.

Just save the hero bullshit for the movies.

Fine.

But if Brognola was required to play the pacifist, it didn't mean that others might not take the field on his behalf. One other, in particular. One *man*.

One hero who had never saved it for the movies.

3

"He'll see you now."

Brognola had been waiting twenty minutes, and he didn't care for Chatsworth's tone. He followed the aide past the secretary's desk and on through tall familiar doors that opened on the Oval Office, waiting as they closed behind him silently. Brognola waited stoically while Chatsworth crossed the navy carpet that was decorated with a giant presidential seal, and stood before the desk.

The President was winding up a phone call, speaking in monosyllables, his face set in a stormy frown. Whatever he was hearing, it had not improved his temperament.

"Keep me informed," he said at last, and hung up. He swiveled his chair toward Chatsworth and stood up.

"Brognola, Mr. President."

"I see him, Emil."

He was circling the desk when Hal moved forward, grateful for the outstretched hand, but still alert to the apparent weariness—the sadness?—etched in his commander's face.

"Sit down, Hal."

The sweeping hand included Chatsworth, and they settled into chairs positioned near the desk. The President was silent for a moment, drifting toward the windows where he stood, arms folded, staring off across the White House gardens and the broad expanse of lawn.

"How are you, Hal?"

Brognola searched for hidden meanings in the question, came up empty. "Well enough, sir."

"And the family?"

It took a moment for Brognola to respond. A sudden tightness in his throat was threatening to strangle him, but he was more concerned with studying the President, his tone. It wasn't like the Man to play at cat and mouse. Brognola felt himself beginning to relax. He didn't know. The early-morning summons was concerned with something else.

"They're well."

Please, God.

"I'm glad to hear it."

Silence stretched out between them like a steel garrote, uncomfortable, tense. Beside Brognola, Chatsworth made a show of studying his wing-tip shoes.

At length the President declared, "We've got a problem, Hal. I need your input."

Chatsworth snorted, covering belatedly with an exaggerated coughing fit. Brognola didn't waste the energy to glance in his direction.

"Yes, sir?"

"We've received persuasive circumstantial evidence to indicate you've got a leak at Justice. A mole. High placed."

Brognola's mind was racing, trying to digest the President's announcement. Always on alert for leaks, for any vestige of corruption, he was not aware of any ongoing investigations. There had been some trouble—plenty of it—with the FBI and NSA last year, but that had been wrapped up by Christmas, all the leaks securely welded tight. Or all the leaks they *knew* about, at any rate.

The President returned to sit behind his massive desk, eyes locked with Hal's, ignoring Chatsworth for the moment.

"Word is that it touches Phoenix."

Something dark and dangerous was stirring in the shadows of Brognola's mind. If there was a connection with his family's abduction, something to provide him with a handle...

"Sir, I have to say this comes as a complete surprise. I've had no indication from my staff of an investigation under way. If you could let me have specific information..."

"Chatsworth?"

Seated on Brognola's right, the aide de camp was riffling through a thin manila folder, nodding to himself and clearly looking forward to the game now that the coach had called him in to play.

"Let's call our suspect 'Mr. X'," he said dramatically. "We were apprised of his alleged involvement with a leak by an informant who has furnished reliable information in the past."

Brognola knew the line by heart. "Reliable informants" might be bugs or wiretaps, documents obtained through shady means, or any one of countless snitches trading in the vital currency of information. Confidential sources were the backbone and the lifeblood of the vast intelligence establishment. Access to their secret information was the key to power, sometimes to survival.

It would do no good to ask for the identity of Chatsworth's source. Brognola knew the presidential aide would keep the information to himself and lie, if necessary, to preserve the source's confidentiality. A name would not add anything of substance to his understanding of the case, Hal realized. The President seemed satisfied, or very nearly so, and for the moment that was good enough.

"Our source relates that Mr. X has been in contact with a list of ranking orgcrime figures, under circumstances that remain unclear." As Chatsworth spoke, his eyes were fixed upon Brognola. He did not consult the folder in his lap, and Hal surmised that he had found the information interesting enough to memorize. "Pursuant to his information, an investigation was initiated, and—"

"I should have been informed," Brognola said, ignoring Chatsworth, speaking to the President.

"We didn't think it wise, all things considered."

Brognola was chewing over that as Chatsworth cleared his throat, resuming as if Hal had never interrupted his report.

"Pursuant to his information, an investigation was initiated, and material collected implicates our Mr. X in covert dealings with the syndicate."

"What kind of information?"

"Stills and videos. Accumulated phone logs. Affidavits from recipients of classified material. The whole nine yards."

Brognola frowned. "I'd like to take a look at what you've got."

"It's classified at present."

"I've got clearance."

"Not for this," Chatsworth replied smugly.

"Since when?"

"Since your department has been compromised."

"Goddammit, Chatsworth—"

"Gentlemen."

They both turned toward the President and found him leaning forward, elbows planted on his desk, his dark eyes boring into each in turn.

"Excuse us for a moment, Emil."

Chatsworth seemed about to protest, but he reconsidered instantly, unwilling to let momentary anger pull the plug on job security. He spent another moment glaring at Brognola, then retreated from the Oval Office, the manila folder tucked beneath his arm.

"I'm sorry, sir."

The President was not concerned with his apology. "I understand your feelings, Hal. There were compelling reasons for excluding you from the investigation."

"I'd be very interested in an explanation, sir."

"Security was paramount."

Alarms were going off inside Brognola's brain now, but he forged ahead. "You indicated that the problem touches Phoenix?"

"Intimately."

Hal made no attempt to mask his rising irritation. "Mr. President, I cannot hope to offer any meaningful advice if I am kept in ignorance."

"I didn't call you in to ask for your advice."

Brognola spread his hands. "Then, what?"

Behind his massive desk, the chief executive was scowling like a man beset with sudden pain. "I've got no stomach for this double talk and innuendo," he declared at last.

"I called you in because our information indicates that *you* are Mr. X."

Brognola felt as if someone had sucker-punched him, hard, below the heart. For just a moment he was stunned. The Oval Office seemed to shrink around him. His stomach did a sluggish barrel roll, and throbbing pain erupted in his temples, keeping perfect time with his accelerated pulse.

"There must be some mistake." It sounded lame, the desperate defense of an embezzler or adulterer confronted with his secret sin.

"As Chatsworth said, we have the tape, the stills. Your phone logs have been triple-checked."

A momentary sense of outrage kindled in his chest, extinguished instantly as Hal digested the apparent situation. It did not surprise him that his phone calls had been monitored, his movements filmed. He had been fingered as a mole, and SOP surveillance had been instituted automatically. He had helped to set the system up himself in the wake of the disastrous raid on Stony Man, and he could not complain if it had worked efficiently.

Except it hadn't worked. There was no proof of his complicity. There couldn't be.

The President had settled back into his chair, regarding Hal with mingled sadness and a sort of morbid curiosity.

"I thought we'd better talk it over one-on-one."

Brognola's mind was racing, searching for connections, links between this latest bombshell and the disappearance of his family. Discounting any possibility of mere coincidence, he sought some common thread between the two events.

"I can't respond to any charges without looking at the so-called evidence."

"You'll have that opportunity, of course."

"And the informant?"

"Will remain anonymous," the President replied. "For what it's worth, we don't know who the hell he is. There have been two communications, written, both unsigned. Both posted here in Washington."

"That's pretty thin."

"The letters won't be used as evidence. They put the wheels in motion, nothing more. Whatever Justice has collected came through channels, SOP."

"I see." Brognola was astounded by the sudden calm that settled over him, as if he were a mere observer to a drama that concerned some other life, some other idiot's career. "Is Justice moving for indictment?"

Frowning back at him, the President appeared confused. "I wanted to consult with you before it got that far. I'm interested in hearing your impressions, your response."

"I've been set up," Brognola told him flatly. "It has all the earmarks of a classic frame."

"It crossed my mind," the President conceded. "But the film, the phone logs . . ."

"Can be doctored, manufactured or explained," Brognola said. "I want a polygraph as soon as possible."

"You have that right, of course, although the end results are inadmissible."

"I'm not concerned about admissibility. *I* know this thing is bogus. It's important to me now that *you* believe I'm innocent."

The President seemed touched. "I understand," he said. "But there are statutory guidelines to be followed. I cannot involve myself before judicial findings have been made." There was a momentary hesitation as he pondered something privately. "If we could single out a motive . . ."

Trapped, Brognola was confronted by a pair of odious alternatives. He could inform the President of his family's abduction, thereby risking interference that might jeopardize their lives, or he could stonewall, risking summary suspension or incarceration, which would render him incapable of helping them in any case.

And finally it was no choice at all.

He told the President his story from the top, omitting nothing, ending with the order that he be available by noon. It was five minutes past eleven when he finished, settling back to wait for the President's reaction.

"Jesus Christ."

Brognola swallowed hard. "Whoever has my family . . ."

"Might want to frame you. Yes, I get the picture." For an instant Hal imagined that he heard a tremor in the famous voice. "What does the Bureau say about all this?"

"I haven't spoken to them yet."

"Of course, I understand. But in the interest of your family's safety, you should try—"

"My family's safety may depend upon the Bureau staying out of it," he told the President emphatically. "The last thing I need right now is fifty college boys in three-piece suits obscuring the evidence."

"There must be someone. Able Team or Phoenix Force?"

Brognola shook his head. "I had another source of aid in mind."

The man behind the desk mulled that one over for a moment, furrows of concern etched deep across his forehead, eyebrows creeping in on each other till they met above his nose.

"You can't be serious."

"I'm deadly serious," Brognola said. "In my opinion no one else could pull it off."

"Could *he*?"

The question had been nagging Hal almost continuously since the call at 4:00 a.m. He knew the answer now, or part of it, at any rate. He had no choice except to try.

"I think so, yes."

The President was clearly worried now. "I can't approve this."

"Sir, I haven't asked you to approve of anything."

"The man's an outlaw, dammit."

"He's my friend."

"A pardon is impossible."

"He wouldn't take it if you offered."

"Mmm."

"I'm speaking off the record now—or on the record if you like, it doesn't matter. From the looks of things I'm finished anyway."

"See here, Hal . . ."

"My family is all that matters to me now. Whatever happens with the job and Chatsworth's 'evidence,' I have to see my wife and children safe at home. My resignation can be on your desk this afternoon.''

"Hold on a second. Don't go flying off the handle."

"I don't have a second, sir. My time is running out. I need to make that contact now."

"As I recall, your man is marked as hit on sight."

It was a startling admission from the chief executive, committed as he was on paper to defend the Bill of Rights.

"That is my understanding, yes, sir."

"Makes it sticky, eh?"

"It's where he lives."

"You understand that I can offer no assistance if you should pursue this course of action."

"I'm not asking for assistance, sir. I just don't want an army on my heels the next few days."

"All right, the Bureau's out. I still think Able Team could help."

Brognola shook his head again.

"They're in Miami and heavily involved. A disengagement now could be disastrous. Anyway, they couldn't make the trip in time."

"And Phoenix Force?"

"In Bogotá. They couldn't pull out at the moment if they wanted to."

"I see."

"One man," Brognola said again. "One special man is all I need."

"Goddammit."

"Yes, sir."

"This could blow up in our faces, Hal."

"In *my* face, sir. As far as I'm concerned, we never had this conversation."

"Mmm. As for this other business . . ."

"I assume I'm on suspension, sir."

The President was bristling. "Dammit, I'll decide who's on suspension. You have time off coming?"

"I'm on holiday through Monday."

"Fair enough. If anybody asks, you're still on holiday. Through Monday."

There was no mistaking the significance of that. He had two days to see his family safely home, wrap up his problems on the side, before he had to deal with Chatsworth's "evidence" directly.

"Thank you, sir."

"For what? We never had this conversation."

"Right."

"There's one more thing."

"Yes, sir?"

"I want a meeting with your friend."

Brognola felt the short hairs rising at the back of his neck. "I don't know if that's possible."

"Hell, anything is possible," the chief executive replied. "I leave it in your hands."

"I'll see what I can do."

"I know you will."

He didn't care to ask what was behind the President's request. It would not be an ambush, he was sure of that. The Man had never worked that way. But setting up the meet could be a problem, all the same. The President's command was good enough for most men, but there were a few—or one, at any rate—who might not be impressed.

One man who might decline the invitation from on high.

One man whose aid now meant the difference between survival and annihilation for Brognola's family.

One man named Mack Bolan.

4

Leo Turrin waited while the officer on duty checked his ID card against the master list and finally returned it with a laminated clip-on pass marked Visitor. Although he was a paid employee of the orgcrime branch at Justice, ranking just below Brognola in the bureaucratic scheme of things, his name and face were not well-known around the beehive office complex at Ninth and Constitution Avenue. No more than a half dozen people in the whole department knew his function, which was fine with Turrin. If his name became a household word in Wonderland, his usefulness would instantly evaporate. Security was everything, and so he was content to be a "visitor" among the staffers who, in actuality, were his subordinates.

The privileges of rank meant little to the stocky veteran lawman. He had seen enough of chiefs and Indians in Vietnam and later, as a "mole" for Justice in the upper echelons of the Cosa Nostra. Rank, which was bestowed by others, could as easily be swept away, and Turrin put no faith in others.

No, that wasn't strictly true. There were several individuals, a handful, really, whom he trusted with his life. His wife and family, of course. Brognola, who had signed him on at Justice in the first place, serving as his personal control and only contact while he burrowed from within the Mafia, ascending through the ranks to find a seat on La Commissióne before the end. And Mack Bolan.

Always Bolan.

Turrin rarely passed a day without some thought of his clandestine comrade, once a lethal enemy and now his closest friend. Their first encounter had been touch-and-go, before the hellfire warrior was apprised of Leo's double role within the Mob. But they had worked some minor miracles together once they understood each other. Turrin owed his life, his family's survival to the man from Pittsfield, and he knew that there was nothing he could ever do to balance out that debt. Of late, they had been out of touch, the soldier fading into limbo after all the shit came down at Stony Man, but Leo tracked his exploits through the media, and through confidential files that found their way across his desk.

The Executioner was labeled "hit on sight," a designation normally reserved for CIA defectors and the sort of mad-dog psychopaths who roam cross-country, killing for the hell of it. In fact, the soldier did not fit in either category, and to Turrin's mind it was a goddamned shame that he had made the hit list in the first place. Still, his unofficial "resignation" from the Phoenix program, his rejection of the deal that had supplied a covert pardon for his other "crimes" had marked him as a renegade in the official view, unstable, dangerous to anyone and everyone.

It was a lot of bullshit, Turrin knew, but there was nothing he could do from his position. Nothing, anyway, unless the soldier got in touch and asked for information or assistance in his next campaign. When that occurred, it would be Turrin's duty to report him, set him up, if possible, and see him dead before he had another chance to cut and run. His duty, sure. Except that he would rather kill himself than help to bring the soldier down.

Goddammit, what a fouled-up world they lived in! Money-grubbing bastards were enthroned in politics, in giant corporations, sometimes with the blood still fresh and dripping on their hands, while heroes were reviled and hounded to their graves. Sometimes Turrin wondered if society had received its just deserts: besieged crime, inflation, chaos in the streets . . . and then he thought of Angelina, of the kids.

The momentary introspection was depressing Turrin, as it always did, and he dismissed the morbid thoughts, intent upon his morning's mission. He had called ahead and found out that Hal Brognola was, in fact, expected in his office on this Saturday. The girl had seemed confused; Brognola had been scheduled for a holiday through Monday, but his early call had let them know that he would be available by noon. To Turrin that meant Hal would probably be in before eleven, poring over files and working angles on a dozen operations simultaneously, and he timed his own arrival to connect with Hal before he broke for lunch.

His covert probe of cocaine sources serving certain senior congressmen and senators had borne surprising fruit, and Turrin knew that he should check with Hal before he forged ahead. There might be profit in avoiding scandal for a chosen few, providing they agreed to work with Justice on uncovering the pipeline. If they tried to stonewall, well, there were a host of ways to get the message out before election time, regardless of admissibility in court. No friend of politicians for the most part, Turrin theorized that some could still be salvaged, turned around in time, but he would need Brognola's go-ahead before he made the overtures. He half expected Hal to grumble at the interruption of his crowded morning schedule, but he had been grumbled at before by experts, and eleven months of digging gave the project top priority in Turrin's mind.

The elevator reached Brognola's floor, and Turrin moved aggressively along the corridor, a quarterback in motion, carrying the ball for one more touchdown.

He reached Brognola's office, brushed on through the open door and found two uniforms emerging from the inner sanctum, laden down with cardboard boxes full of files. It looked like moving day, and Turrin was about to challenge them when he made out the figure of a ranking Justice staffer bringing up the rear.

The staffer's name was Erskine DeVries, and Turrin knew him as a yes-man, recognized for his ability to kiss up the appropriate superiors. Adept at sniffing changes in the winds of office politics, he had survived three administrations, wobbling from left to right at need, a humanoid chameleon intent upon survival and advancement. Leo didn't like the type, and in his fleeting contacts with DeVries, there had been nothing to incline him toward an individual exception.

"Leo, hey! Long time, no see."

Turrin pumped the boneless hand and let it go, suppressing a desire to wipe his palm against the nearest wall.

"What's going on?"

DeVries was grinning at him like a cat about to belch canary feathers.

"Mean you haven't heard? Brognola's checking out. The guy's as good as gone." DeVries was on a roll, unable to contain himself. "He's history. Got one foot out the door, and one on a banana peel. I mean, he's out of here."

"Since when?"

"Since someone figured out the guy was doubling his bets. You feature that? The asshole was a sellout."

Turrin felt the angry color rising in his cheeks, and he suppressed a sudden urge to drive his fist through De-Vries's face. Instead he slid an arm around the weasel's shoulders, lowering his voice to indicate a bond of confidentiality between them, drawing him away and to one side.

"Hey, this is news to me," he said. "I was supposed to see the guy this morning. What's the skinny?"

Favored with an audience, DeVries waxed professorial.

"I can't go into too much detail here, you understand, but someone tipped us that Brognola has been playing footsie with the Families in Baltimore, New York, some other places. We got phone logs, videos, you name it. Primo stuff."

"What's in the boxes?"

"Cases, this and that. You know the drill. Whatever's pending, plus a few selected oldies for comparison. And this."

From underneath his coat, DeVries produced an address book that might have been procured in any dime store, bound in imitation leather.

"So?"

DeVries looked pained.

"So, buddy, this is just his trick book here, that's all. It's full of names and places, dates. Amounts."

"You're saying you've got evidence of payoffs?"

"Hey, what can I tell you, Leo? Some jerks like to write it down. It's like the Nixon syndrome, eh? That Watergate fiasco might have had a happy ending if he hadn't got a tape recorder for his birthday."

When he laughed out loud, DeVries reminded Turrin of a braying jackass. Wincing, Leo forced a grin and waited for the moment of hilarity to pass.

"So what's the deal?" he asked when he could get a word in edgewise. "Is the guy already out, or what?"

DeVries dismissed the question with a shrug.

"Nobody's briefed me on the disposition yet. They'll have to wade through all this shit before they file, I guess, but if the bastard owed me money, I'd collect it while I could."

The braying laugh, abrading Leo's nerves like fingernails across a blackboard, was suddenly cut short as Hal Brognola crossed the threshold.

"Hey, I'll catch you later," DeVries mumbled, steering wide around Brognola, eyes averted as he navigated toward the door.

They stood alone in the reception room, deserted by the vultures now, communicating silently with eyes that never wavered. It was Hal who broke the ice a moment later.

"Perfect timing."

"Hal—"

Brognola raised a hand to silence him.

"In here," he said and nodded toward the inner office. Leo followed on his heels and closed the door behind himself.

"We might not be alone," Brognola told him simply, stooping to check beneath his desk, the swivel chair. There was no way to search a modern office thoroughly with naked eyes and empty hands, but they spent twenty minutes going through the basics, checking furniture and fixtures, lifting artwork off the walls and rummaging through drawers. Hal unscrewed the earpiece and the mouthpiece of his telephone receiver, slipped the base plate off and poked around inside before he satisfied himself that it had not been tampered with. He riffled through the sparse remaining files while Leo checked the heater ducts. When they were finished, Hal sat down behind his desk and motioned Leo toward a chair directly opposite.

"I'm in a bind," he said, presenting Turrin with the understatement of the year. "Somebody's got me marked as a mole."

"If I can help—"

"We'll get to that," Brognola interrupted. "First, I want to put you in the picture. When you've heard me out, if you're inclined to take the chance, at least we'll both be going into it with open eyes."

"All right."

There was no doubt in Turrin's mind that he would offer any possible assistance, but he recognized Brognola's need to fill him in before accepting a commitment. Hal would no more let a friend expose himself to unknown risks than he would sell out his own department. It was unthinkable.

In short, clipped sentences, the big Fed told him everything. The disappearance of his wife and children. The communication from their obvious abductors. His return to Washington, the Oval Office meeting, and his confrontation with the manufactured "evidence" of personal corruption. He was waiting for another call at noon, some thirteen minutes off.

"What have they got, exactly? Did you see this so-called evidence?"

Brognola shook his head. "I'll have to let the lawyers hassle that," he said. "Right now my top priority is Helen and the kids."

"It's got to be connected," Turrin said unnecessarily.

"Of course. I just can't bother with the job right now."

"Were you suspended?"

"Not exactly. I'm on holiday, through Monday."

"Well, that's something, anyway."

"It's all I'm going to get."

"Okay, so let's run down a list of possibles."

"I've got till Monday, Leo, not till New Year's."

"We can make a start...."

"No time," Brognola said again. "I'm going to hear the bastards out and play along with them until I find an opening."

"It's too damned risky."

"Well, I hadn't planned on going in alone."

"All right. Just tell me when and where. We'll roll these scumbags up and shake 'em till they rattle."

Hal was watching him through narrowed eyes. "Not us," he said. "I'm looking for a specialist."

Turrin had been half expecting it, and still the statement, voiced aloud, had come as a surprise.

"Well, sure . . . I mean, you've got some top-notch talent in the program."

"I can't touch it, Leo. Ground rules. I've got sixty hours, tops, and I'm required to go outside the house."

The answer had been looking at him all along, but Turrin was reluctant to suggest the only viable alternative. He waited for Brognola, letting him take the initiative.

"I need to get in touch with Striker."

Once spoken, it became a problem they could deal with logically, deliberately. Both men were fully conscious of the risks involved, the dangers to themselves, the precious hostages and to the man they called Striker. Turrin knew that he could walk out now, refuse to put his future on the line, and no one—least of all Brognola—would think less of him for his decision.

No one but himself.

The former capo mafioso understood his duty, as defined by printed guidelines, and he also recognized a deeper obligation to the man who faced him across the empty desk. Brognola had defended Turrin countless times, had saved his ass from the congressional investigators and from leaks inside his own department, keeping him alive while he fulfilled his mission in the syndicate. When he emerged to claim his rightful place at Justice, Hal had been his sponsor, fending off the others who believed that Leo was a risk, his motives suspect by the very fact that he had spent so many years inside the Mob. He owed Brognola everything he had, and short of sacrificing Angelina or the kids, he was prepared to pay that debt with any means at his disposal.

"I can make some calls," he said.

Brognola didn't answer for a moment. He was staring at the clock, as if he could advance the minute hand to noon by force of will alone. When Leo checked his watch, he found that five minutes were left before the scheduled call.

"I'd better get to work on it," he said, already on his feet before Brognola could respond.

"Take care."

The big Fed's voice was soft and faraway, the normal gruffness tempered by a sorrow that could never be described at secondhand. It had to be experienced—as Leo had experienced it for himself in Pittsfield during Bolan's early war against the Mafia. A faction of the Marinello Family had taken Angelina from him, looking for a handle that would make him crawl, ideally blow his cover and reveal Turrin as a mole. For a brief eternity he had been faced with the destruction of his life, the loss of everything he cared for in the world. There had been nothing Hal could do from Washington, no magic tricks tucked up his sleeves. The mission had required a specialist.

Like now.

A hellfire warrior who could bend the rules or break them as he chose, with the impunity of one who stands outside the system, looking in. A dedicated soldier who was ready to commit himself and risk his life on behalf of others without thinking twice about the costs.

Their situations were identical, and Turrin knew that Hal had used up his other options before he mentioned Striker's name. The guy was like a frigging doomsday weapon—you could not control him; you could only point him in the general direction, turn him loose and pray. There were no guarantees that he would finally succeed, no guarantees of any kind—except that he would do his best, use every means at his disposal to prevent unnecessary harm from coming to the innocent, to any noncombatant.

As he closed the office door behind him, Turrin wondered what had happened to the noncombatants, anyway.

Increasingly the lines were blurred, and he could not distinguish friend from enemy, civilians from belligerents. Increasingly, he had begun to share Striker's view, which held that there were battle lines on every front, insidious opponents waiting for an opportunity to strike on every side. Your enemy might be the syndicate, a clutch of terrorist fanatics or the homicidal boy next door, and any man committed to the preservation of society who, once he relaxed his guard, could count upon no mercy from the opposition.

Turrin knew where Bolan could be found—if not precisely, then at least in general terms. His means of making contact were distinctly limited, but there were ways, and he would spare no effort on behalf of Hal Brognola's cause. The soldier would respond, if he could get in touch before it was too late. If Bolan had an opportunity to extricate himself from the campaign in which he was involved. If he had not become a casualty by now.

Too many *ifs*.

It was the only chance Brognola had, and Leo meant to play it out, whichever way it went. If he could not touch base with Striker, Leo was prepared to stand with Hal and face the enemy alone, no matter what the risk.

It was his duty to a friend, no matter what the rule book said. Some moral obligations never found expression in the printed guidelines, but the lawman knew precisely where they lay.

It was a trait he shared in common with the soldier known as Striker. There were too few like him in the modern world, but one could be enough.

One man with skill, determination and a will to win.

One man like Bolan, sure.

If he could find his way to Wonderland in time.

5

Mack Bolan had been in place since shortly after dawn, and he was stiff from lying in the same position, scarcely moving for a period of hours. Immobility and patience were a sniper's special skills, as much a part of ultimate success as the selection of a weapon, calculation of the drop and windage on a given shot. But stakeouts bore a certain risk, as well. New York was not the Southeast Asian jungle, where a man could disappear ten paces from his comrades, swallowed by the forest undergrowth and shadows. In Manhattan, eyes and ears were everywhere, although they sometimes opted not to see or hear.

The soldier had already staked his life on urban uninvolvement, praying silently that people who might take notice of his rooftop vigil would ignore him, go about their business without giving him a second thought. A call to the police might ruin everything, assuming the police responded to a noontime prowler call with any alacrity. Positioned so that he could see and hear the squad cars coming, Bolan waited for his target to reveal itself.

The condo he had chosen for his sniper's nest had been a lucky find. Unoccupied for weeks, and likely to remain so as the focus of a bitter palimony suit between two headline actors, its position on the northern fringe of Central Park was perfect for his needs. In fact, the park meant nothing to Mack Bolan; rather, he was interested in the neighbors who lived two doors down—one neighbor, to be strictly accurate. Together with her frequent visitor.

The woman's name was Marilyn DuChamps. She did not interest Bolan personally. Rather, he was drawn to her companion, an eccentric businessman who drove around Manhattan in an armor-plated limousine and had his hair cut daily to eliminate the fresh-trimmed look. Two nights a week—and every Saturday—the businessman arrived at Marilyn's expensive condominium to pass some time in solitude, away from workaday concerns. Most times the limo's driver and another man would wait outside, regardless of the visit's length. The men were being paid to sit and wait as Marilyn DuChamps was being paid to satisfy the businessman's peculiar tastes in "relaxation." No one questioned his prerogatives, his right to keep them waiting, use them as he wished. He owned the limousine, the condominium in which he sought his pleasure and a dozen others on the street. He owned them all.

The businessman was known as George Fratierri—he had dropped the Giorgio years ago—and since the New Year he had gained a great deal of prestige around Manhattan. On New Year's Eve his nominal superior, one Paul Castigliano, had been rather forcefully removed from competition while alighting from his armor-plated limousine outside a favored restaurant. Flanked by two "accountants" who were said to be more comfortable with calibers than calculators, Castigliano had been ventilated by a burst of automatic-weapons fire that erupted from a passing car. The two accountants as well, DOA. His driver, bending down to tie his shoe, had been protected by the limo's armor, but he hadn't seen the attackers nor their vehicle. So sorry.

Fratierri had been no more helpful when questioned by police. Castigliano had been like a brother to him, guiding him in business, helping him to prosper. Who would wish to harm a saint? The city was an open sewer, populated with the dregs of humankind. If Fratierri hadn't had his business there...

What business? Real estate, of course. Some wholesale outlets in the garment district. Restaurants. In case they hadn't noticed, Paulie was about to enter one of George's eateries when he was ambushed. All those ugly rumors—the narcotics, gambling, prostitution—were a slander on Fratierri and his family's honor. He would gladly file a lawsuit if the source of his humiliation could be readily identified. As for this talk about Five Families...what man could cope with more than one? The Boss of Bosses? Someone had been spending too much time on penny dreadfuls and the late show. They should give up watching *The Untouchables* and get in touch with modern-day realities.

It was an act that George Fratierri had perfected over thirty years of dress rehearsals, fending off the questions of police and federal officers, congressional investigators and the media. His injured innocence routine was easily the longest-running joke in town, but so far prosecutors had been unsuccessful in connecting him with any of his extra-legal enterprises. Members of the DA's staff were absolutely certain that Fratierri held controlling interests in cocaine and heroin for south Manhattan, that he dominated out-call prostitution city-wide and that he had been personally responsible for twenty-seven homicides since 1980. The hit on Paulic Castigliano and his two body-guards was the latest in a series of strategic murders that had placed Fratierri in position to unite the city's powerful Five Families beneath his own umbrella...and the DA couldn't prove a thing.

Mack Bolan, for his part, did not require corroborating evidence prepared in triplicate. He recognized Fratierri for the animal he was, and in the instant of that recognition had decided on the means of coping with his evil. Years might pass before the government prepared a solid case for prosecution, if they ever got that far. In the meantime, Fratierri's sordid empire would be growing, fattening upon the flesh and blood of citizens from coast to coast. The Executioner already knew of the Mob chief's ties with the narcotics syndicate out west, his plans for squeezing out the Cubans and recapturing control of cocaine traffic nationwide. The money earned from coke and skag would strengthen his position in the East, and let his morbid influence expand from sea to shining sea.

Unless he was eliminated.

Castigliano's sudden death had left the New York Families confused, disoriented, just the way Bolan liked to see them. If he could not finally eradicate the enemy, at least he could perpetuate dissension in the ranks and turn the cannibals against themselves, devouring their brothers in a struggle for the throne. Fratierri's sudden rise to power threatened to impose stability upon Manhattan's Mafia, and Bolan did not choose to let that happen. On this Saturday the soldier was prepared to use his veto, coolly and decisively, before the coronation could become accomplished fact.

New York was a familiar battleground to Bolan. He had visited the Families from time to time, before and since the interlude at Stony Man, reminding them as necessary that their chosen life-style had a price attached. A more impatient warrior might have given up, become frustrated with the New York syndicate's refusal to collapse, but Bolan recognized his private war as something of a holding action, a containment of the enemy. No victory was guaranteed forever in the kind of war he fought; no threat was finally eradicated while a single enemy survived. The capo that he killed today would be replaced next week, next month, and he would have to do it again. But the reality of everlasting war did not discourage Bolan. Going in, he had known the long odds and there could be no turning back.

Today at least he had the opportunity to make a difference, and the streetwise soldier took his opportunities as they arose.

Downrange, an armored Lincoln nosed along the boulevard, its driver and the shotgun rider scanning windows, cars parked along the curb. They didn't bother with the rooftops, trusting years of grim experience to let them spot an ambush on the street as they had spotted others in the past. A lurking Cadillac was trouble, or a curtain drawn too hastily, but no one put his shooters on a roof. Invisible behind the tinted glass, their passenger was confident that he had hired the best available, that they would see him safely to his rendezvous and back again. Three days was three damn days too long, and he did not intend to keep the lady waiting.

Bolan shifted slightly, reaching for the Marlin lever-action rifle with its massive twenty-power scope. At fifty yards, the scope was hardly necessary, but it would allow him to shake hands with Fratierri, look him in the eye and count the fillings in his teeth before he squeezed the trigger. Chambered in .444, the weapon held six rounds and hurled the big 240-grain projectiles at 2,440 feet per second. At his present range, the slugs would spend 2,000 foot-pounds of explosive energy on impact with the target. Bolan could have dropped a charging elephant at twice that range, and George Fratierri had no chance at all.

All things considered, it was more than he deserved.

The shotgun rider scrambled clear and stood beside the Lincoln for a moment, scanning empty sidewalks in a ritual that had become routine. His face filled Bolan's telescopic sight, an angry pimple clearly visible below the jawline, flecks of dandruff clinging to his sideburns like an early fall of snow.

The soldier grinned.

"You need some Head and Shoulders, guy."

Bolan scanned along the Lincoln's roofline, followed the shooter as he backtracked and opened the door for Fratierri. There, the salt-and-pepper hair and ruddy ears, a flash of profile as the would-be Boss of Bosses muttered something to his bodyguard. The shooter grinned and nodded, eagerly confirming that the boss was always right.

He waited, letting Fratierri clear the Lincoln, straighten his jacket, smooth wrinkles from the ride uptown and double-check cuffs to verify that they revealed the proper quarter inch. Another comment to the shotgun rider, and capo turned away, proceeding up the steps to Marilyn DuChamps and momentary freedom from the worries of an emperor-in-waiting.

Bolan brought the cross hairs of the scope to rest on Fratierri's collar, just below the hairline, at a point where vertebrae connected with the skull. He eased the Marlin's safety off, inhaled to fill his lungs, released half of the breath and held the rest. Another second now, just one more step...

He squeezed and rode out the rifle's massive recoil to verify the hit. The telescopic sight put Fratierri almost in his lap, and Bolan saw the capo's skull explode on impact, spewing blood and bone and brains as if the dreams inside had grown too grandiose to be contained. It took a heart-beat for his headless body to receive the message, fold in upon itself and slump to the sidewalk, but the soldier was already tracking in search of secondary targets.

Gaping at the mess, Fratierri's bodyguard was having trouble with reality. It wasn't every day that you saw your boss decapitated on the street, and by the time he recognized the heavy-metal thunder of a big-game rifle, it was far too late to save himself. The gunner swiveled toward the Lincoln and thought of the armor plating, knowing he could never draw his piece and find a target in time to make a difference. Bolan shot him in the face, round two impacting on his upper lip and crumpling his face like something sculpted out of Styrofoam. The gunner vaulted backward, sliding on the pavement in a slick of blood and bile before he came to rest against a decorative hedge.

The driver had already disappeared beneath the dash-board—what had been good enough for Paulie Castigli-ano's wheelman should be good enough for George Fratierri's—and the soldier left him there, intent on disengaging before some startled neighbor got around to calling the police. The urban noninvolvement syndrome worked in the expensive neighborhoods as well, but here the paranoia was sufficient to produce a phone call—possibly anonymous—when gunfire broke the stillness of a sleepy Saturday.

Fratierri's seat was henceforth up for grabs, and Bolan smiled as he imagined the subordinates responding to another sudden vacancy. Their eagerness might lead to war, and Bolan wished them well. It would be helpful if the savages would kill one another for a while, and leave him to strike on other fronts, at other enemies.

He stowed the Marlin in a camo duffel bag, retreating through the access hatch that he had used to reach the roof and slipping out through finely manicured backyards the size of postage stamps to find his rental car. He dropped the rifle in the trunk and put the place behind him, satisfied for now.

But somewhere down the line, the soldier knew, he would be called upon to do it again. If not here in New York, then in Chicago, or Los Angeles, or Philadelphia. No victory was constant in his everlasting war. You kept the lid on tight by hammering a few nails every day, year-round, as need arose. His next stop might be San Francisco or Miami, Vegas or Duluth. When he had cleared the present battle zone, it would be time to test the wind and see where he was needed.

He could have used some R and R, and for a moment, Bolan thought of his brother, Johnny, and the security provided by his strongbase in San Diego. He could call ahead or just show up on Johnny's doorstep, and either way he was assured of being welcome, being safe for the duration. It had been too long since he had seen his brother, shared his company and yet . . .

A homesick warrior was in trouble from the start, he told himself. Besides, the San Diego basin wasn't home. For Bolan, "home" meant memories of blood and pain, all mingled with the good times and the laughter from his childhood. Home was Pittsfield, Massachusetts, where the syndicate had squeezed his father dry and turned his sister out to work the streets, where Bolan's father had eventually cracked beneath the strain and turned the family home into a slaughterhouse. It was a miracle that Johnny had survived, and Bolan had refused to let his brother have a piece of warfare everlasting, until the war had come to Johnny independently. Once blooded, there had been no turning back for Johnny Bolan, and the brothers were together now, in spirit and in fact.

The elder Bolan liked the sound of San Diego at this moment, had almost decided on a visit to his brother when he spied a phone booth. He had a call to make before he left New York, and this would be as good a time as any.

Bolan punched the private number up from memory and waited until Leo Turrin answered in D.C.

"I'm calling for La Mancha," Bolan told him.

"Go ahead."

The breach of regular security, the sudden tension in his contact's voice, alerted Bolan to a crisis in the making. Normally, the man from Wonderland would take his number, find a different phone and call him back within five minutes, thus evading any possibility of taps or bugs. For Leo to accept the call unscrambled on his private line could only mean that he, or someone close, was in a world of trouble.

For a fleeting instant Bolan nearly hung up, breaking the connection before a trace could be established. But he fought the urge and stood his ground. Leo Turrin would never knowingly betray him, and it would be virtually impossible for agents in D.C. to mobilize a New York team in any case. Secure in the thicket of red tape, he forged ahead.

"What is it, Sticker?"

Turrin hesitated then cleared his throat, as if asking for help was an ordeal for him. And in retrospect the Executioner would realize that it had been precisely that. Reluctantly, the former mafioso laid it out.

"Hal's in deep. He needs a specialist."

"Explain."

"His family's been taken, and the brass at Justice have him figured for a mole."

"That's bullshit."

"Hey, *I* know that, but they're talking evidence. Like phone logs, videos, the whole nine yards."

It was preposterous. Brognola was completely, scrupulously honest, and he should have been above suspicion. But the soldier knew that *no one* was above suspicion in the last analysis. Because the enemy was everywhere, he might have allies even in the halls of Justice. And the Executioner had dealt with crooked cops before.

But not Brognola.

No.

It was unthinkable.

What happened next would logically depend upon the quality of evidence against the man, but courtroom machinations could not be the Executioner's immediate priority.

Hal's family took the honors there, and while their lives were hanging in the balance, Bolan could not rest. He had a job to do.

"I'm coming in."

"Be careful, Striker. Someone thumped the hornet's nest, but good."

"What else is new?" He grinned into the mouthpiece of the telephone. "You still around the same old place?"

"Things never change."

"I've noticed."

"See you?"

"Bet on it."

Bolan cradled the receiver and returned to the rental car. As he sat behind the wheel, he spent a moment pondering the strange events in Wonderland. More details would be needed before he even tried to put the pieces together to complete the puzzle. At the moment he was sure of two things only: that Hal Brognola's family was in danger, and that Hal himself was being framed, set up to take a mighty fall for something he had never contemplated, let alone achieved.

The notion of Brognola working with the enemy was laughable, ridiculous. In other circumstances, Bolan would have seen the humor in it instantly. But with "evidence" behind the accusations, there was nothing funny about his friend's predicament. Hal needed help—a "specialist," damn right—and Bolan fit the bill precisely.

Wonderland was calling him to come and join the dance of death. For once he would not be the guest of honor, but the Executioner would not have missed it for the world.

6

Brognola pounced on the telephone before it had the chance to ring a second time. His palm was moist and sticky as he lifted the receiver to his ear.

"Hello?"

"You made it. Good."

"My family can't help you."

"They already have. We're talking, aren't we?"

"If you harm my wife or children—"

"What?" There was a challenge in the tone. "You gonna track us down?" The caller chuckled to himself. "That's bullshit, man. We're on your back like white on rice, and you *will* do exactly what you're told."

Brognola took a breath and held it briefly, finally allowed it to escape between clenched teeth. He had been on the verge of threatening this faceless enemy, a foolish move that could have jeopardized his wife, his children. Already chilling out, he recognized the need to take things easy, without provoking any violence on the other end.

The caller was correct, of course. Hal's bluster had been that and nothing more, an empty challenge, totally devoid of substance. He could never hope to find them on his own, retrieve his family and dole out retribution single-handedly. Even if he knew the bastards' names and their whereabouts, there would be little he could do. As long as Helen and the kids were held as hostages, his hands were tied.

"I'm listening," he said at last.

"That's better." Triumph, gloating in the other's tone. "We're going to need a meet."

"Just tell me where and when."

"Relax, old man. Don't be too eager. You've got chores to do before it gets that far."

"What kind of chores?"

"We need some information from you. You've got sources and it's time to share."

"Be more specific."

"Names and places ought to do for openers, okay? Protected witnesses, your people under cover, shit like that."

The pit was opening beneath his feet. He had to stall. "I don't have access to that kind of information."

Sudden anger. "Bullshit, man! You set the system up yourself. I've done my homework, see?"

"You didn't study long enough. I've been suspended, as of ten o'clock this morning. They only let me in the office to retrieve some personal belongings."

"What the hell—"

A hand was clapped across the mouthpiece, muffling a heated conversation, and the man from Justice knew that he had scored. Whatever the apparent link between his dual calamities, the gunners who had snatched his family appeared to have been kept in ignorance. That could be good or bad, Brognola realized, depending on their boiling point and how he handled things from here on out.

Another moment, and the sullen voice was back, the tension evident in every spoken word. "You'd better not be shitting me, old man."

"I'm not about to play that kind of game with all I have to lose."

"I find out that you're jerking me, you're gonna have a triple funeral to arrange, and then we're coming after you."

"It's straight," Brognola told him. "If you don't believe me, check it out yourself."

"I just might do that."

There was a momentary silence while the gunner pondered fresh alternatives, another way to work his scam. When he resumed, his tone was thoughtful, introspective.

"What the hell, your problem, right? We want that information. It's your price for momma and the kids."

Stall the bastard.

"It's extremely difficult—"

"That's tough."

"—to get the list you want. If you could pin it down to one or two specific names . . ."

The names might offer him a starting place, a point of reference toward unveiling his opponents. If the opposition wanted a specific witness, he would have a fair idea of who had let the contract in the first place. Given that, he would possess a pressure point.

The gunner thought about it for a moment, or pretended to, before he spoke again. "No good. It's all or nothing, man."

"I'll need some time."

"You've got six hours, starting now. You'll get a call at . . . let's say 6:15. Be home, or you can kiss it all good-bye."

"Hold on!" Brognola's heart was hammering in his rib cage. He could scarcely form the words. "How do I know my wife and children are alive?"

"You don't."

"Not good enough."

"Hey, listen, man—"

"*You* listen, *man*," Brognola snapped. "In case you missed the point, I'm not in this thing for my health. The minute that I don't believe my family's safe, we've got no deal at all." He waited for a silent heartbeat, letting that sink in. "Now, do you put them on the line or shall I pull the plug right now?"

"You're bluffing."

"Try me."

Another hesitation, and Brognola half imagined he could see the gunner fuming, weighing odds and options, struggling to a decision that would let him save some face. His voice was taut with anger when he spoke again.

"Hold on, goddammit!"

As he waited, Hal Brognola switched the telephone receiver to his other hand and wiped his sweaty palm against his slacks. The risk had been a calculated one, but he was dealing with an unknown quantity. It had been possible that his demand, his very tone, would spark a homicidal fury in the caller, push him into acting out his anger and frustration on the hostages. If it had come to that, Brognola would have been compelled to live with precious blood upon his hands, devoting every moment of his remaining life to the annihilation of the animals who had been hired to destroy his world.

But it had worked, at least so far. His reckless gamble had paid off—or would, if he could hear the voices of his family. As long as they survived, he had a reason to play along with their abductors. And the moment that he doubted their survival, as he had informed their captor, then he would have nothing left to lose.

There was a muffled rustling as the other telephone was lifted, passed from hand to hand. Something broke inside him at the sound of Helen's voice as she pronounced his name.

"Hal? Are you there?"

"I'M HERE."

She heard his pain and longed to reach for him, to clasp his big hands tightly in her own and make him smile. For now, though, it would have to be enough to hear his voice and answer when he spoke to her.

"Are you all right? The kids?"

"We're fine." The lie caught in her throat. "We miss you."

"Jesus, Helen—"

"Hal, be careful."

Even as she spoke, the blonde was reaching out to twist the telephone receiver from her trembling hands. His face was livid as he snarled into the mouthpiece.

"There, you satisfied?"

From where she sat, Hal's answer was inaudible, but Helen could guess the content from the furious expression on her captor's face.

"Forget it, Jack. You've wasted too much time already with this bullshit."

Another momentary silence as he listened, and his face had grown so dark that Helen thought he might be on the verge of apoplexy.

"Shit!" He held the telephone away and swiveled toward the nearest ape, on station at the bedroom door. "Bring out the others, Gino."

"Huh?"

"I said bring out the frigging others. Are you deaf, or what?"

"I hear you, man."

"Then move your ass."

The thug looked sullen as he moved to do his boss's bidding, reemerging in a moment with Eileen and Jeff. He herded them in the direction of the telephone and waited, watching, as they each communicated with their father in the fleeting time allotted. Jeff went first, projecting grim bravado, glaring at the blonde with hatred in his eyes while listening to Hal. Eileen, in turn, could barely speak at all. Fresh tears were glistening on her cheeks, and she avoided looking at her captors, whispering for Hal to please take care and watch himself. She was her father's daughter, after all, and she would not allow herself to break while he was listening.

"That's it," the blonde announced as he reclaimed the phone. "You wanna talk to anybody else, call Dial-a-Prayer. And keep the number handy while you're at it, guy. You try an' fuck me over on this deal, your little family's gonna need some prayers."

He banged the telephone receiver down and spent a moment glaring at the silent instrument, as if it might be thinking of another way to challenge his authority. When he was satisfied that he had finally achieved the final word, he turned again to Gino.

"I'm goin' out awhile, to see some people, eh? Get Carmine in here an' the two of you keep both eyes open. I don't want no fuck-ups while I'm gone."

The ape looked bored.

"Bring back some burgers, will ya?"

"Yeah, don't worry. Just remember what I said. No fuck-ups."

"Stop worrying, for Chrissake."

"I get paid to worry."

After he had gone, the import of his words hit home to Helen. He had called his two companions by their given names, uncaring that she might have heard him. That presented her with two alternatives: the names were either aliases, which struck her somehow as unlikely, or the blonde had no concern that she would later be in a position to identify his comrades. And with sudden, chilling certainty, she realized that there was only one way to ensure her silence.

He did not intend to let them live.

When he was finished with her husband—sooner, if he could persuade Hal to proceed without the reassurance of a phone call—they would be eliminated. Having served their purpose, they became disposable.

The prospect of a violent death had haunted Helen's dreams for years, but in relation to her husband, sometimes to her children. Hal had placed himself in killing situations countless times, and all his reassurances had failed to put her mind at ease, although she had become adept at hiding what she felt. In later years, as she had watched their children grow, the fears had broadened to encompass Jeff and Eileen. There were so many terrors in the world outside her home, which ranged from lethal accidents and drunken drivers to the random, senseless violence now pervasive in America. A child, especially a girl-child, was constantly at risk.

But Helen had harbored no concerns about herself until this moment, realizing now that she was marked to die. It was the rough equivalent, she thought, of having a physician look you in the eye and solemnly inform you that your tests were positive, the lump was malignant and your hours were numbered. But an illness could be treated, life extended artificially through chemotherapy and, in the last extremity, by hardware. In her present circumstance, there was no treatment to prescribe, no possibility of a remission.

It would take a miracle to save them now, and Helen's faith would not admit the possibility of intervention from an outside source. If there were any miracles, they would be manufactured by her husband . . . and she wondered for the first time in their married life if Hal was equal to the task.

For Jeff's sake, for Eileen's, she hoped that he could pull it off. There was so much of life in store for each of them, so much ahead, if they were only given half a chance.

If not, there might be something she could do herself, provided that an opportunity arose. And if all else failed, she knew she would be forced to try.

It was a mother's instinct to defend her young at any cost. While life remained they had a chance, and she would not surrender meekly to the fate these bastards had in store. Whatever else they wanted from her family, they would have to take by force.

BROGNOLA DIDN'T WASTE A MOMENT cleaning out his desk. The photographs of Helen and the kids were stowed inside his briefcase when he left the office, as were certain documents selected from the jumbled ruin of his files, but the rest was standard issue, items he could say goodbye to without regret. If he returned at some point in the future, everything would be there, and if not . . .

He found that job security, pension, carried little weight where the survival of his loved ones was concerned. If he was finally suspended, fired—if he was ultimately jailed on manufactured evidence—Brognola knew that he could live with it, provided that his wife and children were protected, safe. If they were harmed in any way, if he could find the sons of bitches who had damaged any one of them, the charges filed against him would extend beyond the fine points of corruption and into homicide.

If he could find the sons of bitches.

And he was working on a lead already, something he had picked up on the telephone. When he demanded evidence that Helen and the kids were safe, the caller had relied on someone else to fetch them, and he had called the second man by name. Though muffled, the name had sounded very much like Dino, Gino—something on those lines. It wasn't much—there had to be at least ten million guys with either of those names—but at least it was a start. He could tap into the computer, run a list of names, cross-indexed to the orgcrime files, and see what filtered out.

At least he would be doing something while he waited on the call from Leo, telling him that Striker was in town. There was a possibility that Bolan would not come. If he was caught up in a campaign, if Turrin couldn't reach him, if the enemy had finally tagged him in that endless, lethal game of hide and seek . . . God knew the soldier had sufficient problems of his own without Brognola heaping another burden on his shoulders.

But Bolan would come, if he was able. Hal was certain of it in his heart and in his gut. The Executioner would come for friendship's sake, for Helen, Eileen, Jeff, because the guy was made that way. He could no more stand back and watch an old friend's family be sacrificed than he could voluntarily desert his private war.

Hal felt a pang of guilt at using Bolan to secure and protect his own. It was Brognola's job to keep them safe from harm, and his enlistment of Mack Bolan's help was the same as confessing that he couldn't do his job. Another man might have approached the situation differently, but Hal was hemmed in by his sense of duty. He could not provide the information that his family's abductors had demanded. Hundreds of protected witnesses and scores of undercover officers would be exposed to certain death if he revealed their names or whereabouts. If he was stripped of viable alternatives, Brognola knew he would be forced to sacrifice his family in lieu of giving up those others, violating their collective trust and ruining so many lives. If it came down to that, he would accept the loss as best he could, and learn to live with grief while he spent every waking moment on the track of bittersweet revenge.

But he was counting on the Executioner to grant him some alternative, an escape hatch from what appeared to be a hopeless situation. Bolan had a knack for turning circumstances upside down, attacking hopeless problems with unique solutions. Given any chance at all, the soldier would retrieve Brognola's family—or wreak such awesome vengeance on the enemy that Hal might find some private solace in the ashes.

Gruffly he dismissed the morbid thoughts and concentrated on the image of a family reunion. He could not afford to write his family off so early in the game, when there was still a fighting chance of their recovery. He had until six o'clock, and in that time he would be scanning the computer files for any Dino/Gino sound-alikes who fit the bill.

The operation reeked of Mob involvement, and he had already put the several groups of active terrorists out of mind. Despite their tendency toward violence and abduction, none had any use for the existing roster of protected witnesses. The rare defectors, others who were brave enough to testify in trials resulting from the recent wave of urban terror, were too well-known already, marked for death on sight. As far as undercover operatives, there had been slim success at infiltrating terrorist brigades, and Justice had no agents currently in place.

It would be syndicate or nothing, and the thought did not restore Brognola's confidence. He knew the kind of talent readily available for jobs like this and realized that any one of—what, a thousand mercenary guns?—might whack his family for the hell of it, regardless of his acquiescence to demands.

So many enemies, and every one a proved killer. He could never hope to see his family alive again without a killer of his own to even up the odds.

A killer like Mack Bolan, sure.

An Executioner.

tion would be enough to ruin him if anyone was tapping in. By the very nature of the risk involved he had communicated desperation, and it wasn't Leo's style to overdramatize.

The Executioner recalled another time, in Pittsfield, when the undercover Fed had sounded equally upset. On that occasion, Turrin's wife had been abducted and held hostage by a group of renegades within the Marinello Family. The hostiles had him pegged for an informer and were planning to exert the kind of leverage that never failed. But they failed disastrously by omitting Bolan from their calculations. They had not prepared themselves for hell on earth, and in the end they were unable to stand hard before the flames.

Bolan knew Hal and Leo would brief him when they met. For now, his sole objective was to arrive at the contact point. Before he flew, a call from Kennedy had netted him the address of a town house in Georgetown, and he stopped again in Hyattsville to phone ahead, confirm that he was on the ground and homing in. The traffic worsened mile by mile, became a snarl as Bolan crossed the line from Maryland to D.C. proper. The final run to Georgetown was a short six miles, but it took the soldier forty minutes, hitting every red light on the way.

The neighborhood was quiet, stately, home to senators, diplomats and cabinet members. Turrin's safe house, purchased in the early days of the protected witness program, was a condo overlooking the Potomac, with a striking view of Arlington across the water. Bolan found a parking space and locked the Ford, secure in the knowledge that police patrols would keep the average car thief off those cloistered streets. Avoiding the flamboyance found in certain areas of Southern California, for example, the neighborhood still exuded affluence and style. His car, big enough and new enough to pass a rough inspection, would no doubt remind the neighbors of a poor relation visiting from out of town.

He crossed the sidewalk and climbed a flight of steps with decorative hedges on either side. Another moment and he would be swallowed up, invisible to neighbors on the north and south. Behind him, at a distance of some fifty yards, the

7

The charter flight dropped Bolan at an airport near the University of Maryland, three miles from Hyattsville. It offered him the dual advantages of light security and close proximity to Washington, his final Georgetown destination only ten miles as the crow flies. Bolan tipped the pilot from his war chest—heavily enough to keep him happy, not so heavily that it would set him talking in the local bars—and headed off in search of a rental car.

He would have saved an hour with a scheduled direct flight to Washington, but Bolan wasn't interested in taking chances with security. His luggage held enough assorted hardware to ignite a minor war, and he would be needing it if Leo's problem was as serious as it had sounded on the phone. Hal's problem, he corrected as he spied the Avis window. Either way it cut, he was needed, and the knowledge of a friend in danger left him no alternative.

He took a midsize Ford and stowed his luggage in the trunk then retrieved the Beretta 93-R with its shoulder rigging, tucking it beneath his jacket as he slid behind the wheel. A roadside turnout halfway into Hyattsville provided Bolan with an opportunity to slip on the rigging, and he felt better as he nosed the Ford back into traffic. Whatever happened next, he was prepared to answer fire with fire. No longer feeling naked, vulnerable, Bolan focused upon his mission in D.C.

There had been no time for elaboration on the telephone, no inclination for Sticker to discuss his business on an open line. The urgency was obvious, and Bolan knew it was not in Leo's nature to exaggerate. The open conversa-

dark Potomac swept along its timeless course, conveying passengers and cargo toward the sea.

The town house was defensible, he saw at once, its proximity to the adjoining structures limiting the opposition's angle of attack. Determined shock troops, striking with the full advantage of surprise, could storm the place, but they would pay a price in blood before they cleared the windows. Aside from that, the first barrage would send the neighbors into shock and have them reaching for their telephones to call the police.

The uniformed response to any shooting call in Georgetown would be swift, decisive. Washington had heard enough of senators attacked while walking to and from the parking lots around the Capitol. Determined to survive with dignity, despite the proximity of reeking ghettos and a violent crime rate equal to some cities twice her size, the seat of government was going hard.

The soldier wondered if it might be too late.

He knocked and waited for a moment, hearing footsteps from within and standing tall before the unobtrusive spy hole mounted in the center of the door. Leo fumbled with the double lock then stood before him, grinning weakly.

"Hey, long time."

They shook hands warmly, then the soldier followed him inside.

"Looks cozy."

"It'll do." He hesitated, finally beckoning the Executioner to follow him. "I'm glad you could make it."

"I'll pretend I didn't hear that, guy."

The sunken living room was on their left as Dolan followed Leo down a narrow hallway. Hal Brognola rose to greet them, setting down his whiskey glass. Bolan shook his hand then sat down beside him on a sofa facing picture windows, which were curtained now against the threat of prying eyes.

"You made good time," Brognola said.

"I caught a charter." Bolan cleared his throat, aware that there was no time to be wasted on preliminary small talk. "So, let's have it."

And Brognola gave it to him, everything that had happened in the hours since he signed off work on Friday evening. Bolan took it in, refraining from the vacuous commiseration that does nothing to relieve the suffering of the bereaved. He understood Hal's pain, had been there—and beyond—on more than one occasion, and he knew that what Brognola needed at the moment was decisive action to retrieve his loved ones. Platitudes and sympathy were useless in the present situation. If he couldn't get the big Fed's family back, his most sincere condolences wouldn't be worth a damn.

"No progress on the name?"

It was a long shot, almost laughable, and when Brognola shook his head, the Executioner felt no surprise.

"It's hopeless. I've got seven different guys who might be 'Gino' in the local Family alone. That's seven guys we know about, and never mind the other Families from coast to coast."

"You have some reason to believe it's national?"

"I haven't got the faintest fucking notion *what* it is," Brognola said, disgusted with himself. He downed his whiskey and started for a refill, then thought better of it and pushed back the empty glass.

The Executioner relaxed a bit. Despite his pain Brognola was maintaining self-control. A lesser man, with booze at hand, might have been verging on unconsciousness by now.

"Let's call it local for the moment," Bolan said. "What's going on that might provoke this kind of action?"

Leo glanced at Hal and answered for his boss.

"I'm running down a drug connection that involves some congressmen. It's youngbloods, mostly, but we've locked in on a heavy name or two along the way."

"How strong is the connection?"

"That's the problem. We can prove possession based on what we have right now. I've got a junior senator set up to fall for dealing. As for the supplier..."

"Is there any doubt?"

He shook his head.

"No doubt at all, except we haven't got a thing to hang indictments on. This time next month we might be ready for arrests."

It was a tantalizing lead, but years of jungle warfare had conditioned Bolan to search for hidden traps before he forged ahead.

"I understand that Gianelli's still in charge."

"You called it."

"And he has some difficulties at the moment?"

Turrin smiled.

"What Nicky has right now are multiple indictments charging tax evasion, a subpoena for the President's commission and the makings of a shooting war with Cuba's finest."

"Plus your own investigation."

Leo nodded.

"Right."

"So there's a motivation. With your witness list, he has the chance to plug some leaks and maybe win some points with other Families."

"I know a dozen capos who would kiss his ass on Pennsylvania Avenue to get those names," Brognola growled.

"And with the names of undercover officers..."

"He cripples out continuing investigations," Leo finished for him.

"So."

"It fits."

"All right, it fits," Brognola snapped. "But what about this other bullshit at the office?"

Bolan spread his hands. "Somebody wants that information," he reiterated. "Call it Gianelli for the moment. But he also wants you out, discredited before you have a chance to blow the whistle. As it is, you'll be suspected of delivering the information for a price. Two birds with one stone, Hal. Case closed."

"Okay, so what's the answer?"

Bolan's smile was thin, devoid of warmth. "The shortest route is still a straight line," he replied. "Remember Boston?"

Something dark and fearful flickered in Brognola's eyes. "It's not the kind of thing you're likely to forget."

"I'm turning on the heat, beginning now. Let Gianelli simmer for a while and see what comes up to the top."

"I may not have a while," Brognola told him earnestly. "They're calling me at six, remember?"

Bolan checked his watch. "Go home and wait. Hang tough. No matter what they say, you need more time. If the snatch and frame-up are connected, then they have to know you're working with a handicap."

"My family..."

"Is safe until you make delivery."

And even as he spoke, the soldier wondered if his words were true. There was no guarantee that someone on the firing line would not get hinky, blow it in an angry moment. Hal Brognola knew it too, but in the absence of alternatives he would be forced to follow Bolan's lead.

"All right."

"With any luck, I should have time to make a tag or two before you take that call."

Brognola cleared his throat, his weathered face a study in anxiety. "You've got another stop to make," he told the soldier haltingly. "Somebody wants to see you."

Bolan stiffened. "Come again?"

"The Man is anxious for a face-to-face. He's waiting for my call."

The soldier shook his head. "No good. We've played that scene before."

It was as if Brognola's frown were etched in stone. "He's given me two days. The sit-down was his price."

"You made the deal. You call it off."

"I can't do that. Considering the so-called evidence, this meeting is the only thing that's kept me on the street. You need me on the outside if we're going to make this work."

And Bolan couldn't get around his logic. The abductors would not deal with intermediaries if Brognola was arrested. Bolan needed time in which to rattle cages, turn the heat up under Nicky Gianelli and his outfit, but the time could only be obtained through Hal's negotiations with the enemy. If he should disappear, break contact suddenly, his family was as good as dead.

The news of an impending sit-down with the President had taken Leo Turrin by surprise, as well. Before the Executioner could grudgingly consent, the former mafioso blurted out a cautionary warning.

"I don't like it," he declared. "It's got the makings of a setup."

Bolan smiled. "I don't think so," he said at last. "Okay, confirm the meet and give me the coordinates. I want it somewhere public, where I won't get claustrophobia."

"No problem." Hal was on his feet, already moving toward the kitchen and the telephone. He hesitated in the doorway, cleared his throat again. "Uh, Striker..."

Bolan heard it coming, moved to squelch the words of gratitude. "It's premature," he said. "Let's see what happens."

With a thoughtful nod, Brognola disappeared. A moment later they heard his muffled voice in conversation on the telephone.

"I didn't know about this meeting," Turrin told him.

"Forget it. If the Man was working on a scam, he'd have the troops outside right now. I'm just concerned about the wasted time."

And time was one commodity that they were short of at the moment, Bolan realized. Within the hour, Hal would be receiving his instructions for delivery of the information, stalling if he could, and listening to threats against his family. The Executioner had never seriously entertained the thought that Hal would fold, deliver names of undercover officers and witnesses in hiding, but he was afraid of the alternatives. The guy might crack, agree to the delivery with an eye toward laying hands on someone he could squeeze for information. In his emotional state, Brognola might react with violence that would doom himself and seal his family's fate—unless he had the nerve to sit and wait, ride out the threats and anything that followed, placing all his faith in Bolan and the Executioner's ability to turn the heat on his enemies.

There was an outside chance that Gianelli's family had no hand in the abduction, but it didn't matter in the long run. Nothing on this scale could happen in a capo's jurisdiction if he had not granted his approval. Gianelli was the key, regardless of his personal involvement in the plot. If he was innocent, so much the better; it would make him that much more inclined to cut his losses and reveal the guilty parties once he felt the heat of Bolan's wrath.

Whoever was behind the scam, they had been making use of Gianelli's Washington connections, and from all appearances the tentacles at Justice had been long enough to touch Brognola where he lived. It would be part of Bolan's mission to identify those tentacles, to search them out and sever them before their probing grip became a stranglehold.

If he was not too late.

The recent revelations of corruption in the FBI and NSA had shaken confidence in national security, but random spies imparting information to the Soviets were few and far between. The greater risk by far was the domestic threat of infiltration and subversion by the native cannibals who had so much to gain by undermining honest government: the lobbyists who lavished cash and gifts on pliant legislators; corporation presidents who kicked through with illegal contributions in the nick of time; the manicured mobsters standing ready with their payoffs and assorted favors in return for service rendered—venal politicians, outlaw businessmen, and gangsters fattening on both.

But it was not the soldier's mission to reform a nation, overhaul a system that had sheltered corruption from the start. His war was limited in scope, his moves restricted to the possible, and for the moment it would be enough if he could save three lives. Achieving that goal in itself might be the death of Bolan, but he meant to give it all he had.

He owed Brognola that. For all the times when Hal had risked his pension, his life, to offer aid and comfort in a lonely soldier's war against the odds. For offering an opportunity to make his war official, and for maintaining contact when the roof fell in. Beyond all that, the warrior felt a gut responsibility to strike against the cannibals wherever and whenever possible. It was his life, his reason for existence and the driving force behind his endless war.

He did not share Leo Turrin's fears about a meeting with the President. The Man would not have given Hal two days without some sense of what was happening behind the scenes. Brognola would have been in jail by now, his home and office under guard, if he had not convinced the Oval Office—at least to some small degree—that he was being framed. The President's support would soon evaporate if Hal could not produce substantial evidence.

In the meantime it was simply that the meeting struck Mack Bolan as a waste of time. He owed the President a certain debt of gratitude for setting him up in the Phoenix program, giving him the freedom to conduct his war world-wide. But any debt had long been paid in blood. He forced his mind away from April and the others, wondering precisely what the White House wanted from him. In the end, he finally decided that it would be best to wait and see.

No matter what was said or offered, Bolan's obligation of the moment was to Hal Brognola and his family. If he could not retrieve those gentle souls, his mission would be ultimately counted as a failure, and the measure of his vengeance would be nothing in comparison with Hal's traumatic loss.

If he could not secure the safety of Brognola's wife and children, scourge the animals who had abducted them, his presence in D.C. was nothing but a hollow mockery.

And he was wasting precious time.

But before he moved against the enemy, he had a date to keep.

Mack Bolan braced himself to meet The Man.

8

Susan Landry pushed her chair back from the computer keyboard, stretching as she double-checked the paragraph that she had just completed on the monitor. She caught a typo and deleted it, reentered the proper spelling of the word and thanked her lucky stars again that she had purchased the machine. With its many functions, the word processor had taken half the effort out of getting stories ready for the wire. The other half, of course, was still the digging—good old-fashioned legwork, phonework, or whatever—and she doubted whether any new technology would ever help reporters cover that end of their beat.

In fact, she loved the work involved in digging out a story. Though she would complain about it with the best—comparing blisters, insults, the occasional menacing letter—she thrived on the research, the intrigue involved in rooting out corruption, searching for the dirty laundry. It was something she excelled at, and the knowledge of her own ability provided confidence required for tackling the tough—and sometimes dangerous—assignments.

There might be nothing dangerous per se about her latest story, but it was important to her all the same. It had begun with scrawled, anonymous complaints, alleging criminal mistreatment of the residents at certain D.C. nursing homes. A string of interviews with residents, beneath the watchful eye of smiling nurses, had done nothing to substantiate the stories. But an off-the-record conversation—and a strictly off-the-record payment—with a member of the cleaning staff at one facility had cast a different light upon the scene. Provided with a suitable inducement, her informant had agreed to take a camera inside the rest home where he was employed. His photographic style would never rate a one-man show, but his subject matter spoke to Susan Landry's heart. Police were studying the photos now, together with a tape that her informant had secured while wired for sound, but she was not inclined to wait for the indictments. UPI was waiting for her lead and talking a potential series. The police would have to watch her dust.

The piece was small compared to other stories she had handled. Susan's coverage of the Cleveland underworld had flirted with a Pulitzer, and she had won acclaim for coverage of the Bolan trial in Texas. Still, the subject matter counted, meant more to her than the national exposure she was likely to receive. It mattered when her writing made a difference in the lives of people on the street, in board-rooms where the fear of media exposure made the fat cats think twice before proceeding on their merry way and trampling the little man. But Susan Landry didn't write for glory or for the recognition of a byline. Several of her hottest stories had been quietly suppressed, against her own best interests, and the Bolan trial had been a fluke.

Bolan...

She thought about the solitary warrior often, wishing there was some way she could tell his story to the world. A part of it had surfaced after Cleveland, rising from the ashes of her own irrevocably altered life, but she had so much more to say about the man. So much that she could never say in public.

He had saved her life on two occasions: once in Cleveland, and again in Washington, before the roof fell in on Bolan's supersecret operation with the government. Each time the guy had risked his own life to pull her out of jeopardy created by her innate curiosity. She would be dead now if it was not for the man in black, but there was nothing she could say or do to repay that debt.

In Cleveland he had saved her from the syndicate; in Washington, from strung-out members of a street gang on the payroll of some renegades at the CIA. The shock waves from his D.C. operation had produced some changes in the

Company, but they had also left Mack Bolan once more on the outside, looking in. She wasn't privy to the fine points of his previous arrangement with the government, the price that he had doubtless paid through loss of freedom in return for coming in from the cold. But Susan knew that there had been a hefty price tag on his leaving. She had gleaned from fragments of unguarded conversation that a part of Bolan's heart, a portion of his soul, had been severed, left behind when he was banished from Stony Man.

No, scratch that. The soldier had not been expelled. From all accounts—and there were precious few available—the choice to leave had been his own. If Bolan was in exile now, the penalty was self-imposed, and Susan knew that he would live with it the way that he had lived with being hunted like an animal throughout his early war against the Mafia. From what she gathered off the wires, that war was still in progress, and the Mob was having no more luck at pinning Bolan down today than in the bad old days.

They had come close in Texas with their scheme to put the guy on trial for murder, pin him up in jail where he would be an easy mark for assassination or where he would doubtless find himself condemned to execution for his "crimes." It had been close, but even in a cage, the Man from Blood would never be an easy mark. The trial had been an education in itself, but sudden violence had disrupted the proceedings prior to the delivery of a verdict. Susan wondered what the decision might have been, but the presiding judge steadfastly fended off requests for interviews. If he had come to a decision in the Bolan case, he seemed determined that it would not surface in the headlines.

She thought about the last chaotic moments of the trial in Texas. Bolan had been marked for murder in the courtroom, with assassins salted through the spectators and others waiting on the street outside. But in the final moments he had not been alone. With cameras excluded from the courtroom, there had been no photographs of Bolan's comrade, and the sketchy "artists' renderings" reminded Susan Landry of a Saturday cartoon. She had observed the action from a ringside seat, had passed within ten feet of Bolan's young compatriot as he sat taking notes, a Press badge pinned to his lapel. She had not seen him since, might never cross his path again, but if she did . . .

And maybe Bolan wasn't out there on his own, alone against the overwhelming odds. Perhaps he had a friend— or two, or three—to stand beside him when the flames were licking at his ankles. But she was wrong again, and recognized the fact before the thought was fully formed. The soldier never lost sight of his goals. And if his goals were ultimately unattainable . . . well, he would persevere in any case. It was the very definition of a hero and, in Susan Landry's eyes, Mack Bolan fit the bill.

It wouldn't do for Susan to express herself in print—the wires and major magazines were known to frown on editorials romanticizing "common criminals"—but in her heart she knew that there was nothing common in Mack Bolan's private war. Someday, somehow, she might be able to describe the man as she had known him, make the reading public understand the driving force, the dream, behind his long crusade. Despite their relatively short acquaintance, Susan felt that she could see inside the warrior—one facet of the man, at any rate—and understand what made him tick. The truth was painful in its brutal simplicity.

He was *decent*, nothing more nor less. Too decent for the modern world, perhaps, and certainly too decent to permit the savages, the cannibals to go about their business unmolested. He attacked the enemy because he had to, and because he had the skills required to make it stick. When courts of law broke down and justice failed, when predatory animals were circling their prey, the Executioner stood ready to exterminate the vermin, to restore a measure of security, of sanity to daily life inside the urban jungle. Having seen him work, and having shifted from the opposition's viewpoint to the status of an unabashed admirer, Susan Landry knew that Bolan's contribution was important, even vital to the maintenance of civilized society.

Someday, somehow, the world would see Mack Bolan through her eyes. She only hoped that he would be around to share her vision, and to realize precisely what he meant to one reporter in D.C.

The telephone disturbed her private reverie, and Susan got it on the second ring. She recognized the voice at once, a junior officer at Justice who had given her some leads from time to time. The guy had trouble understanding why her gratitude had never been expressed in bed.

"How are you?" Friendly, but with distance that would let him know his place.

"We're jammed up to the rafters, but I thought you'd want to know about your friend."

Alarm bells chimed softly in the back of Susan's mind. "Which friend is that?"

"Brognola."

"What about him?"

"Hey, I guess you really haven't heard."

"What's going on?"

"Perhaps we could discuss it over dinner?"

"Sorry, I'm on deadline. Now, if you've got something for me..."

"Always."

Angry now. "I don't have time for this. If you have nothing more to say—"

"Okay, okay." A note of petulance, the little boy rejected once again. "Brognola's busted."

"What?"

He sounded satisfied with her reaction. "Well, they haven't reeled him in, but it's inevitable. We've got evidence that puts him in the middle of a major orgcrime leak."

"What kind of evidence?"

"That's need-to-know right now, but take my word for it, he's history. They've got him on administrative leave right now."

Her mind was racing, trying to make sense of the ridiculous. Brognola leaking classified material about the syndicate? Perhaps receiving payoffs? It was ludicrous, yet if Justice was anticipating an indictment...

"Listen, I appreciate the tip. I owe you one."

"Say, that's more like it. We could—"

Susan cradled the receiver, cutting off his pitch and letting him romance the dial tone while she tried to grasp the full significance of what he had revealed. It was bizarre enough for Hal to be suspected of disloyalty, but for the brass to formally relieve him, something more than scuttlebutt must be involved. It would be Susan's job to trace that something else, to run it down and find out what was happening before her competition caught the scent and started nipping at Brognola's heels. With any luck she might find some way to assist him in exposing what was clearly a mistake, or worse.

Except there might be no mistake, she realized. The allegations might be true, and God knew stranger things had happened in the past twelve months, with G-men, military officers, their families, all dealing secrets to the Soviets. She knew that *anything* was possible, and yet . . .

Not Hal.

The lady knew it with a certainty that was rooted in her soul. The only problem now was proving what she knew, unearthing evidence that would support her instincts, her beliefs.

And Susan would begin her search, as always, at the source.

"I DON'T LIKE THIS."

It was as close as he would come to arguing with Bolan once the big guy's mind was set, but Leo Turrin had to air his apprehension as he pushed the station wagon north along Wisconsin Avenue in the direction of Bethesda, Chevy Chase and points north.

"Don't worry."

Bolan's voice betrayed distraction, and Turrin couldn't blame him. He was cruising toward a sit-down with the man who had once pardoned him, and then invoked the hit-on-sight directive that prevailed since Bolan's exit from the Phoenix Program. Anything could happen, and despite his faith in Bolan's judgment, Leo did not share his confidence in secondhand "official" guarantees. They might be walking into one hell of a setup, and in spite of his misgivings—

no, because of them—he had insisted on providing Bolan with some backup for the meet. He wasn't sure what would happen if they should be met by someone other than the President—by marshals armed with riot guns and M-16s, for instance—but the veteran lawman would not let his friend go down without a fight.

In some ways, it reminded Turrin of the old days, walking into danger situations with the man in black beside him, risking everything on some fantastic run against the odds. They had survived, incredibly, to fight again. But it was different now. If there was trouble this time, Leo's enemy would be the very government that he had served since he enlisted with the First Marine Battalion and shipped out to Vietnam. And if it came to killing, Leo knew that Bolan would not fire a shot at any lawman who acted under orders. He would be a sitting target for the firing squad.

And if that happened, Turrin didn't know how he would react. The marshals wouldn't recognize him, wouldn't know that he was on the payroll, and his own reaction might become superfluous if they were shooting first and asking questions later. Leo knew he might be driving toward his death, but he could no more turn his back on Bolan now than he could voluntarily stop breathing. They were in this thing together, both of them for Hal.

A nagging apprehension had already taken root in the back of Leo's mind, subverting his determination with the message that their mission was a bust, that Brognola's family had no chance whatsoever of surviving their encounter with the Mob. They might be dead already, and most certainly they would not be released to Hal, potential witnesses at large who might exonerate Brognola, turn the spotlight back upon the syndicate. It would be lunacy to let them go, and while the leaders of the syndicate were always savage, sometimes less than brilliant, they were far from being idiots. The man who released Brognola's family, with everything to lose and nothing positive to gain, would have to be a fool.

If Bolan bought it in the coming hour, at his meeting with the President, Hal's family was doomed. It would require a special touch to bring them out of this alive, and Bolan had that touch, in spades. The little Fed had seen him shake the very walls of Castle Mafia, not once but time and time again. His reputation was enough to rattle certain ranking mafiosi, and the ones who weren't afraid of him had never seen the guy in action.

It would be Turrin's job to see that Bolan was not betrayed before he left the starting gate. And if his sit-down with the Man turned out to be a gun-down with a troop of marshals in attendance, well, then Sticker would be forced to offer some diversion while the Executioner withdrew, intact. It was that simple.

Sure.

Like juggling bottles full of nitroglycerin, or playing hopscotch on the high wire, minus safety net.

If he was driving Bolan into peril, it was Leo's task to see him safely out the other side, no matter what it cost him privately. It was the least he could do for someone who had saved his life, more times than he could count.

He owed the warrior that.

And if the sit-down fell apart, it would be time to pay his debts in full.

The former capo prayed that Hal was right in his assurance of a safe, protected meet. If he was wrong, how would Brognola live with the knowledge that his plight had sent the soldier to his death? How would he live at all if Bolan bought it at the sit-down, if he never had the chance to attempt to rescue Helen and the kids?

Too late to think about it now. In a few more minutes they would be coasting into range of the rendezvous. Another block, and there would be no turning back. He fought an urge to park the station wagon, or to turn around and power out of there before the trap could close around them.

Too late.

Committed, Leo held the station wagon steady, eyes alert for any sign of tail cars in the rearview mirror. He was in for the duration, and with any luck at all, he would be sitting down with Angelina later in the evening, thankful that his world was safe and sound, his family secure.

But he could not escape the nagging apprehension that his luck was running out.

9

Leo Turrin parked the station wagon on a narrow side street off the western fringe of Rock Creek Park. Directly opposite and half a mile away on the far side of the park, stood the Walter Reed Army Medical Center. Somewhere in between, inside the park itself, Mack Bolan had a scheduled meeting with the Man.

In preparation for the sit-down, he removed the sleek Beretta from its shoulder rigging and handed the weapon to Turrin.

"You might want to think about that," Leo grumbled.

Bolan shook his head. "I'm here to talk."

The little Fed did not appear to be convinced. "Well, listen, if you're wrong..."

"Do nothing," Bolan told him flatly. "If it sounds like I've run into trouble, start the car and drive away."

"Goddammit, Sarge..."

"Whichever way it goes, you're out of here in thirty minutes. Understood?"

"I should be going in there with you."

"Thirty minutes."

"Yeah, all right, I get the message."

Bolan rested one big hand on Leo's shoulder. "Watch yourself."

"Let's try, 'I'll see you later.'"

"Sure."

He closed the station wagon door, waited for a taxi and a family sedan to pass before he crossed the street. The park was green, inviting, but the Executioner could not suppress a certain apprehension. It could be a jungle as easily as it could be a playground, and he knew that Leo could be right. The marshals might be waiting for him, riflemen positioned for effective cross fire. It would be so easy, if the President had set him up.

No altruist, the soldier still believed in certain basic values. Duty. Justice. Honor. And responsibility. Those ancient concepts had determined Bolan's course of action when he had returned from Vietnam to find his family in ruins. Those same ideals had brought him back to Washington, the scene of other conflicts in his never-ending war, and they would keep him here until his job was finished—or until somebody dropped him with a well-placed bullet.

It could go either way, right now or in the coming hours. Bolan knew the odds, and he had been prepared for death since his arrival in the Southeast Asian hellgrounds. Nothing that had happened since had shaken his resolve to see his duty through.

But there were other duties, too. Responsibilities to friends, and to the country that had nurtured him. His parents had deserted other homelands for the shining promise of America, had borne their children here, and they had seen their dreams turn into dust, the promise nullified by savages who lived outside the law. Mack Bolan had a duty to that dream, to generations yet unborn, and he would serve their cause with every fiber of his being.

His meeting with the President was an unwelcome interruption of the soldier's newest life-and-death campaign. Each moment counted now, for Hal Brognola's family. But Hal had called the play and seemed intent on going through with his end of the bargain. Bolan would accommodate his friend to a point, but the Executioner did not believe that anything would come of his discussion with the chief of state. They understood each other well enough, and neither of them would be able to back down, reject his own responsibilities in favor of a compromise.

The President was not Mack Bolan's enemy, per se. He had responded to the Stony Man debacle with restraint, compassion and a willingness to see the Phoenix Program forge ahead once the battle smoke had cleared. It had not been the President's idea for Bolan to sever all—or almost all—official ties. The Executioner had simply realized that he could not wage war effectively beneath the government umbrella, bound to systems and superiors that made his lightning war a clumsy juggernaut.

Early in his war against the Mafia, the media had spoken of Mack Bolan as a "one-man army." There were implications that he thrived on loneliness, existed for the thrill of battle and sustained himself, like Dracula, on the blood of fallen enemies. The truth was rather different, but in one respect, the media reports were accurate. He fought a one-man war—when and where he could—and there had been no room for armies of supporting personnel in Bolan's scheme of things. The vision of an army at his back had been intoxicating, coming off his long last mile against the Mafia and reeling from a week of constant contact with the enemy, and he could not deny the victories that had been captured by the Phoenix Project.

Neither could he venture to deny the costs.

From the initiation of his private war, the soldier's greatest fear had been the sacrifice of allies who enlisted in his fight. The bloody roster haunted Bolan's dreams. So many lives cut short in pursuit of one man's own quixotic quest. How many times had Bolan sworn off the enlistment of another ally in his war? How many times had brutal circumstances forced him to recant that pledge? The list of dead and wounded, from his first campaign in California to the Stony Man disaster, was as long as Bolan's strong right arm. There had been others since his exit from the program, might be more before the day was out, but now the soldier had some measure of control regarding those who joined his war.

The men of Phoenix Force and Able Team, secure and satisfied beneath the wing of Phoenix, had elected to remain and fight their battles from within the system. Bolan could respect their stand, remembering that it had been his own not long ago, but there were always choices to be made. And for Mack Bolan, the decision had been simple, inescapable, inevitable. He was meant to wage his war on private terms, according to the rules established by his enemies.

The Secret Service agents met him fifty yards inside the park. There were three of them, all Robert Redford lookalikes in charcoal suits and mirrored aviator glasses, wearing tiny microphones like hearing aids. The flankers both held mini-Uzi submachine guns underneath their coats and took no pains to hide the weapons from Bolan. Their companion and apparent leader stood before him empty-handed, but his jacket was unbuttoned, granting easy access to the Magnum handgun nestled beneath one arm.

The soldier waited while they frisked him, examined the contents of his pockets and exchanged cautious glances when they found the empty shoulder rigging.

"You alone?"

Bolan smiled. "It looks that way."

If they were watching the perimeters they would have spotted Leo, marked him for an easy drop if he attempted to approach the meeting point or otherwise encroach upon the park. If they were unaware of him, it was not Bolan's job to point him out.

The leader stepped back and spoke into a small transmitter clipped to his lapel. A moment passed before he got his answer, and then he nodded to the gunners flanking Bolan.

"It's all right," he told them, turning toward the Executioner. "Let's go."

The gunners stayed behind, securing their backtrack, while the odd man out proceeded eastward, leading Bolan through some hedges, down a grassy slope, to intersect a narrow, curving drive. A limousine was waiting for them there, with three more 'Robert Redfords' standing watch around it. Bolan recognized the model at a glance, but there was something missing, and it took a moment for him to decide precisely what was lacking from the picture.

Presidential seals.

The limo's occupant was incognito, and while any resident of Washington would recognize the Secret Service escort at a glance, there were too many limousines in town for this one to attract undue attention on the highway. With the tinted windows, standard plates and lack of fender-mounted flags, the vehicle might have belonged to any diplomat or wealthy politician in the District.

Bolan let himself relax a fraction. If the Man had meant to have him taken out on sight, there would have been more gunners in the trees, and he would never have survived this far. He felt the agents watching him, their fingers itching for the draw, but he ignored them, willed his knotted stomach to unwind. It was a simple sit-down.

Except that he would be unarmed, conversing with the President of the United States, surrounded by the palace guard.

The nearest agent cut in front of Bolan, reaching out to catch the door and open it, retreating as the soldier slipped inside the limousine. A sidelong glance through sound-proof glass revealed another agent in the driver's seat, eyes forward, both hands planted firmly on the wheel. Beside him, also facing forward, was a slender, nondescript accountant-type, a heavy briefcase resting on his lap.

"My bag man, so to speak." The President was smiling, but the smile was strained. "I can't leave home without him."

"Mr. President."

"Good evening, Colonel...no, I guess it isn't Colonel Phoenix, is it? Well, good evening, in any case."

Outside, the shadows had begun to lengthen among the trees, but there was still an hour or more of daylight left. Inside Mack Bolan's head, the doomsday clock was ticking, and he longed to be about his business in the capital.

The President seemed ill at ease, uncomfortable in Bolan's presence, and the soldier sympathized. But he had called the meet, and he would have to carry it from here.

"I understand that you've been busy since...the last time we talked."

"Yes, sir."

"I wanted to inform you, for the record, that we weren't behind that business down in Texas."

"I'm aware of that, sir."

"You're aware that I've already spoken to your friend about his family."

Bolan nodded, waiting.

"This is a disgusting business. Women, children placed at risk. I've offered full assistance in recovering the hostages."

"Too risky," Bolan told him. "It's a one-man job."

The presidential frown showed more concern than irritation. "So I've been informed, and I accept the judgment of professionals. But you must realize my options are severely limited." The frown was growing deeper, cutting furrows in the famous face. "Considering the other circumstances, evidence of impropriety..."

"A frame-up, sir."

"I understand your feelings, and your loyalty does you credit. Blind faith is a luxury that I'm unable to afford."

"I've got my eyes wide open," Bolan told him, "and my vision's fine. It doesn't take an analyst to see the circumstances are related."

"I agree. But in the absence of supporting evidence on Hal—your friend's behalf..."

"You'll have the evidence you need. What *I* need now is time."

"And there's the rub." The President was looking past him, through the tinted windows, studying the trees. "I would anticipate that your solution to the problem may involve...extraordinary incidents?"

"It's possible."

"Extraordinary incidents produce extraordinary coverage by the media. Demands for action, for results. A public outcry, condemnation of police officials."

Bolan spread his hands. "I couldn't rule it out."

"That kind of bad publicity could be disastrous for your friend. It wouldn't do to clear him of corruption charges and convict him of consorting with a fugitive."

It was the soldier's turn to frown. "I only know one way to play the game and get results," he said. "I haven't got a lot of time to spare right now, and anything I do is going to happen fast. You've set a Monday deadline?"

"I've done nothing of the sort. Officially, I haven't spoken to your friend, and I most certainly have not been here with you today. If everything is status quo when he returns from holiday on Tuesday morning, fine. If not . . ."

"Whichever way it goes, it shouldn't take that long," the warrior said.

And in his heart he knew it must not take that long. Once he began to rattle cages in the capital, the enemy's reaction would be virtually immediate. Whichever way it went it should all be settled by this time tomorrow. Any effort to prolong the siege would only jeopardize the hostages, increase the odds against their safe return. Those odds were long enough already, Bolan realized, becoming impatient.

"I'm on a schedule," he informed the President, "so if there's nothing else . . ."

"Just one more thing." The voice was solemn, soft, almost a whisper now. "For some time now, I've wanted to express my personal condolences about . . . what happened in Virginia."

"That isn't necessary, sir."

"I think it is. I feel a sense of shared responsibility for . . . everything. The lapses in security—"

"Were not your ultimate responsibility," the soldier finished for him.

"Dammit, I reject that categorically. The ultimate responsibility will always rest with me, my office. I make no attempt to shirk that burden."

"Fine, if that's the way you want it." Bolan felt his irritation creeping closer to the surface.

"I believe you should reconsider coming back to Phoenix."

He had been expecting it from the beginning, and he didn't have to think about his answer. "That's impossible."

"I understand your feelings, but—"

"No, sir," the soldier cut him off, "I don't believe you do."

"All right, I had that coming. But I also have a reason for suggesting that you reconsider your decision at this time."

"There's nothing that would change my mind."

"Not even if I told you I have reason to believe that some of Farnsworth's friends are still among us? Still at the CIA?"

The warrior stiffened, one hand on the door handle. Lee Farnsworth was the ranking Agency official who had set the wheels in motion for the strike on Stony Man. He was—had been—responsible for April's death, for all the others, and upon identifying Farnsworth as his enemy, the warrior had eliminated him without compunction. After handing in his resignation from the Phoenix Program, he had executed Farnsworth in the Oval Office, with the President and Hal Brognola looking on.

"Who are they?"

"No names yet, unfortunately, but if you were back in-house..."

"That's negative. I've got a job to do already."

"Well, if you should change your mind, the option's open—but distinctly limited in terms of time."

He got the message loud and clear. If Bolan chose to spurn the offer of another governmental sanction, he could not expect a free ride over and above the business with Brognola. Fair enough. He had been warned, and it was more than he had any right to expect in the circumstances. Bolan recognized the President's dilemma, knew that he could not appear to countenance a wild-assed vigilante tearing up the streets of Washington and sniping at the CIA. Once he had settled with Brognola's enemies, if he was still alive, it would be open season on Mack Bolan once again.

"Good day, sir."

There was something close to anguish in the eyes that met and held his own. "You think about it, son. Don't throw your life away for nothing."

"Sir, it never crossed my mind."

The Secret Service agents watched him closely as he climbed out of the limousine, their shades incongruous in the descending dusk. They let him pass, but Bolan cleared the trees before he began to relax completely, part of him expecting lethal rounds to slam between his shoulder blades at any instant.

He was clear for now, but in his heart and mind the Executioner was far from being free. The mention of Lee Farnsworth and his friends at the CIA, had opened wounds and stirred old ghosts to life again. Those spirits traveled with the soldier, reaching out to touch him, whispering their message as he cleared the park.

Their message of revenge.

And there was suddenly a great deal more at stake in Wonderland than Hal Brognola's family, his twenty years at Justice. Suddenly, the memories of Stony Man, of April Rose, Konzaki and the rest were back full-force. He could not shake them off, and there was only one way that he knew of to appease their hunger.

They would need an offering of blood, and once he had secured Helen, seen Brognola's children safely home—God willing—he would turn his full attention to the hunt for Farnsworth's cronies in the Agency.

10

There is another Washington concealed behind the spit and polish of the nation's capital. In place of monuments to presidents and heroes, shabby houses testify to broken dreams; children run the streets by day and night, collecting into gangs for self-protection, striking out in anger at society's indifference. The alternate reality of Washington is rich in violence, boasting crime rates that have placed the seat of government among the ten most lethal cities in America. From time to time the mayhem overflows its teeming reservoir and laps against the steps of Congress, leaving bloody stains on Pennsylvania Avenue.

The "other Washington" does not appear in tourist guidebooks or society reviews. It may be found more often on the local nightly news in living color: scenes of savagery and desperation broadcast into stately homes ten blocks— and worlds—away. But for the most part, it is locked away behind the television screen, securely penned inside the magic box. Its horrors are transitory, simply and efficiently eradicated with a touch of the remote control.

Mack Bolan's blitz began within that other Washington. He nosed the rental Ford through streets where garish neon scarcely seemed to touch the shadows, hostile faces swiveling to watch him pass. A decade earlier, the faces would have been predominantly black, but there were Hispanics sprinkled in among them now, and Orientals, cast-off exiles from the island states of the Caribbean. A ghetto still, the other Washington had lost its ethnic unanimity, and with the change had come another rise in violent crime.

One thing about the ghetto had not changed. Its vice was still controlled by absentees who pulled the vital strings on gambling, narcotics, prostitution and pornography. The masters of corruption still went home at night to Georgetown, Arlington, Bethesda, leaving ethnic underlings to bear the heat of periodic crackdowns by police. It was a one-way street as far as profits went, the money flowing out and fattening the coffers of the syndicate. The ghetto was a major source of gangland income, and the Executioner had opted to begin his blitz by striking his opponents where it counted. Directly in the pocketbook.

The numbers bank was one flight up, above a pool hall christened Whitey's by some long-forgotten wit. Bolan drove around the block and parked the car in an alley, underneath the pool hall's rusty fire escape. No passersby had taken notice of him yet, and Bolan planned to have his business finished well before the vagrant street waifs could search out and strip the car.

He spent a moment double-checking armament before he locked and left the car. The silenced Beretta was primed and ready, nestled in fast-draw leather under Bolan's arm. The silver .44 AutoMag, Big Thunder, rode his hip on military webbing, canvas pouches stuffed with extra magazines for both guns circling his waist. He was in blacksuit, having shed his street clothes prior to strapping on the pistol belt, and hidden pockets held stilettos and garrotes, the tools of an assassin's trade.

The soldier was anticipating trouble, counting on it, but he meant to choose the time, the killing ground. There would be lookouts in the pool hall proper, ready to blow the whistle if a strange white face appeared. They would immediately realize that he was not from Gianelli's stable, and while Bolan was secure in his ability to handle sentries, he was hunting bigger game this evening. A firefight in the pool hall would delay him long enough for his primary targets to escape, and so the Executioner was opting for an alternate approach.

The fire escape was fitted with an access ladder, hinged to let it fold up underneath the bottom landing, but the rust of years had covered everything, and Bolan could not risk the screeching noise the ladder would produce on being lowered into place. Instead, he scrambled atop the rental's trunk and leaped to catch the platform overhead, suspended momentarily in space before he found the railing with his fingers, pulling up and over with the agile movements of a jungle cat. The hardest part behind him now, he knew the only other problem would be getting out alive.

Secure from prying eyes until he reached the lighted window that he had selected as his point of entry, Bolan took the metal steps by twos, the lethal 93-R in his hand, prepared to meet all challengers. When he was halfway up, the soldier hesitated, scanned the alley one more time in search of errant witnesses, found none and forged ahead.

The target window stood half-open to the night, and Bolan watched the men inside, taking stock and catching fragments of their conversation. They were four in all—three black, one white—and there could be no doubt as to the man in charge. Without a second glance, the warrior knew that Whitey's was precisely what the name implied, regardless of the clientele downstairs.

A burly mobster sat behind the battered desk, counting stacks of money, riffling the bills between his fingers, thick lips moving as he verbally kept track. His shirt-sleeves were rolled up around his elbows, baring massive forearms bristling with hair and mottled with tattoos. His sport coat had been draped across the back of a chair, and he wore a snub-nosed Smith & Wesson .38 beneath his arm.

His three companions lounged in straight-backed chairs and watched the count with hungry eyes, unspeaking. They were dressed like sideshow hucksters: velvet coats and wide-brimmed hats, pegged trousers tapered at the ankles over pointy patent-leather shoes. Draped in chains of gold, the black trio fairly sparkled in the light from naked ceiling fixtures, their fingers glittering with diamonds in a tribute to conspicuous consumption. On the streets they would be viewed with awe as masters of the brute survival game, the men to watch and emulate, but they had come to see their master here, and they kept silent as the mafioso struggled to laboriously count his tribute.

Bolan crouched to take advantage of the partly open window, bracing his Beretta in a double-handed grip and sighting down the slide. Four targets, but he meant for one of them to live and carry word of his encounter with the Executioner. It mattered little to him which one of the runners should survive. But Bolan had already taken stock of who should die.

The hood behind the desk was his immediate concern, the holstered .38 most easily accessible of all the weapons in the room. His runners would be armed, but they would have to fumble under jackets, their reactions hampered by the Executioner's advantage of surprise. And Bolan had another reason for selecting their superior as first to die: it would be doubly galling for a thug like Gianelli to receive the news of his impoverishment from a subordinate outside the Family.

The Executioner's finger tightened on the trigger. The Beretta sneezed, and he was tracking on in search of other targets, wasting no time on assessment of the shot. Round one impacted on the mafioso's upper lip and punched on through, the fleshy face imploding like a rotten gourd, a spout of blood erupting from the wound.

The runners recoiled, scrambling from their chairs and digging under velvet coats for hardware. One of them had spotted Bolan in the window, pointing dumbly, struggling to voice a warning. Round two exploded in his face and pitched him backward, long legs flailing as his wide-brimmed hat took flight.

The second runner had a weapon in his hand, but no time left to use it. Bolan shot him twice, in the chest and throat, before the guy could bring his gun to bear. He saw the life wink out behind dull eyes, the lanky carcass folding in upon itself, and he was tracking onto number three before the second runner's legs gave way.

The final target had already opted for retreat, no longer trying for his side arm as he pounded toward the door. A parabellum round behind the knee was all it took to break his stride, but the momentum sent him into crushing impact with the door. The guy rebounded, leaving bloody traces of himself behind as he collapsed onto the threadbare carpet.

Before he could recover, Bolan entered through the window, crossed the office to unlatch the door and peer outside. A murky stairwell granted access to the billiard parlor below, and he could hear the voices of the regulars, their laughter floating up the stairs. No sign of any scouts attempting to investigate the noise upstairs, no indication that the troops had heard a thing.

He closed the door again, relieved the sole survivor of his .38 and backtracked toward the desk. Between the leaking mafioso's feet he found an empty satchel and began to fill it with the greenbacks from the desktop. He was nearly finished when the wounded runner groaned, a signal that the guy was wrestling his way to consciousness.

The soldier knelt beside him, waiting for his eyes to focus on the face of death. The runner's eyes crossed as the Beretta's muzzle came to rest upon his nose.

"I'm back," the warrior told the trembling thug. "Somebody has the merchandise I want. Somebody should deliver while they can."

"Hey, man, I swear to God—"

"Shut up and listen!" Bolan punctuated the command with his 93-R, tapping it against the guy's forehead. "Your job is to spread the word. You start with Gianelli, and you tell it straight. Somebody should deliver while they have a chance."

"I got it, man, I swear." The beads of sweat were standing up like marbles on his forehead now. "I'll tell 'im."

Bolan left as he had entered, scrambling down the fire escape until he reached the bottom landing, swinging out across the rail and dangling a moment prior to letting go. He stowed the satchel in the rented car's trunk and locked it down, secure as it could be while he was on the warpath.

There was something like a quarter-million dollars in the satchel, no big thing to Gianelli, but still substantial when considered on its own. The capo could afford it, Bolan knew; what he could not afford would be the loss of face, the sheer indignity of being ripped off. The insult would be worse than any loss of income, any loss of life. And Gianelli would receive his message, the Executioner was sure of it.

The would-be boss of Wonderland would read him loud and clear.

FRANCESCO SCOPITONE HAD NOT answered to his given name in twenty years. His friends, acquaintances, police detectives and the like all knew him more familiarly as Frankie Scopes. And sometimes when he wasn't listening, the more courageous or foolhardy called him Frankie Scars.

The nickname was a natural, but its careless use could lead to fatal accidents. No matter that the history of Frankie Scopes's disfigurement was common knowledge. He preferred to act as if the scars did not exist, and his associates who planned on staying alive had grasped the wisdom of incurring temporary blindness in his presence.

Frankie Scars had been a handsome boy in childhood and on through adolescence, but like countless other boys his age, he had been drawn to the fraternity of street gangs, petty crime that sometimes escalated into brutal warfare. On the evening of his eighteenth birthday, Frankie's clique, the Gladiators, had collided with the Saracens—a rival gang— in mortal combat. Three boys died before police arrived, and Frankie had been slashed across the face, bone deep from ear to ear, emerging with a grisly, twisted smile that wrapped halfway around his skull.

The county doctors had advised him to consider plastic surgery, but Frankie's family had been poor. With seven mouths to feed and frequent bouts of unemployment, Frankie's father had ruled out expensive medical procedures. By the time he was old enough and rich enough to make arrangements on his own, it had become a point of honor to retain the scars and challenge any living soul to mention his disfigurement. Within the syndicate and on the streets, his brute ferocity was legendary. Homicide detectives in New York and Washington suspected Frankie Scars of intimate involvement in at least a dozen homicides, but witnesses were an endangered species, and the mutilated thug had never come to trial.

In recent years his business was narcotics. Murder was a necessary adjunct to the business or, some said, a sweet fringe benefit that Frankie Scars enjoyed. Unauthorized competitors could normally expect a single warning, often painful and humiliating; if they failed to take the hint they were assassinated publicly or else they simply disappeared.

Lately, Frankie was considering a war against the Colombians. Conveniently amnesiac concerning his own roots, he hated foreigners with an evangelistic zeal more common to the 1920s than the mid-1980s. Frankie loathed the Cubans, the Vietnamese, the Haitians, Arabs, Mexicans and Puerto Ricans. He *especially* despised Colombians because they held a stranglehold of sorts on premium cocaine, and they refused to quake in fear at his approach. The nervy bastards seemed to thrive on violence, dealing out sadistic punishment to traitors and informers, littering the streets with bodies in a style that Frankie Scars was forced to view with grudging admiration.

Two weeks earlier he had dispatched a pair of gunners to eliminate the leader of a ring that was importing flake direct to Washington from Bogotá. His soldiers had been missing for three days before a jogger was attracted by the odor rising from the trunk of an abandoned Chevrolet in Hyattsville. Authorities had found a human jigsaw puzzle inside the trunk, bits and pieces severed, trimmed and rearranged with what appeared to be a chain saw.

It was time to teach the Indians a lesson, and the only question left in Frankie's mind concerned the where and when of the instruction. There had never been a question in his mind concerning how to do the job. Such foolish insolence could not be cured, it could only be annihilated, and the problem now was pinning down the clique, securing an address, a location, where his gunners could surprise a group of them. Nicky wouldn't like the bad publicity, but once he had a chance to think it over, he would realize that there had been no other choice. So sure was Frankie in his mind, that he had already decided to proceed without the capo's blessing.

But in the meantime there was business, product to be moved and money to be made. The world kept turning in spite of the Colombians or anybody else, and Frankie Scars was not about to let life pass him by.

Phase one of his campaign to purge the Indians was economic. In the short run he could undercut their prices, take a loss on street sales while he waited for phase two, the military phase, to coalesce. He had connections in Bolivia, and while their product couldn't hold a candle to the pure Colombian cocaine, its lower quality allowed for lower prices on the street. When the Peruvian was advertised as pure Colombian, the budget rates were even more astounding, and the customers were lining up from Constitution Avenue on back to Arlington with hands out, nostrils flared. He could supply them at the discount rates for two or three more weeks before the costs became prohibitive, and in the meantime he had spies and gunners scouring the city, searching for a target that would put them on the map.

He was expecting a delivery tonight, in fact, and had arrived an hour early at the warehouse to ensure security. The flake was coming in by truck, a dozen hefty plastic bags sewn into the upholstery of tacky furniture, three loaded chairs concealed within a shipment of two dozen. On arrival, Frankie's men would strip the chairs, retrieve the bags of crystal, stuff the chairs with pre-cut foam and ship the whole lot off to one of Frankie's discount shops in Delaware. The flake would stay behind, and by this time on Monday it would be fulfilling fantasies for congressmen and bureaucrats across the city.

Frankie checked his watch and nodded to the lookouts posted on the loading dock. The truck was due, and he would give them fifteen minutes more before he closed the warehouse, rerouting to the backup drop.

A sudden glare of headlights cut across the loading dock, and Frankie heard the truck now, engine growling, air brakes hissing as the driver put it in reverse and backed it in. The stevedores, all armed in case of unexpected trouble, were proceeding toward the dock, and Frankie followed, one hand wrapped around the roll of cash he carried in the pocket of his trench coat. He was passing through the giant doors, had one foot on the concrete apron, when the world exploded in his face.

The moving van appeared to swell before his eyes, as if it were inhaling monstrous breaths somehow, and then it detonated, roof and sidewalls peeling back along the welded seams, a fireball rolling outward and sizzling across the dock. The flames consumed his lookouts and a couple of the stevedores before the rest could scatter, left them dancing on the platform like burning puppets wreathed in flames. He was driven backward by the shock wave and the sudden heat. Automatic-weapon fire erupted from the firelighted darkness of the parking lot, precision bursts dispatching fiery dancers.

It would be the Colombians, he knew, and Frankie Scars was cursing, digging for his side arm, searching for a target in the firelight. From the shadows of the warehouse, several of the stevedores were firing blindly from the cover of a forklift, spraying useless rounds. Frankie Scars was braced to make a run for their position, take his chances with the unseen gunners in the darkness when a larger weapon coughed out there, beyond the margin of the firelight, and the forklift suddenly exploded into flames. He saw two bodies airborne, others wallowing across the pavement in a lake of fire, and something snapped inside of Frankie Scars.

He bolted, giving up his meager cover, and pounded back into the warehouse toward the distant sanctuary of his office and the weapons hidden there. He would surprise the bastards yet, if only he could get his hands on some of the artillery he kept in case of an emergency.

Before he made a dozen strides, the mobster's legs were cut from under him. He did an awkward belly flop and felt the pistol skitter from his fingers, lost before he could react. It took a moment—too damned long—for Frankie to regain the feeling in his legs, and when it hit him, there was nothing he could do but scream.

From out of nowhere one of the attackers loomed above him, reaching out and rolling Frankie over with his foot. From where he lay, the big bastard didn't look like a Colombian, all dressed in black that way, but you could never tell. The mobster's full attention focused on the cannon in his hand, and Frankie recognized it at a glance. It was a frigging M-16, with something like a stovepipe mounted underneath the barrel. He didn't have to ask the bastard what it was—not after sitting through selected clips from *Scarface* seven times.

"What the hell..."

He knew precisely what the gunner wanted, but he was intent on buying time. One of his own hitters might emerge from hiding, pop the bastard where he stood.

But no one came to rescue Frankie Scars.

The man in black crouched beside him with the muzzle of his cannon smack in Frankie's face.

"Somebody has a package that belongs to me," he said. "Somebody should deliver while they can."

"A package?"

"Spread the word."

The guy was rising, leaving. Frankie Scars could not believe that he was going to survive. He didn't understand a fucking word the guy had said, but he would spread the word, yes. They would be hearing him from hell to Sunday once somebody got him out of there, tried to save his legs. He had no wish to spend the rest of his forsaken life as Frankie Stumps.

It was eternity before he heard the sirens, heralding the swift approach of fire trucks, with an ambulance, and at the sound of their arrival, Frankie Scars wondered where he went wrong in his life.

11

Susan Landry had tried Brognola's office first and had been
advised that he was "on holiday," but she could not let it go
that easily. She had his private number, legacy of her encounter with "John Phoenix" and the Stony Man debacle,
and she dialed it from a roadside booth, surprised when Hal
had answered on the second ring. His voice was tense and
strained; he fairly snapped at her before she had a chance to
speak. Afraid that he would deny the interview immediately, she had mumbled something incoherent, hastily
apologizing for her error, hanging up and racing for her car.

The address had required more effort than Brognola's
private number, but she had a contact with Ma Bell, and she
had marked Hal's street for reference on her map before she
left the office. He would be surprised to see her, certainly;
he might demand to know how she had found him. Long
experience had taught her that it was more difficult for men
to dodge an interview in person. Even if he slammed the
door in Susan's face, there was a decent chance that some
remark would point her toward another source of information. Susan Landry recognized her personal effect on
men, and she was not ashamed of using any means at her
disposal to secure a story. She had never bargained sex for
information, but if femininity could open certain doors, so
much the better.

Everything she knew about Brognola told her he was a
devoted family man, conservative, traditional, and Susan
knew that she would have to be discreet in her approach. If
nothing else, his tone of voice had flashed a warning signal
to her, urging caution. Something had Brognola on edge,

and whether it was a suspension from his job or something else entirely, Susan realized that she could not approach the subject like a scandalmonger who wrote for one of those newspapers found at supermarket checkouts. Some sophistication was required, and Susan felt that she was equal to the task.

She found Brognola's street and made a single driveby to confirm his car was parked outside before she doubled back and nosed her Honda in against the curb. She double-checked her equipment—the compact recorder in her purse, the notebook, pens—then climbed the concrete steps to Hal Brognola's porch.

She pressed the doorbell, waited, tried a second time before she heard the cautious sound of footsteps from within. The door swung open and Brognola stood before her, looking older than the woman had remembered him from Texas, a few months earlier. The wrinkles—worry lines?— were deeply etched into his face, around his mouth, his eyes. It was the eyes that struck her hardest, peering out from under bushy brows and looking cornered, trapped.

He should remember her from Texas, from the Phoenix flameout, but the lady wasn't taking any chances.

"Susan Landry, with the—"

"Yes," he interrupted her, "I know."

"I wonder if you might have time to answer several questions."

"Questions?"

Susan noted that his eyes had shifted past her, scanning along the street in both directions. Perhaps he was expecting camera crews to spring out of the shrubbery.

"If I might just step inside . . ."

"What kind of questions?"

Fair enough. She dropped the smile and forged ahead. "It's been reported by a confidential source that you have been suspended from your post at Justice, pending an investigation into certain charges of administrative impropriety."

Brognola's smile was crooked, bitter. "I'm on holiday," he told her. "Three-day weekend."

"Any comment on the charges? The investigation?"

She was on the edge. It would be simple for him to deny the rumor, close the door and leave her standing there. It would not put her off the track, of course, but it could slow her down, and he must know as much. Another visual sweep up and down the street, and then Brognola stepped aside to clear the doorway.

"Come with me."

He closed and double-locked the door behind her, led the way along a corridor that seemed to more or less divide the house, with bedrooms on the right, the parlor, kitchen, dining room to Susan's left. He steered her toward the breakfast nook and found a stool on one side of a counter topped in decorative tile. She sat across the counter, facing him.

"What do you want to know?"

Presented thus, devoid of shadowboxing, the inquiry took her by surprise.

"I'm interested in your side of the story," Susan told him simply, settling back to wait.

Brognola mulled it over for a moment, glancing at his watch as if the time held great importance for him, and again the lady felt that he was worried by something more than the potential ruination of a proud career in law enforcement. When he spoke, the big Fed's tone was curt, his phrases clipped and economical.

"There have been certain leaks at Justice," he informed her. "Some of them in my department, some in others. You're aware of recent cases that have made the papers."

It was not a question, but she answered anyway. "Of course."

"Investigations are continuing," he told her cautiously, "and someone thinks they've got a handle on a leak inside my office."

"Your response?"

"I haven't had a chance to see the so-called evidence."

She frowned. The man was stalling, playing games. "Your personal response?"

His scowl was withering. "I categorically deny releasing any confidential information from my files at any time, except through channels duly authorized. If someone's holding evidence that points the other way, let's see it in a court of law."

"And have you been suspended?"

"Like I told you, I'm officially on holiday. Unless somebody serves a warrant, I'll be clocking in on Tuesday morning, as usual."

She tried a different tack. "How is your family reacting to the charges?"

She was startled by the sudden change in Hal, his stiffening, the pallor in his cheeks. His answer seemed to take more energy than he possessed.

"I have their every confidence," he said at last, his voice remote and somehow very sad.

Susan's instincts told her that she was within a hairbreadth of another story altogether, but she couldn't find the handle, and she had no way inside. Instead, she doubled back to the investigation.

"Any comment on the evidence compiled so far?"

He shook his head. "As I've already said, I haven't seen it yet. It will be subject to intensive scrutiny." Brognola checked his watch again. "Now, if you'll please excuse me..."

She was poised to ask another question, but her train of thought was interrupted by the telephone. Brognola jumped, and Susan would have been amused by his reaction under other circumstances. As it was, she noticed the anxiety that surfaced on his face, the hesitation as he reached for the wall phone close at hand, then stopped himself.

"Excuse me, I'll take this in the other room."

He fairly bolted from the bar stool, disappearing along the corridor in the direction of his den. The door swung shut behind him, and the telephone's third ring was severed halfway through.

Susan felt an urge, suppressed at once, to listen in on the extension. It would be an insult to Brognola and his hospitality, of course, but she was equally convinced that he would catch her at it, recognize the sound of the receiver being lifted in the breakfast nook no matter how distracted he might be.

She checked her watch and found it was one minute past six o'clock. Brognola had been waiting for a call; she realized that much from the compulsive study of his watch, his shock-reaction when the telephone had finally rung. Her reporter's instinct told her that the call had less to do with problems at the office than with something more immediate, more intimate. More painful, if it came to that.

The man was hurting, and from what she knew of Hal Brognola, it was not his typical reaction to a challenge on the job. Brognola would be angry, even outraged, at a challenge to his personal integrity, but he would come out swinging. There had been a trace of the anticipated anger in his grim determination to confront the recent charges in a court of law, but underneath the surface there had also been a trace of . . . something else.

The call was more important to Brognola than his job, and that sudden certainty left Susan Landry with a narrow range of viable alternatives. What might produce the symptoms she had witnessed in a man of proved courage and determination? Office politics was out, as well as any effort to indict him for a crime that he had not committed. The reverse side of the coin—his actual involvement with a leak of confidential information—never seriously entered Susan's mind. And what was left?

A threat against his life?

She couldn't buy it. Hal had doubtless been in dangerous situations countless times before, and from the information readily available in public files, he had revealed no trace of cowardice.

A threat against his wife and family?

The silence of the house, its emptiness, struck Susan like a fist above her heart. Hal's children would be grown, of course, away at school or off with families of their own by now, but Susan suddenly realized that she had seen no sign of another woman on the premises since she had entered.

And what was that supposed to prove? Was she expecting an Italian housewife to appear and dog Susan's footsteps through the house, encumbered by a tray of coffee, tea and cakes? So many women worked these days, so many others had a bustling schedule of activities outside the home. Why had she automatically assumed that there was something sinister about the seeming absence of Brognola's wife?

It was the kind of argument a raving chauvinist would use, where two plus two made five . . . and still, she couldn't shake the nagging apprehension fostered by the empty house. If there had been some kind of threat against Brognola's wife, he might have moved her elsewhere, seen her safe before he turned to face the enemy.

It was the kind of thing Mack Bolan would have done.

But Bolan wasn't here, she told herself, and he had no connection to the story that was brewing in her mind. If there had been a threat against Brognola's wife, his family, and if the threat could be related to his other problems on the job . . .

Before she had a chance to chase it any further, she was interrupted by the sound of footsteps in the hallway. Hal had left the study, covered half the distance to the breakfast nook before she heard him, and the lady was surprised that he could move so quietly, despite the deep-piled carpeting.

Brognola's face was haggard, drained, as he regarded Susan from the open doorway of the breakfast nook. The hasty question she was struggling to frame escaped her in an instant, and she let it go.

"Is everything all right?"

A stupid question on its face, it was the best that she could manage for the moment.

"I have things to do," he told her, speaking with the tone of someone half again his age. "If you'll excuse me now . . ."

"Of course."

There had been nothing else to say, and she was off the stool, picking up her purse and preceding Hal along the hallway toward the door. From nowhere she was stricken with a sudden sense of claustrophobia, a need to put the house behind her. Brognola's sadness and anxiety surrounded Susan like a shroud and left her feeling stifled, short of breath. She thanked him for the interview, flashed a plastic smile and had to restrain herself from bolting as he held the door.

Inside the Honda she took a moment to compose herself. There was a story here, she knew that much, but she would have to find another handle, someone other than Brognola who would grant her access to the secret. Hal was being driven by some demon he could not, *would* not reveal—but there were always other ways to crack a story, raise the stone and flush out whatever huddled underneath in darkness.

Susan Landry was a pro at lifting stones, exposing secrets. Brognola had intrigued her, put her on the scent of something dark and dangerous. His possible suspension from the post at Justice was a portion of the story, but Susan sensed that there was more. A great deal more. And she would find no peace until she knew the rest of it.

It was her job, what she did best in life. Brognola knew that much; he would expect it of her. Susan would endeavor not to hurt him, but the truth demanded periodic human sacrifice, and if a choice should be required, she had a sacred duty to perform. Exposure of the world beneath the stones, at any cost.

She gunned the Honda into life and aimed it toward the heart of Washington. Her answer, or the clues to finding a solution, would be waiting for her there. Brognola might not know it yet, but Susan Landry meant to help him if she could. And failing that, she meant to share his story with the world.

THE GUNNER'S LAST INSTRUCTIONS had been brief and to the point: "We've set the meet for midnight. It's at Arlington. You're visiting the Unknown Soldier. Bring the lists. You miss this meet, you've missed it all."

Just that. No chance to speak with Helen or his children, to verify their safety. Then a kind of menace to the buzzing dial tone until he slammed down the receiver with enough force to crack the plastic. It had taken several moments for

Brognola to recover his composure, or what little of it still remained, and he was certain Susan Landry had been picking up the bad vibrations loud and clear.

He put the reporter out of mind. Someone had obviously tipped her to the stink at Justice, and she had been following her nose. Brognola hadn't thought to ask her how she had acquired his address, and he didn't care. He had too many more important things to think about.

Like Helen, Jeff and Eileen.

They might be dead already, discarded as a hazard to security. If they were still alive, their hours would be numbered now. He could not think of any reason for the gunners to let them live past the midnight drop. Once Hal delivered—once he pulled whatever damned fool stunt his fevered mind was able to devise—they would be so much excess baggage, useless to their captors and a certain liability to any clean escape. They could be dead before he made the drop, assuming always that the gunners didn't plan to kill him, too.

It was entirely possible, of course, although the scheme struck Hal as too elaborate for an assassination. There were countless opportunities each day for a determined hitter to score: at work, in transit, at the supermarket or at home. The syndicate had never lacked in opportunities to kill Brognola, and he had to think that there was something more involved. The murder of a ranking Justice officer would generate tremendous heat, and anyone involved would have to insulate himself sufficiently before he risked the flames.

Unless the sudden shadow over Hal's career might prove sufficient to diffuse the heat, convince a cynical establishment that he had gotten only what he bargained for in dealing with the Mob. But what of his family? If he was murdered while apparently cooperating in delivery of the secret witness list, how would annihilation of his wife and children be explained?

Brognola couldn't crack the riddle, and he finally gave it up, convinced that there was some other motive in the move against his family. If only he could crack the riddle...

But he didn't have the time for puzzles now. Six hours, give or take, before he was expected to present himself at Arlington, to do or die with everything that mattered to him in the world depending on his choice of a reaction.

And the man from Justice realized that he had been engaging in some artful self-deception. Everything depended on Mack Bolan now, and nothing Brognola did would matter in the least if Bolan muffed it. The Executioner was every hope and prayer Brognola had, and the guy was out there at that very moment, kicking ass and taking names. He would be raising hell with Gianelli's troops, with anybody else who tried to block his path, and Hal could almost feel a grudging sympathy for Bolan's human prey.

Almost.

The soldier's enemies were now Brognola's enemies, as well. The violent world outside had forcibly intruded on his private space, and only a strategic escalation of the violence could secure his family's safe release. Brognola's world was resting in Bolan's hands tonight, and if the soldier fell, Brognola's universe would tumble down around him.

There was nothing he could do but wait and chart the grim alternatives that would remain if Bolan failed. If something happened to the warrior, if Brognola was compelled to face the enemy alone, he knew that he would keep the midnight rendezvous prepared to die. With nothing left to lose, aware that Helen and the kids were doomed whichever way he broke, it would be left for Hal to track the bastards on his own. He might not ever see the members of his family again, but if he lived past Arlington, if he was able to secure the identities of their abductors, he would have a short-range motive for survival till the job was finished.

As for the future... He couldn't focus on the days and weeks beyond. Reality had shrunk to the here and now; there was no future after midnight, nothing tangible beyond his scheduled face-to-face with death.

Brognola meant to keep that grim appointment, take his private pain and ram it down the throats of those who had already traumatized his world. And if it was the last thing that he ever did, well, he could live with that—or die with it—and screw the rest.

But for the moment there was Bolan, out there in the darkness, stalking.

Hal Brognola said a silent prayer for all concerned and went to clean his guns.

12

Raenelle Gireau had not been blessed with beauty. The ugly duckling of her class in any given year, she waited patiently at first, and then with mounting irritation, for the transformation that would make her into a graceful swan. Her parents and a host of doting relatives made light of her concerns, assuring her that she was a "late bloomer," destined to achieve a beauty all her own . . . in time.

But time had not cooperated, and at twenty years of age, Raenelle had finally decided that the hand of nature needed some assistance from the hands of man.

Raenelle admitted to herself that she was plain, and early on she had determined to be beautiful. What she had lacked in glamour, the young woman more than compensated for in keen intelligence, and she had found a way of earning money for the magic transformation she desired. In junior college, she had introduced herself to half a dozen independent prostitutes in Buffalo, New York, and offered them her services as manager, accountant, general troubleshooter. With her knowledge of computers, she had organized a thriving out-call service, booking contacts in advance and reinvesting income for "her girls" at only ten percent commission. Word had spread like wildfire on the streets, and at the end of Raenelle's second year in business, she was managing a ring of more than sixty girls full-time.

She had been able to afford the plastic surgery that had turned her into someone her parents wouldn't have recognized. It scarcely mattered, since they had already learned of her activities at college and had disowned her. They would not take her calls, her letters were returned unopened and she finally stopped trying to secure their approval. She had finally blossomed, but no thanks were due to them, and when Raenelle lost her virginity at twenty-three, it was the first completely happy day of her life.

In time, the out-call service had attracted more than customers. The local Family was interested in anything that turned a profit on the far side of the law, and after an examination of the books, their representative had made an offer that Raenelle could not refuse. The syndicate absorbed her operation, bought her out at a substantial profit and installed her in the nation's capital. In three short years, she had become the ranking madam in a three-state area, with roots in Washington itself. Her girls had serviced diplomats from half the countries of the world, and they had not been overlooked by the domestic crop of politicians, either.

Raenelle's base of operations was the Venus Spa and Health Club, a retreat with membership reserved for an exclusive clientele. No member of the club had ever lifted weights or done aerobics on the premises, but that is not to say that they refrained from working out. Raenelle employed a staff of nubile "therapists" who were adept at handling the kinks their clients had developed in the course of diplomatic service. Stressing hands-on therapy and frequent repetition of procedures that produced the best re-
_____, her staff had never failed to satisfy.

_____ourse, the operation had not been her own since she
_____d her contract with the syndicate, but when she
_____t it, Raenelle told herself she didn't mind. The
_____t, the hours flexible and at her own discre-
_____ve among the girls herself, receiving from
_____tion and affection that had been denied
_____id not concern herself with the affairs
_____ although she was aware of hidden
_____the rooms, she asked no questions
_____o came at intervals to change the
_____was involved, if certain guests
_____participate in profit-sharing

enterprises, she was not involved. The fault could not be hers.

The Venus always had a decent crowd on Saturdays, and today was no exception. Raenelle surveyed the parlor from the doorway of her office on the second floor, counting nationalities. She picked out Africans, a pair of military officers from somewhere south of Texas, here a clutch of Orientals, there a group of Arabs in their flowing robes. At times like this, Raenelle imagined she was queen of the United Nations, studying her subjects from on high. But it was better this way; she had never heard of any queen receiving bonus pay for overtime and holidays.

She picked out the handsome stranger a moment after he arrived. One of her girls—a redhead, Stacy—was attempting to attach herself and work some action, but the guy was having none of it. He scrutinized the crowd with narrow eyes, and from her lookout post Raenelle could recognize him now.

The guy was trouble.

She caught him halfway to the bar, put one hand on his shoulder and he turned to face her with the fluid motion of a cat.

"What can I do for you?"

"You run this place?"

"That's right. I haven't seen you here before." She put on her best smile in case he might be one of Gianelli's men. "If I can get you something special . . ."

"You've got sixty seconds to evacuate this place befo[re it] blows," he told her, looking past the plastic smile and [look]ing at her soul.

"What?"

"You're wasting time. We can't afford to let yo[ur cus]tomers get singed."

It finally came across that he was warning her.

"Who are you?"

"Never mind, I'll spread the word myself."

He took a backward step and hauled out an [automatic] pistol from beneath his coat, unleashing two s[hots at the] ceiling. Even with the ringing in her ears, screams from somewhere at her back, she heard him loud and clear when he addressed the customers and girls assembled in the lounge.

"We've had a bomb threat. Everybody out! Right now!"

As if on cue, a hollow thunderclap erupted from the general direction of the kitchen, rattling the walls and tinkling the chandelier above Raenelle's head. She smelled the acrid smoke before it started wafting through the parlor, and the crowd broke as a second, closer blast reverberated through the nearby dining room.

One of the Africans collided with Raenelle, and she staggered, would have fallen if the handsome stranger hadn't snaked an arm around her waist and kept her upright. He retreated toward the bar, and from that vantage point they watched the crowd stampede toward double doors that could not possibly accommodate them all at once. A shoving match erupted, and she watched as an Arab was pummeled to the ground by two Latin military types.

"My God, what's happening?"

"You're going out of business," he informed her.

Still carrying the pistol, he was fishing inside his jacket with his free hand, coming out with what she took to be a highway flare. He twisted off the plastic cap and swung it wide as sparks and colored smoke poured forth. A looping overhand, and Raenelle watched it sputter through the doorway of her office, out of sight. As she stood, dumbstruck, he removed two more of the incendiary sticks from hidden rigging worn beneath his coat, and lobbed them both across the railing of the second-story landing toward the bedrooms. Within a moment, more of Raenelle's girls and customers were scrambling toward the spiral staircase, breaking for the exits, most of them abandoning their clothes.

A shout from the direction of the dining room, and one of Gianelli's soldiers staggered through the drifting purple smoke, one hand still raking at his eyes, the other wrapped around an Army-issue .45. He was the token gesture toward security, superfluous until tonight and generally ignored. But he had Mr. Trouble's full attention now.

Before she had a chance to shout a warning, Raenelle saw the stranger pivot on his heel, the automatic in his fist already rising. At a range of twenty yards, he triggered off two shots in rapid fire, and Gianelli's soldier took them both directly in the face. Raenelle could feel her dinner coming up as blood and bone exploded from his cheeks, the impact lifting him completely off his feet and slamming him against the kitchen doorjamb.

The stranger stood beside her, waited while she finished retching. Then he drew her upright, pulling her in the direction of the nearest exit. As she followed him, Raenelle could hear the hungry crackle of the flames behind her, felt the glowing heat against her back. When they were clear and standing side by side on the lawn, he placed one hand beneath her chin and raised her eyes to meet his own.

"You're out of business," he repeated. "Permanently. Spread the word to Gianelli. Someone has a package that belongs to me. The heat stays on until I get it back."

Somehow, impossibly, she found her voice. "Who are you?"

"Gianelli knows. You see he gets the message."

"Yes."

And he was gone, a shadow merging with the other shadows. She couldn't tell for certain, but it seemed that everyone had gotten clear, except for Gianelli's soldier. He was roasting in the middle of it now, and Raenelle felt her stomach turning over once again.

She had a message for the boss, and she would pass it on as soon as she was finished with the fire department, the police and whoever else might be attracted to the fire like moths. She could predict the *don*'s reaction in advance, but she would tell him all the same. Raenelle Gireau had no intention of allowing Gianelli to escape without some notion of the terror that she felt inside.

A survivor at the best, or worst, of times, she realized that she might have the opportunity to rebuild something for herself. As for the boss, he would be needing every bit of luck available when Mr. Trouble finally met him face-to-face.

Raenelle would not have traded places with Gianelli, not for all the money in the world. He was already marked, except he didn't know it yet.

THE ANACOSTIA WATERFRONT was dark as Bolan nosed his rental car northeast along the riverside. Due south, the sprawl of Bolling Air Force Base was brightly lit around the clock, prepared for any airborne menace to the capital. Across the water, Fort McNair and the Washington Navy Yard represented other branches of the service, each on constant standby for emergencies. The soldier had no business with them now. His target was a different sort of fortress, and the occupants conducted their primary business in the dark of night.

The Smithfield Export warehouse was designed for maximum security. No windows opened on the outside world, and giant loading bays had long been welded shut, mute testimony to the bankruptcy proceedings that had closed the warehouse three years earlier. Within the weeks immediately following its closure, Smithfield Export's one and only piece of real estate had undergone dramatic—though invisible—revisions. Stripped of merchandise, it had been labored over night and day by workmen whose continued silence was ensured by lavish overtime, the cavernous interior divided into smaller rooms, each soundproof, insulated from the rest. Whatever might transpire inside those cloistered rooms was strictly private. Members of the closed fraternity had paid for privacy, and it had been elaborately guaranteed.

The warehouse was a "lockbox," in the parlance of the street, a house of prostitution catering to savage needs that other brothels could not—would not—satisfy. The customers were guaranteed complete security, but it was not for their protection solely that the building had been turned into a fortress. There was "merchandise" to be protected, also, and the human cattle of the lockbox were no ordinary prostitutes, recruited by the profit motive. Forcibly obtained and forcibly restrained, the lockbox residents were chosen for the needs of "special" customers, the johns—

and janes—who needed "something extra" in their sexual diet. Catering primarily to "chicken hawks"—the pederasts who dote on brutalizing prepubescent children—the lockbox also served a small but wealthy clientele of sadists, necrophiles and other aberrants. No fantasy was too bizarre, too grisly for the management to entertain, and in three years of constant service, they had never failed to satisfy.

The man ostensibly in charge was Girolamo Lucchese, a.k.a. Gerry Lucas, a soldier with the Gianelli family who had served several prison terms—for rape and sodomy, molesting children, pandering, contributing to the delinquency of assorted minors. The recipient of pay beyond his lowly rank, Lucchese wore the label of a button man without complaint. He understood that it was insulation for the capo, something in the way of guaranteed security in case the lockbox should be penetrated. If and when that happened, Lucchese would be on his own, but through continued silence he could guarantee himself the best in legal talent, a continuation of his salary regardless of the outcome and a ready-made position in the Family upon release from jail. It was an offer he could scarcely have refused, since the alternative—providing testimony for the prosecution—would have meant his very painful death.

Lucchese was a man who valued pain. Infliction of it granted him the sort of sexual release that he had never found through normal channels, and he realized that pain was also educational, a useful tool for discipline. *Receiving* pain was something else entirely, though, and he knew that he could do a lot of time before he cracked and spilled the secrets of the Gianelli family. Hell, life would be a piece of cake compared to death the way that Gianelli's contract butchers dealt it out.

Mack Bolan knew Lucchese through his files at Justice, though the two of them had never met before tonight. Lucchese would have known Bolan by his reputation, but the Executioner would not be on his mind this evening. Having found a means of merging business with his pleasure, profiting from both, the mobster would be concentrating on his clients and their special needs.

The Executioner was counting on it.

The lockbox had no roving guards outside; Lucchese had decided that invisibility was preferable to an army on the street, and his exterior security was unobtrusive. Bolan's single pass was all it took to make the nondescript sedan, two passengers. The vehicle had been parked a half block down and faced the fortress warehouse, waiting for a danger signal that had not been used in three years.

The operation was protected at many levels. There were payoffs to be made at local levels, but Lucchese's customers themselves provided further insulation. Many of them crawled from under diplomatic rocks to seek their pleasures in the lockbox, representatives of European, Asian, African or Middle Eastern countries on duty in the nation's capital. Immune themselves to any charge of criminal behavior, they exerted a collective pull beyond their individual capacity, ensuring that authorities along the waterfront remained myopic, deaf and dumb.

The Executioner knew of the Lucchese-Gianelli alliance, and knew that it would never stand in court. If he had been a prosecutor or detective, Bolan would have busted Lucchese's operation anyway, preferring short-term gains to lasting victories. But as it was, he had a different goal in mind.

The Executioner was not obliged to prove his case before a jury, satisfying all the rules of evidence, maneuvering among the countless technicalities that made the legal system work halfheartedly at best. His mission was retrieval of Brognola's wife and children, and his modus operandi was the Gianelli squeeze. His other scattered thrusts would have the capo fuming, anxious to retaliate.

Bolan parked his car in a narrow alleyway and shed his topcoat, taking time to double-check his weapons prior to going EVA. He was a shadow gliding through the darkness as he backtracked toward the plug car, moving close enough to make a positive ID of hardmen on the job before his silenced Beretta sent them to eternal sleep.

The lockbox stood before him, undefended. All he had to do was get inside and get back out again. Alive.

He used a compact grappling hook and nylon line to reach the roof, and said a silent prayer of thanks that soundproof insulation worked both ways. As he had expected, there was a skylight, plate glass painted black against the sun and any chance of outside scrutiny. Whoever did the painting, though, had done it from the outside, standing where the soldier stood, and Bolan had no difficulty flaking off a dime-size chip of paint to provide him with a peephole to the room beneath.

An unoccupied bedroom, Spartan in its furnishings. He marked the cot and mattress, straight-backed wooden chairs, a folding table. Access to the room was through a single door and it would be from that direction that the danger would come, if any came at all.

He eased around the skylight, found the location where he figured the latch would be inside, and spent a moment clearing paint away to verify its placement. Pockets of his skinsuit surrendered strapping tape, a slender glass cutter, and the soldier went to work, etching a circle the size of a softball, inserting cautious fingers, feeling all along the sill for an alarm that wasn't there. When he was satisfied, he turned the simple latch and eased back the skylight retrieving rope and grappling hook for his descent.

The Executioner landed like a cat, the mini-Uzi in his hand almost before he had released the nylon line, alert for any sight or sound of danger. He was in, but that was only half the battle—less, if Gianelli had his troops in residence. Somewhere within the lockbox, he would find Lucchese, and the ghoul would take a message back to Gianelli for him, if the Executioner could find a way to spare the bastard's life. If not, well, he would write it off and find some other way to get the message through. It might be worth the extra effort just to see Lucchese die.

Fire and thunder were the ticket now, and Bolan braced himself, prepared to make the move that would begin his sweep—or end it, very suddenly. He threw the door back, glanced both ways along the empty corridor and moved out to his left. There were three doors on either side and at the end of the narrow corridor, a stairwell led down to other chambers and the street.

He tried the first door on his left and found it open. In a carbon-copy bedroom, Bolan stumbled upon a scene that made him feel like retching. He fought the urge to find a tap, wash the faint away. He drew his combat knife and severed the bindings that restrained a teenaged girl to the bed. The other occupant of the room, a gray-haired matron in leather mask and corset, spluttered in protest at the interruption of her "pleasure." Bolan backhanded her across the face and she toppled unconscious to the floor. He helped the former captive to her feet, retrieved a sheet to preserve what was left of her dignity.

"Wait five minutes," Bolan told her, when he had convinced himself that she was not in shock, "then make it to the street. That's left, and down the stairs. You'll have some company by then."

"Okay."

"You've got one chance," he cautioned her. "Don't blow it."

"I won't." He was already moving when she caught her voice and reached out to catch him in the doorway. "Hey...I mean, well, thanks."

The Executioner held up an open palm. "Five minutes."

He moved across the hall and took the next door in a rush, recoiling from the empty room without a break in stride. Three down, and now he realized that none of them were equipped with locks. The customers were paying for their privacy, but there was no way any one of them could barricade himself inside one of the rented rooms, creating sticky problems for Lucchese and his crew.

The next door on the right swung open under Bolan's hand, and one glance made him wonder if there really was a God. A young boy, with a terror-stricken face sat cowering on the bed. His puny arms were raised, body tensed and braced against the descending leather strap held by a middle-aged accountant type. The soldier ripped the man with a burst of automatic fire and left him writhing on the stained linoleum, already crossing to the youth as doors sprang open on the corridor and startled voices babbled their confusion. The cells were not quite soundproof, after all.

"Are you all right?"

It was a foolish question, but the best that he could summon in the circumstances. Shock had drained all color from the young boy's face, and now his pallor showed the welts and bruises off in stark relief. He needed medical attention, but the soldier couldn't interrupt his strike before he found Lucchese, not before he passed the message.

"Can you walk?"

"Uh-huh."

The youth recoiled as Bolan tried to lift him from the bed, then gave up, unable to resist effectively. The soldier ripped a sheet in two and wrapped half around the boy, tucking folded ends into his hands. That done, he led the kid outside and back along the corridor until he reached the bedroom occupied by one unconscious woman and one frightened teenage girl.

"It hasn't been five minutes, mister."

"No. I've got somebody for you to look after. He could use a doctor when you're clear."

"Oh, Jesus."

But she took the youth, held him to her like a mother holds her injured child, instinctively.

"I'll get him out okay."

"I know you will. Keep counting."

Now that he had lost the slim advantage of surprise, Bolan merely glanced inside the three remaining rooms, made sure that they were empty, predators and prey abandoning the ship. Downstairs, a fierce commotion had erupted as Lucchese's troops, attempting to investigate the shooting, ran headlong into a stampede of their clientele and captive slaves.

Bolan hit the stairs before the bastards could recover, lining up on the hardman who stepped out to intercept him. The guy was hauling out a pistol from beneath his arm, and a 3-round burst was all it took to shred his face, the corpse preceding Bolan in an awkward tumble down the stairs, upending stragglers and dumping all together in a tangle on the bottom landing.

He spied Lucchese in an instant, flanked by two more gunners and surrounded by perhaps a dozen customers. They were all jostling for the door in varied stages of undress. The thugs were shouting, trying desperately to separate their human merchandise from patrons, having trouble with it now that all had been reduced to their birthday suits. He saw Lucchese tangle fingers in a young girl's hair and drop her with a hard right cross. The backup gunners had their hands full with a pair of wiry youths who looked like twins, intent on breaking for the exit.

Bolan switched the mini-Uzi to his left hand and hauled out Big Thunder with his right. He let the little stutter gun unload at 700 rounds per minute, riddling the insulated walls and ceiling, showering the room with glass from overhead fluorescent fixtures. Below, Lucchese and his guns reacted as they should, releasing captives, digging for their hardware even as they sought a living target, and the moment gave Bolan all the edge that he required.

The AutoMag slid out to full extension, locking on the nearest target, bucking once and moving on. Downrange, 240 grains of death impacted on the torpedo's nose and punched on through, collapsing cheeks and chin like so much tissue paper, blowing him away.

Before the thunder had a chance to fade, round two was hurtling toward impact with the second gunner's forehead. The gunner vaulted backward and slithered out of range.

Lucchese had his .45 in hand, but Bolan wanted him alive. Round three ripped through the child molester's shoulder, separating his right arm from its socket in a sloppy bit of surgery. Staggered by the impact, Lucchese would have fallen, but Bolan couldn't let the bastard go. Another screaming .44 impacted on his kneecap, detonating bone and muscle, ripping tendons from their moorings. The guy sat down, the bloody ruin of his leg tucked underneath him.

They were alone, the tiny lobby empty now. The Executioner approached Lucchese, crouched beside him. Fear and agony were mingled in the mobster's eyes, and unaccustomed tears were etching tracks across his cheeks.

"I call the cops in fifteen minutes, Gerry. You could crawl a block by then, or maybe two, if you've got the guts."

And through the pain, a latent trace of curiosity survived.

"Who are you?"

"I'm the guy who could've blown your head off, Gerry. Maybe next time, eh? Right now, I've got a job for you to do."

"A job?"

"Tell Nicky that I want the package back. Tonight. If it's been damaged, he can kiss his life goodbye."

"The package?"

"Tell him, Gerry. Next time I might aim a little higher."

Bolan jammed the muzzle of his AutoMag against Lucchese's groin and twisted, satisfied with the impression that it made. He left the bastard there, to drag himself away as best he could, secure that Gianelli would receive his message. If Lucchese died, it wouldn't matter in the long run. Bolan's destruction of the lockbox would be instantly connected with the other strikes, and Nicky G. would get the message, loud and clear.

The soldier had another call to make before he touched base with Brognola, this time on the other side. Before he rattled any more cages, Bolan wanted to assess the "evidence" against Brognola, slip the pieces into place and look for any gaps he might exploit. And he already had a source in mind.

Let Gianelli stew for now, devouring his own insides with questions that he could not hope to answer on his own. The Executioner had other business in the seat of government, and he was moving on.

To Justice.

He meant to see if any still survived.

13

Cameron Cartwright killed the Porsche's engine, listening to it tick for several moments as it cooled in the night. It was not cold outside, but he could feel the gooseflesh rising on his arms, betraying agitation as it did each time he was compelled to meet with Gianelli. So much at risk, so much to lose, and still he had no choice. When Gianelli called a meeting, Cartwright would be there with hat in hand.

It galled him, catering to common criminals this way, but, then again, there had been nothing common in the threat from Gianelli. At a single stroke, the mafioso could erase a quarter century of faithful service to the government, leave Cartwright's long career at the CIA in smoking ruins. Gianelli could destroy him if he chose to, and until he found a way to break the mobster's stranglehold, Cartwright was at his beck and call.

The Watergate Hotel provided anonymity, though Cartwright scarcely would have chosen it with tight security in mind. He still remembered Hunt and Liddy, the deliberate shambles of a burglary, the months of hearings that had toppled Nixon. It had been a foolish stunt from the beginning, amateurish, pointless, and the analysts at the CIA had recognized a shaky hand behind the half-baked plot. It wasn't burglary that put them off, but rather wasted effort, risking personnel to gather information that was readily available from countless other outlets. Farnsworth had been quick to sense the shifting winds and, with Cartwright's help, had moved to blow the silly scheme wide open. They had weathered out the shitstorm side by side, emerging with the scent of roses while so many others fell around them.

Even Gianelli didn't know of Cartwright's secret meetings with Bob Woodward, from the *Post*, although the mobster might have guessed that Cameron's sense of humor, coupled with his fondness for pornography, had prompted him to choose the contact code name of Deep Throat.

So long ago, but he could not approach the Watergate, could not drive by it in the Company's armored limousine without the images and memories returning, just as if it all had happened yesterday. You're getting old, he thought, and knew it wasn't true. Still vigorous at fifty-one, the CIA agent could hold his own against the best—he'd proved that much when he outlived Lee Farnsworth—but the carelessness of others placed him under Nicky Gianelli's thumb, and Cartwright ruminated constantly on methods of escape. If it had not required such careful planning, so damned much finesse . . .

As always, he had parked the Porsche himself, avoiding the valets who might remember faces, license plates, if anyone should ask about him later. Cartwright's passion for selective anonymity had marked him as a bit of an eccentric with the Agency, so many years beyond his final field assignment, but the up-and-coming staffers had no inkling of his background, everything he stood to lose through indiscretion and exposure.

In the wake of Farnsworth's death, the bloody business in Virginia, he had spent a frenzied weekend purging records, reaching back across the years to Southeast Asia, Cuba, the Dominican Republic, Chile, shredding anything and everything that might incriminate him. It was simpler now than in the old days, with computers to assist him in the search, and Cartwright hadn't missed a thing—except for Gianelli's copies, secretly collected since the sixties, stored against the day when Nicky needed extra weight to throw around in Washington. The bastard had it all, in triplicate, complete with names and dates, securely tucked away where Cartwright couldn't reach it.

Yet.

A quarter-century in the clandestine services had taught him that no secret was eternally secure. It had only taken one professor to reveal the Pentagon's most treasured secrets in the early seventies, and whistle-blowers were a dime a dozen in official Washington. The kind of information Cartwright needed from inside the syndicate would be more difficult to come by, but where there was a will...

The doorman nodded courteously to the suit, ignoring Cartwright's face. The man had seen him here before as he saw thousands every night five days a week, but Cartwright worked at leaving no impression on the minds of strangers and remote subordinates. He fit "the type" that would be calling on the Watergate for business meetings of an evening: three-piece suit; salt-and-pepper hair, now mostly gray around the temples; wing-tip shoes. He was unarmed and had not carried guns with any regularity in a dozen years. But there were times like now when he still missed the reassuring weight beneath his arm. Its absence caused a pang, like sending a favorite child off to college in the fall or breaking with a mistress who had been particularly skilled.

The danger lay within connections, and he hoped to break the link with Gianelli soon, perhaps when they were finished with the current project. In the meantime he was on for the duration, and there was no viable alternative to absolute success.

He waited for the elevator with an older couple, tuning out their conversation, concentrating on the purpose of his visit. Gianelli had been agitated on the phone and with good reason. There were indications that his plan might be unraveling around the edges, but they had no other options now. They were committed, and the mafioso would be waiting for suggestions, ways of nailing down the battle plan before it rolled up in their faces and was blown away.

Cartwright had no answers for him yet, but it was in his own best interest to secure the game before it slipped away. He had as much at stake—and more, perhaps—than Gianelli. Everybody knew that Gianelli was a thug; they simply couldn't prove it in a court of law. In Cameron Cartwright's case, however, there were reputations to protect, an image to preserve, and he could not—*would* not—allow the present freakish circumstances to destroy what he had worked to build since he had come of age in Washington.

He loved the town, and hated it, the feelings sometimes surfacing together simultaneously. The nation's capital had nurtured him, allowed him to become the man he was, and it would just as cheerfully destroy him. It would be Cartwright's task to see that no such opportunity was granted to any of his enemies. Or any of his friends, he added silently, relieved by the arrival of the elevator. There were no such things as friends in Washington, not since Lee Farnsworth, and he was reminded of that fact each time he spoke to Gianelli. In emergencies allies would betray you at their leisure once the danger to themselves was past. It was a lesson that America had failed to learn in 1941, in 1945, in '59 and '63 and on and on. It was a lesson Cartwright only had to suffer once before he read the writing on the wall.

Trust no one but yourself. Reveal no weakness to your "friends" or enemies at any time. Permit yourself no public indiscretions and confess no errors of judgment. Stonewall to the end, and cut another deal beneath the table if you have to, anything to save yourself.

He disembarked, abandoning his elderly companions on the fourteenth floor. He took no pains to hide his face from other men and women passing in the corridor as he approached Gianelli's suite. They didn't know him, had no reason to remember him. As perfectly anonymous as any man alive, he reached the door that was numbered 1425 and rapped twice against the polished wood.

The door was opened by a six-foot-eight behemoth, decked out in a suit that seemed about to split along its seams. He held the door for Cartwright, closed and double-locked it when he was inside, and frisked the Company operative for weapons. Cartwright kept the grimace from his face, inured to the embarrassment by now, convinced that Gianelli's private paranoia was a sign of weakness. That could be useful knowledge in the future when the time was ripe for eliminating Gianelli's shadow from his life. Soon.

The ape conveyed him through a narrow entry hall into a sitting room with bedrooms opening off either side. The doors were open, the bedrooms vacant. As soon as Cartwright was delivered, his companion ambled back in the direction of the door to stand his watch.

"You're late."

"I'm never late."

Still, Cartwright ignored the urge to check his Rolex. It was one of Nicky's favorite ploys, Cartwright knew, a childish bid to knock the other side off balance, prior to opening negotiations. It was stupid of him to be playing games with Cartwright at a time like this, and Cartwright made another mental note regarding Gianelli's ego. The fanatical one-upmanship could be a fatal weakness, leading him to reckless action when the chips were down, and it was good to know.

"You want a drink?"

"No, thanks."

"So, sit."

Cartwright sat and waited for the mobster to begin, examining his adversary for perhaps the thousandth time since their association had begun. He might not fit the profile of a mobster, with his stylish haircut, understated suit and jewelry, but there was something oily in the mafioso's mannerisms, even in his voice, that had a way of setting Cartwright's teeth on edge. He felt contaminated any time he came into contact with the man who held his past, his future, in those manicured hands.

"Your end all right?"

"It's covered," Cartwright told him. "I understand you've got the target marked."

"You understand exactly right." There was a shadow of uneasiness behind the mobster's smile. "The bastard's here, and I can tell you that he's hot as hell."

"You were expecting that."

"Damn right. I didn't think he'd take it this fast off the mark, but I was counting on some losses here and there."

The capo's tone betrayed his anger, faint bewilderment at what was happening on the streets of Washington. From quiet sources, Cartwright knew that Gianelli had been taking hits all evening, from the ghetto to his favorite pleasure palaces. It was the price he had to pay for setting up an operation in his own backyard.

"I set the meeting with Brognola as you asked. It's Arlington at midnight."

Gianelli frowned. "I wish we'd set it earlier, the way this bastard's tearing up the town, but what the hell. It's just a few more hours, right?"

"Four hours, thirty-seven minutes."

"Yeah, all right. You mentioned something on the phone about another problem."

Cartwright nodded, drawing cautious pleasure from the mobster's agitation.

"It's the media. Specifically a free lance by the name of Susan Landry. Someone tipped her to the move against Brognola, and she's pressing for supporting evidence."

"Goddamn it. Was it Landry? Why's that name familiar?" Gianelli's scowl was carving furrows in his cheeks. "I know that name from somewhere, dammit."

Cartwright gave it to him on a platter. "She's the one who broke the story on that little business in Virginia. Prior to that, she had alleged connections with your target's Cleveland operation. Someone in the Family up there should have the details."

"Shit, I know the score on Cleveland," Gianelli growled. "The bitch was there, all right. Goddammit, what's she up to now?"

"An educated guess would say that she's attempting to corroborate—or to expose—the evidence against Brognola."

"Christ, that's all we need. The frigging media. How badly can she hurt us?"

Cartwright didn't even have to think about it. "There's a single source of information she could tap, outside this room."

"DeVries."

It hadn't come out sounding like a question, but he nodded all the same, confirming Gianelli's choice of the potential leak.

"We'll have to take him out. You wanna set it up?"

It was the CIA man's turn to frown. "I think it's better handled out of house. Less chance of comebacks in the long run."

Gianelli chuckled. " 'In-house,' 'out of house,' what the hell's the difference? *I'll* handle it, and we won't have no fucking comebacks, neither. Shit, you cloak-and-daggers kill me."

Not a bad idea, thought Cartwright, but he kept the icy smile in place. The time was not yet ripe for dumping Gianelli. Later, when the present mess was all behind them.

"While we're on the subject, Nick, I think you should be covering the meet in Arlington."

The mafioso dropped his smile, bent forward, elbows planted on his knees. "Why's that?"

"My ass is hanging out a mile for no good reason on this thing. I laid the groundwork, got your target here. It's your show now."

"My show? Your ass is hanging out for no good reason? Maybe you should take another look around and find out who your friends are, Cam. Think about the shit you'd have to wade through if Brognola tied you in with Farnsworth and that fuck-up in Virginia."

"He was nowhere close. You know that."

"What I know is that it only takes a phone call, and your little world goes up in smoke. *Capisce?* Somebody ties you in with Farnsworth, and you wouldn't have a pot to piss in by this time tomorrow."

Cartwright bristled.

"This has never been about Brognola, dammit. It's about his contact."

"What's the matter, you can't say the name? It's *Bolan*, asshole. Say it."

"This is childish."

"Say it!"

The explosion took him by surprise, the dark contorted face reminding Cartwright that the mobster might be capable of anything. Behind him in the entryway, he heard the hulking gunner sucking wind and waiting for the order to attack.

He said it.

"Bolan."

Gianelli rocked back in his easy chair, retreating from the brink of detonation, and the sudden shift confirmed for Cartwright that he had been dealing with a psychopath these past two years.

"See there? It's easy when you try."

"I've got no argument with Bolan."

"Oh? Well, I'd lay money on it that he's got an argument with you. He lost some people in Virginia, just in case you don't remember, and the bastard has been known to hold a grudge. He finds out you were in the deal with Farnsworth, chances are that you'll be dead before you come to trial."

"It wouldn't stand in court," the Company man responded. "Nothing ever went on paper, and the principals are dead. Assuming that you wanted to involve yourself with federal juries, any testimony you presented would be hearsay."

"You want evidence on paper, pally? Think about the notebooks Farnsworth left behind. Dumb move for such a cagey bastard, huh? He wasn't stingy with the names, I'll give him that. And all those memos that he cycled through the Xerox for a rainy day. I'd say it's raining pretty hard right now."

"The statute's run on that by now. It's ancient history."

"So, tell me why you're sitting here right now? Could be that you're embarrassed by the thought of all that shit resurfacing? Could be the statute doesn't run on murder... or should I be calling it assassination?"

Cartwright couldn't answer. He was rooted to his chair, jaws locked, his mind racing back across the years and miles. He flashed on Dallas and the motorcade turning off Houston, running west on Elm Street toward the triple underpass, the grassy knoll. There was a telltale puff of smoke behind the fence, an echo from the book depository, thunder in his ears... And he was instantly transported to Los

Angeles, amid the crush of campaign workers at the great Ambassador Hotel. It was congested, even claustrophobic in the kitchen, but he saw the slender figure edging forward, reaching with the pistol to bestow his special blessing, firing blindly toward the ceiling while another shooter closed on Bobby's flank to pop the lethal caps at skin-touch range, secure in his silent weapon, the invisibility of his policeman's uniform.

For Cartwright, the recovery of here and now was the emotional equivalent of diving naked into icy water. For an instant, impact with the present took his breath away.

"All right."

"What's that?"

"I said *all right*."

"That's better. Arlington is your show, and you'd better get it right the first time, 'cause you won't get any second chances, dig it? I'll take out DeVries, and if the Landry bitch gets burned, we can consider it a bonus."

"Anything you say."

The mobster flashed a savage grin. "I like our little chats, don't you? Let's keep in touch."

He turned away and ambled toward the bar, dismissing Cartwright like a servant, carving one more notch out of his dignity. The man from the CIA retreated through the entryway, ignoring the gorilla's smirk, and took the elevator down.

For now he would be forced to play along, but there were ways of breaking Gianelli's stranglehold when this was finished. He had written history before, with Farnsworth, and he would again. It mattered little that no authors had recorded their achievements for posterity; it was enough that Cartwright knew and understood.

For now it was enough that Gianelli felt self-satisfied, his confidence inflated to the bursting point, assured that Cartwright was his stooge. When it was time to break the news, it would hit him that much harder.

Cameron Cartwright would be looking forward to that moment when he saw the recognition dawn in Gianelli's eyes. The recognition that it cut both ways, that nothing in the world was settled while you had an enemy still living.

But there would be other business first. With Hal Brognola and his batboy out in Arlington. The Bolan reputation did not frighten Cartwright. He had lived through Vietnam, the Bay of Pigs, Grenada, and the enemy had never laid a glove on him. Not yet.

It wouldn't be a piece of cake in Arlington by any means, but it would not be Armageddon, either. When the dust had settled, there would be time enough for Gianelli and his files.

Cartwright was taking first things first and keeping his priorities in order. It was the mark of a professional.

14

A string of well-placed calls had finally provided Susan Landry with the name of the investigator handling Brognola's case. She had been forced to call in some markers, to promise favors where she had no running line of credit with the source, but it would all be worth it if the story broke as large as she expected. Hell, if she could document her own suspicions of a tight sophisticated frame against Brognola, she was sitting on the local story of the year.

Her target was a Justice middle-ranker named DeVries. She didn't recognize the name, but that did not surprise her. Quiet sources told her that DeVries was on the inside, well-positioned on the ladder for a shot at bigger things if he could earn a reputation for himself. Brognola's scalp would be a step in that direction, provided that the case was strong enough to stand in court or force a resignation. Hal would never quit, she knew that much, and so DeVries would be expected to produce substantial evidence of criminal complicity, enough to validate the frame and send Brognola to the penitentiary.

She stopped herself, aware that she was running on emotions instead of facts. She had not seen the evidence against Brognola. When she had seen and heard it all, she might be calling for Brognola's crucifixion as well.

But no. Her reading of the man was accurate. Susan trusted her innate ability to see through falsehood, smell a lie that festered under the veneer of partial truths. Brognola wasn't giving anything away, might well be hiding something of importance, but he wasn't covering a guilty conscience. Susan would have staked her reputation on the fact that he was clean. In fact, she was prepared to do exactly that.

Which left her with DeVries. His office had been closed, but further digging had disclosed an address in the northwest section of the city. Susan tried his number—she had been surprised to find him in the book—and he had answered on the second ring. A strong voice, tinged with self-importance, radiating confidence. He had surprised her once again by readily agreeing to an interview; in retrospect, she thought that he had almost sounded eager for the chance to share his information with the media.

There are at least a million information sources in the nation's capital. Perhaps two-thirds are open to the public, occupied around the clock with grinding out releases, statements, broadsides and position papers. The remaining third are lumped together in the trade as "leaks," the unofficial sources of official information that was not designed for publication in the first place. Congressmen and senators, their secretaries, members of the bar, policemen, countless bureaucrats and civil servants. Each possessed a private ax that he or she would grind at carefully selected moments for the benefit of friendly ears. Their motives varied widely, from the purest altruism on through every shade of gray and black, but there was always something in it for the leak.

Before she met DeVries, Susan knew that she would have to ferret out his motive for revealing information that was surely classified. His willingness to talk supported her belief that Hal was being framed; a solid case would be preserved in secrecy until the prosecution had its day in court, while weaker evidence might do more damage in the headlines than before a jury. If DeVries was talking now, she realized, he might not have sufficient ammunition for a public showdown where the rules of evidence were rigidly enforced.

The lady stopped herself before her own imagination could betray her. She could not assess DeVries until they met, until she saw his evidence against Brognola. Only then would she be able to expound upon his case with any real authority.

She overshot his street, a cul-de-sac three blocks from
Stanton Park, and doubled back. The condos that surrounded her were not especially elaborate, but Susan knew
the price range and she was surprised DeVries could meet
the payments on his salary from Justice. Something else to
think about when she began assessing motivations and intent.

She parked the Honda, locked it and made her way
among the condominiums that were arranged like scattered
children's blocks around a common green and swimming
pool. DeVries was on the ground floor, separated from the
pool by thirty yards of lawn. She punched the bell, and he
was there before the tinny echo of the chimes had died away,
all smiles, inviting her inside. She realized he had been
waiting, watching for her since she called him on the phone,
and something sour settled in her throat.

Too eager.

"Come on in." He took her hand and pumped it ener-
getically. "DeVries. Just call me Erskine."

"Susan Landry."

She distrusted him at once, the plastic smile, the way his
eyes slid over her like groping hands. In any other circumstances she would not have spent another moment in his
company, but this was business. He had information that
she needed, and he would not be the first man who had un-
dressed her with his eyes.

"Sit down." He gestured toward a brace of chairs that
clearly were designed for decoration more than comfort.
Susan settled into one of them. "You like a drink? I'm
having Scotch."

"No. Thank you."

"Hey, I'm easy."

I'll just bet you are, she thought, but kept it to herself and
waited while he poured a double, settling in the chair that
matched her own and scooting closer, so that their knees
were almost touching. She resisted an instinctive urge to pull
away.

"So, shoot."

She tried to meet his eyes, but they were fastened on her chest and finally she gave it up, referring to her notebook and a list of questions she had jotted down in preparation for the interview.

"As I explained before, I'm interested in background information on the case against Brognola. Assuming that there *is* a case."

His eyes quit mauling her just long enough to meet her gaze, a flicker of uneasiness behind the washed-out gray, and then they dropped back to her hemline, inching up her thigh.

"Oh, there's a case, all right." He sounded cocky, certain of himself. "We've got the bas— We've got him cold."

"And what, precisely, will he be accused of?"

"Well, they haven't drawn the charges yet. Somebody might decide to let him bargain down. From what I've seen, he's in the bag for multiples on bribery, releasing classified material, consorting, perjury, the works."

"As far as evidence . . ."

"We've got it up the ying-yang, babe. The guy is very photogenic, if you get my drift."

"I wish there was some way—"

"For you to see it? Well, I really oughta make some calls, but what the hell? I've got some things you might be interested in right here."

He jerked a thumb across his shoulder toward what had to be the bedroom, and his smile was crooked, sloppy from the liquor, hungry like his eyes. *Too eager.* It was not supposed to be this way, and she could feel her hackles rising, the alarm bells going off inside her skull.

"You wanna come with me . . . ?"

Her smile was ice.

"I'll wait."

"Hey, suit yourself."

She kept the frozen smile in place while he unfolded from the chair and walked toward the bedroom. As far as he could tell, Susan wryly thought, he had her hooked, and it was time to reel her in. She wondered why the men behind DeVries had not invested time in acting lessons for their star performer. Or was he precisely what he seemed to be: a horny jerk prepared to barter information for an hour's dalliance?

She put the second option out of mind. It was too pat, a tired cliché that probably could still be found in action anywhere outside official Washington. The penalties for whistle-blowers were increasingly severe, and no one but an idiot would risk his job, his freedom, on the off-chance of an unexpected one-night stand. Perhaps if she had known DeVries for weeks or months, if she had implied availability as her part of a working contract...

No. The guy was obviously hoping for a shot, but he was far from stupid. Still, a third alternative was nagging at her. Suppose DeVries was acting on his own, assuming that his sponsors would appreciate some free publicity to nudge Brognola, turn the heat up. There was just a chance De-Vries might use his own initiative, and hope for something on the side.

He reappeared a moment later, carrying two slim manila envelopes. Before he sat, she noticed that he nudged his chair some inches closer to her own. Without a word he opened one of the manila envelopes and handed her a stack of glossy eight-by-tens.

"We never could've tagged him this way two, three years ago," he said. "You wanna know the truth, I think the guy is getting senile."

Silently she scanned the photographs. Each one depicted Hal Brognola in the company of men she didn't recognize. One face recurred in half a dozen of the shots, and Susan memorized it: wavy hair, thick brows and brooding, deep-set eyes, a classic Roman nose. The other men were nondescript.

"Okay." She could not let DeVries know that the faces held no meaning for her. She would play it out and take the information as it came.

"Okay? That's it?" He shook his head and tapped an index finger on the Roman nose. "This guy's a major power with the Family in Baltimore. That ring a bell?"

DeVries was shuffling through the stack of photographs and ticking off credentials for the men who had been captured with Brognola in the camera's eye. A shooter from Toledo. Numbers bankers from Manhattan. A Chicago politician. Cocaine cowboys from Miami. A Las Vegas businessman whose interests ranged from legal gambling to child pornography.

The list went on, and Susan Landry felt a numbness spreading from her stomach, threatening to paralyze her limbs. Could she have been so radically, completely wrong about Brognola? Had the man been fooling everyone for years? She stopped herself before the train of thought could gather perilous momentum. There were still too many things that could not be explained away: Brognola's record of arrests, investigations that had rocked the syndicate and packed its leaders off to prison, his relationship with Bolan in another sort of war against the Mob.

It seemed impossible, and yet...

"When were these taken?"

"We've been dogging him full-time the past three months. That's ninety days of around-the-clock surveillance. I don't even wanna think about the deals that he was pulling off before we got our tip."

"What kind of tip?"

DeVries put on a thoughtful frown. "I really can't go into that, at least until we get indictments. If you call me in a week or two..."

She didn't take the bait.

"What's in the other envelope?"

"Oh, this?" He passed it over. "There, you've got the phone log on Brognola's private line. The past three months, he's gotten a dozen calls from Mr. Baltimore alone, and there's a couple dozen others from around the country. All from members or confirmed associates of Cosa Nostra Families."

She was unfastening the envelope, betrayed by fingers that had suddenly begun to tremble, when the doorbell sounded, causing her to jump.

"Relax," he said, grinning. "I'll lose whoever, and we'll have a drink, okay?"

He was away before she had a chance to veto the suggestion, and she concentrated on the list of numbers in her hand. The digits held no meaning for her; she would have to copy them and check them on her own, but she was worried, afraid that any further digging might reveal that she had been mistaken in her judgment of Brognola. And if she had so misjudged the man from Justice, then what else, *who* else, had she been wrong about? Was *any*one precisely what he seemed in Washington?

The gunshots were explosive, thunderous, reverberating through the narrow corridor and bringing Susan to her feet, the photographs and printouts spilling from her hands. DeVries lurched through the doorway, panting, breathless, with an automatic pistol in his fist.

"Get down!" he shouted at her. "It's a hit!"

Behind him, out of sight, she heard the door burst open, slamming back against the wall. DeVries was turning, firing back along the hallway, when the sliding windows at her back imploded, raining shattered glass. She caught a fleeting image of the lawn chair as it bounced across the carpet, recognized the hammering of automatic weapons as she dived for cover, flattening herself behind the couch.

It would protect her for a moment, and Susan had no time for thoughts of Hal Brognola now. Her mind was fully occupied with facing the reality of sudden, violent death: her own.

MACK BOLAN PARKED HIS RENTAL Ford between a Firebird and a family station wagon. He killed the engine and remained behind the wheel for several moments, listening. The cul-de-sac was quiet, sidewalks empty, and he was relieved that there were no apparent parties underway in any of the nearby condominiums. His mission was a soft one here, but crowd scenes added unknown variables, inconvenient witnesses, unnecessary risks.

Brognola had supplied the name of the investigator on his case, and in a hurried phone call he had also tipped the soldier to a scheduled midnight meet in Arlington. The Executioner would be there, standing by his friend, but first there were some questions begging to be answered, and the answer man would be Brognola's nemesis, Erskine DeVries. He had the condo's number, knew the guy was single, that he lived alone and that he wasn't in his office. Odds were good that he would be at home, and based on Hal's assessment of the man—"a loser with the ladies"—it was likely that he would be on his own.

The odds against his making voluntary conversation would be something else entirely, Bolan knew, but he could be persuasive when he tried. DeVries had seen the "evidence" against Brognola, had perhaps collected some of it himself, and with some marginal encouragement along the way he just might share his knowledge with the Executioner. Convinced that Hal was being framed, the soldier was more interested in motives than in manufactured evidence, but any leads might be productive in the end. If he could squeeze some solid answers from DeVries, he would be that much closer to the men behind the frame.

He locked up the car and struck off through the complex, checking numbers as he went and homing on the address that Brognola had provided. A stereo was warming up somewhere to Bolan's right, discordant strains of heavy metal drifting toward him through the darkness, far enough away that Bolan could afford to put it out of mind. He found the numbered building he was seeking, turned the corner—and immediately froze.

Four hardmen, wearing trench coats over suits, were there ahead of him. They picked out the condo's number, huddled briefly, then fanned out to take up their positions. Two disappeared around the back, the others killing time until their backup men were in position, smoking, whispering between themselves. A minute passed, then two, and Bolan watched them grind their cigarettes to ashes on the sidewalk, fanning back their coats to free the automatic weapons holstered in shoulder rigs.

The hardware banished any fleeting thought that these might be detectives setting up a bust. The pincer movement was a classic, crashing in the front while snipers waited to annihilate the target fleeing through another exit, and if nothing else, the soldier knew that someone else was interested in DeVries. No time to ponder the apparent contradiction of a hit upon the man who was cooperating in a major frame. DeVries might be demanding bigger bucks, or suffering the pangs of conscience. At the bottom line he was expendable, and someone had decided it was time to break the chain, remove a crucial link before it could be followed backward to the source of Hal Brognola's troubles.

They were on the doorstep now, one reaching up to jab the bell when Bolan moved, the sleek Berctta filling his hand. Split-second timing was required, and if he blew it there would be no hope of any answers from DeVries.

An endless moment passed while the gunners waited for an answer to the doorbell. The soldier had already covered half the distance, fading in and out of shadows as he ran. With twenty yards between them, Bolan saw the gunners tense, their weapons rising in response to something he could neither see nor hear.

And instead of opening, the door was sprouting chest-high bullet holes, the shooters desperately recoiling, dodging lead and flying splinters. They recovered swiftly, like professionals, the taller of them stepping up and kicking at the door. The impact shattered its lock, opening the way. His partner loosed a short precision burst to clear the entryway, and they were inside before the soldier could react effectively.

He broke for cover, sprinting for the stoop, aware of new activity around him. Cautious faces peered through the curtains of surrounding condos, porch lights winked on, dispelling darkness in an instant. Sharp, staccato gunfire echoed through the open doorway, coupled with a crash of broken glass.

Too late.

The message hammered in Mack Bolan's brain before he cleared the concrete steps, before he reached the doorway and plunged inside.

But he would never know for sure until he tried, until he saw it for himself.

If he survived that long.

15

He came upon the hit team from behind, and even so he almost lost the advantage of surprise. With twenty feet between them, someone in the living room began returning fire, big .45 rounds gouging plaster from the pastel walls. The shooters scrambled backward, crouching, and the nearest of them caught a glimpse of Bolan from the corner of his eye.

He barked a warning, swiveling to bring his Uzi up, the muzzle winking fire at point-blank range. Excellent timing and the shooter's haste were all that saved Mack Bolan's life, a belly slide on blue shag carpeting removing him from the initial line of fire. He heard the parabellums slicing air above his head, impacting on the walls, and he was angling with the Beretta, making target acquisition as the hit man started to correct his aim.

The first round from the 93-R ripped through the gunner's chest and rocked him backward on his heels. The Uzi's snout drifted upward, bringing down a rain of plaster dust as 750 rounds per minute chewed up the ceiling. Bolan's second round bored in beneath the shooter's chin and snapped his head back, opening a jagged keyhole in his skull.

The second gunner was already ducking as the body fell across his line of fire, and Bolan took advantage of the momentary distraction, rolling clear before the automatic rounds came ripping in, peeling ragged strips of carpet back and pulverizing the concrete beneath. He triggered three quick rounds from the Beretta, saw his target jerk, colliding with the wall, rebounding in an awkward pirouette that ended in a sprawl. He didn't have to check for vital signs to know the guy was as dead as hell.

From the direction of the living room he heard male voices hoarse with tension, calling to the dead.

"Zito! Eddie! What the hell?"

On his feet and closing, Bolan left them guessing as he stepped across the leaking corpses of their comrades. He holstered the hot Beretta, then stooped to retrieve the Uzi from his first kill, picking up an Ingram MAC-11 as he passed the second lifeless body. Both weapons were primed and a quick check told him he had sufficient ammo to meet the challenge. He cleared the doorway, searching for another target.

They were waiting for him in the shambles of the parlor, shattered sliding windows open on the night behind them, curtains stirring with the breeze. He was aware of someone stretched out on the carpet to his right, but there was no time now for sizing up the casualties.

Shooters three and four were stationed twenty feet apart, prepared to close the hallway with a lethal cross fire from their automatic weapons at a moment's notice. It was a professional defensive stance that fairly guaranteed survival for at least one member of the team; if any unexpected enemy appeared, he would be forced to choose one target or the other while the odd man out was free to cut him down.

The soldier read their purpose at a glance, together with the heartbeat's indecision in their faces as he cleared the doorway in a crouch. They had been waiting for an answer from their silent partners, still not understanding, when the Executioner unloaded on them with his captured weapons, raking left and right together in a blazing double arc of death.

The Uzi ran its remaining rounds in rapid-fire and swept the starboard gunner off his feet as parabellum slugs ripped his chest to shreds. The impact blew him backward, through the shattered sliding windows, shrouded in the bloody curtains as they ripped free of their moorings and followed him outside.

On Bolan's left, the MAC-11 cut a lethal figure eight between the final gunner's throat and knees, .380 stingers slamming home with enough force to knock him backward in a sloppy somersault.

Bolan dropped the Uzi, tossed the Ingram after it and was turning toward the nearest corpse when furtive movement behind the sofa captured his attention. Bolan hit a combat crouch, the Beretta filling his fist and searching for a target. His finger tightened around the trigger, hesitating only when the numbers failed to jibe.

Four gunners, all of them accounted for. The ventilated body at his feet would be DeVries, already silenced for eternity. He should have been alone among the dead.

"One chance," he snapped. "Throw out your weapon. Let me see those hands."

A woman's voice came back at him from somewhere in the suburbs of hysteria.

"I haven't got a weapon, dammit!"

"Stand," he ordered her, prepared for anything. "And make it easy."

Recognition hit Mack Bolan first, but Susan Landry wasn't far behind. Her mouth hung open for a moment, wide eyes rising from the muzzle of his weapon to the face that she had seen most recently in Texas.

He holstered the Beretta, one swift glance assuring him that she was still intact before he crouched beside DeVries. He didn't need to take the nonexistent pulse, but Bolan did it anyway, and cursed the circumstances that had robbed him of the opportunity to question Hal's accuser.

Susan was beside him now, recovered well enough from her initial shock to make her mind and mouth coordinate.

"You came here looking for DeVries?"

He let the question pass. "I see you found him first."

"Somebody found him." She surveyed the carnage, paling as her eyes glanced off the other riddled bodies. "What the hell is all of this?"

"It's overkill," he answered, holding Susan with his eyes. "Somebody must've thought DeVries was granting interviews."

"You're here for Hal," she countered, sudden understanding in her voice. "I should have known."

"What brings *you* here?"

"Could be the same. I haven't had a chance to make up my mind yet." She nodded toward the body of DeVries. "We never got that far."

Outside, a rising babble had resolved itself into the sound of cautious voices. Bolan didn't have to understand the words to realize that neighbors would be edging closer, gaining confidence as silence swallowed up the echoes of the firefight. Someone was certain to have called police, several calls would be more likely, and the squad cars would be on their way by now. A glance told Bolan that the lady was already putting two and two together, and she beat him to the punch.

"I move we finish off this conversation in a cooler atmosphere," she said, "before somebody else drops in to interrupt."

The soldier didn't argue with her. He was stepping through the shattered sliding windows, past the shrouded corpse of one assailant, when he noticed Susan hanging back, intent on gathering some photographs and papers that were scattered near the couch. She caught up with Bolan on the flagstone patio, in lockstep with him as they put the house of death behind them.

As Bolan led her back circuitously toward the parking lot, avoiding contact with the neighbors who were popping out of condos on every side, his mind was on the papers in her hand. He hadn't noticed them in the excitement of the firefight, the surprise of seeing Susan Landry rise from cover. But if the lady cared enough to bring them with her, shaving precious seconds off their getaway, they might be worth a closer look.

Whatever they contained, they were his only hope of getting information from DeVries now that the man himself had been irrevocably silenced. Scattered papers, glossy photographs . . . and Susan Landry. It made some sense.

Susan had been with DeVries before the raiders struck. There was a chance that he had spilled some measure of the manufactured case against Brognola, speaking carelessly, perhaps, or out of cold deliberation, playing to his audience. Most frames looked better in the media than in court, Bolan knew, and he was betting that DeVries had planned a series of strategic leaks to stain Brognola's reputation. Someone else had vetoed the idea with bullets, and the Executioner could only hope that something might be salvaged from the ruins before it was too late.

Except, he told himself, it might already be too late.

Conditioned toward ignoring hopeless odds, he pushed the defeatist train of thought away. It wouldn't matter what the scattered papers said or who might be depicted in the photographs, if the two of them were swept up by police responding to the shooting call. Before he could protect his friends, the soldier knew it would be necessary to protect himself, to put some ground between himself and five fresh corpses that would have to be explained.

He had no explanation for the carnage yet, but it was coming. He could feel it in his gut. If only he could recognize the answer, seize the truth before it throttled him.

SHE WATCHED HIM as he finished with the printouts of Brognola's phone calls, passed them back and started riffling through the photographs a second time. Was that a frown of recognition? Of concern? The silence stretched between them like a taut piano wire, and Susan Landry clenched both hands together in her lap to keep from gnawing at her nails.

He looked the same... or did he? Finely chiseled features, so unlike the face that she had known in Cleveland, but she recognized him well enough from their encounter on the eve of his defection from the Phoenix Program, from another meeting in a Texas cell block.

She wondered if those eyes had seen so much of blood and fire that they could never smile again. She stopped herself before the maudlin train of thought could take her any farther. She was on a story, dammit, and the man beside her was a part of it. If there had been no solid handle on the thing before, she had it now. One federal officer accused of bribery and worse, a second murdered in his home by contract killers—and the Executioner in Washington. Again.

Despite herself, she felt a certain awe in Bolan's presence and she realized that it could rob her of her objectivity if she permitted it to go too far. The man had saved her life on two occasions—no, three; she couldn't just forget about tonight—and in return she studied him as if he were some kind of laboratory specimen, examining his actions, scrutinizing motive and effect. It was her job, and yet she owed him so much more.

The man's arrival was coincidence, his brisk elimination of the four assassins done before he even knew that she was in the room. It scarcely counted if you put things in perspective properly.

But yes, the man had saved her life. Again.

He finished with the photographs but did not pass them back to her at once. When several heartbeats passed in silence, Susan took it on herself to break the ice.

"Familiar faces?"

"What?" It seemed as if her voice had brought him back from somewhere. He shrugged. "A few."

"I guess they're syndicate."

"Does that come from DeVries?"

She nodded, wondering how much she could afford to give away.

"I don't know how much else he had, but he was banking on indictment and conviction."

"Any names?"

"He didn't have the time. I planned to trace the numbers through Ma Bell."

Had she said *planned*? Why was she talking in the past tense? Nothing she had seen so far tonight had changed her mind.

"I'd like to show these to a friend," he said, so softly that she almost had to strain to catch the words.

"Brognola?"

She had hoped to take him by surprise, but Bolan only frowned, the graveyard eyes unflinching, locked with her own. "I can't go into that."

She felt the sudden anger flaring, made no real attempt to rein it in. "For heaven's sake," she blurted, "I've already spoken to him once. And just in case you missed it, I was almost murdered earlier tonight."

"While working on a story."

"No!" She hesitated, startled by her own response. She *had* been working on a story, hadn't she? When she spoke again it was as if in answer to herself. "Not just a story."

"Oh?"

"I thought I could help...somehow."

"You didn't help DeVries."

"I didn't kill him, either. But I'll bet my life that someone in those pictures did."

"Don't bet with anything you can't afford to lose."

"You think I'm wrong?"

"I think I'd like to run these past a friend and hear him out before I make up my mind, either way."

"Okay, let's go."

There was a trace of humor in his smile. "I'll drop you at a pay phone. You can take a cab back to your car, but you'd be smart to wait awhile and let the bluesuits finish up."

"I'll stick with you."

"It's not an option."

She turned away from him and faced the darkness, concentrating on her own reflection in the windowpane and trying to collect her thoughts.

"You owe me one," she said. "You wouldn't have those pictures if I hadn't gone to interview DeVries."

"I'd say we're even."

"There are ways that I can help you...and your friend."

"If I keep wasting time, you'll have a chance to help me out with an obituary."

"Dammit, I know people in this town! If you need information, I can get it for you."

Susan stopped herself, aware that she was offering to join him, in effect become a part of the mystery and bloodshed that surrounded him. But she had already become a part of it...how long ago? Had she been anything but part of it since Cleveland? Since McLary County?

There was something in his silence that unnerved her.

"So?" she asked.

"What do you know about Lee Farnsworth?"

"I know you killed him."

"What about associates?"

"Inside the Company?"

"That's right."

"Well...I could make some calls. I know some people out at Langley. But it's give and take. You've got to let me in."

Hesitation while he thought it over, then, "It isn't my decision."

Susan tasted victory, a flavor so elusive that she swallowed it at once.

"So, make your calls."

"My friends may not be interested," he said.

"I'll take the chance. They turn me down, I'm out. Case closed."

"And out *means* out?"

"What can I tell you? You've got all my evidence for what it's worth, and there's a little matter of some unsolved homicides."

"They wouldn't hold you overnight."

"They wouldn't give me bupkus for my story, either. Dammit, I need you as much as you need me."

And even as she spoke the words she wondered whether Bolan needed her at all. That line about Lee Farnsworth was intriguing, but...

"I'll make some calls."

She felt like cheering, but she kept it to herself as Bolan put the car in motion, pulling out of the deserted filling station into spotty evening traffic. There was still a chance that she might be rejected by his "friends"—Brognola and whoever else was presently involved—but her acceptance by the soldier was a triumph in itself.

As for Lee Farnsworth, his connections in the Company, there would be ways to tap that well of information—to a point. The CIA was so damned secretive that some directors never knew precisely what was going on within the ranks, but Farnsworth was—had been—a renegade. His lethal games had been a rank embarrassment to veterans in the Agency, inspiring oversight committees that had poked around inside the nooks and crannies. There would be secrets left intact, of course; you couldn't make the Company go public any more than you could make the syndicate go straight. But agents on the right side of the line would be concerned about a repetition of the Farnsworth episode. They might cooperate in weeding out another renegade, if he could be identified.

And where had that thought come from? There was nothing in the circumstances of Brognola's case to indicate an Agency involvement, nothing in the murder of DeVries that smacked of anything but Mafia. If Bolan hadn't mentioned Farnsworth...

But he had, and Susan knew the soldier well enough to realize that he would have his reasons. He had not survived this long by chasing phantoms of his own creation. If he had a lead on some of Farnsworth's cronies, other rotten apples at Langley, and if any of it was connected with the moves against Brognola...

Jesus, it could be the story of the year!

The lady kept her fingers crossed and prayed that Bolan's friends would not reject her offer of assistance, bar her from the game. It was a death game now, and there would be more killing before the final score was toted up and verified. It crossed her mind that she might be among the dead, but she put the prospect out of mind. The risk was part of her profession, and a part of it that Susan Landry secretly enjoyed.

She would enjoy the chance to work with Bolan, and that was no one's secret. Even as she offered up her prayer for personal success, another was already forming in her mind. She prayed for Bolan's safety through this night, at least, and hoped with all her heart that she would not be called upon to watch him die.

Because she needed him a damn sight more than Bolan needed her.

And that was one dark secret she might carry to her grave.

16

The photographs had worried Bolan most of all. Their mere existence proved that Hal was being closely shadowed, and together with the phone logs they presented Bolan with the picture of a tight surveillance that had obviously been conducted over several months. At first he was surprised that Hal had failed to recognize the tail, but with the new equipment readily available to governments and individuals, surveillance had become a whole new ball game in the eighties. Telephoto lenses were the least of it, he realized, and half a dozen agencies might listen in on private calls without a hint of any warning to the person being scrutinized.

The *how* of it was rendered insignificant by Bolan's curiosity about the *who* and *why*. If Hal was truly under government surveillance, then the Feds had not received their money's worth. The evidence against him would not stand in court, nor even bring indictments once Brognola told his side. It was the other possibility—the probability—that worried Bolan now. If the surveillance of Brognola was in fact conducted at the urging of the syndicate, then Gianelli or some other ranking mafioso would have access to the logs and photographs. And that spelled danger.

Because the photographs had captured Hal in covert conversations with a half dozen of his ranking undercover agents working on the orgcrime beat. Selected mobsters, grafting politicians or affiliated businessmen who had "rolled over" on the syndicate, providing vital information on the operations of the Mafia in major cities coast-to-coast. The soldier knew a few of them by reputation, others from the supersecret Phoenix files at Stony Man, and any member of the Mafia's La Commissióne would instantly appreciate the full significance of secret conversations with Brognola. Any capo worth his salt would know that Hal had never taken payoffs, never signed his name on anybody's pad and Family members or associates who huddled with him would be marked for execution as traitors.

But there was more.

Aside from Hal himself, the faces captured by surveillance cameras had been secondhand acquaintances to Bolan, for the most part. He had seen their mug shots, read their Justice files, but he had never met them face-to-face. Except for one.

Besides Brognola's, his had been the only face repeated in a string of photographs, proof positive that his connection with the man from Washington had been no mere coincidence. The pictures damned him irrefutably as Brognola's eyes inside the Mob, and it would only take a glance from Gianelli—hell, from *any* ranking boss—to seal his fate. The soldier felt an arctic chill engulf him as he contemplated the reward that lay in store for recognized informers, once they were identified by fellow mafiosi. He would not have wished that living hell on anyone.

And least of all on Nino Tattaglia.

The guy had been an underboss with Carlos Nazarione's family, out of Baltimore, when he was tagged by federal agents for a double homicide. His choices had been limited, and Nino had rolled over quickly, clutching at the opportunity to save himself from prison. Granted, it had been a matter of expediency, but the mobster had been going through some private changes since recruitment by Brognola's strike force. Over time, Tattaglia had been transformed from grudging mole to something else entirely, his perspectives gradually evolving from the savage state to something that approached the altruistic. He had already taken Leo Turrin's place as Hal's primary source of inside information on the Mob, and Bolan—ever cautious in his dealings with "converted" mobsters—came to realize that

Nino was the rarest of all jungle predators: a leopard who could truly change his spots.

Worse yet, if they could capture Nino, if they had the capability of trailing Hal that far without his noticing, then it was possible that they—whoever in the hell *they* were—might breach the Phoenix Program soon. The soldier would not let himself believe that it had been exposed already; it was possible, of course, but contemplation of another Stony Man fiasco was too much for him to deal with at the moment. Able Team and the others would have to watch their own back door, while Bolan did the job that he had come to do in Wonderland.

He watched Brognola shuffle through the photographs once more, and waited till the big Fed dropped them on the coffee table.

"So?"

Brognola's gaze went from Bolan to Leo Turrin, back again. His tone was cautious, and it didn't take a genius to realize that he was having second thoughts about the presence of the woman in their midst. It had surprised the Executioner when Hal and Leo grudgingly agreed to her suggestion—her demand—that she be dealt into the game. From the expression on Brognola's face he was already having second thoughts, and Bolan understood where he was coming from. He had the most to lose if things went sour, and the lady was a wild-card noncombatant, tested in the press room but completely inexperienced in combat.

Bolan put the problem out of mind and concentrated on the photographs, the evidence that Hal's most sensitive connections in the Mob had been exposed.

"If this is what it seems to be," he said, "you'll need to bring some people in."

Brognola nodded wearily. "I'm way ahead of you on that," he answered. "Jesus, what a mess."

Across from Hal, hunched forward on the sofa, Susan Landry glanced from one man to the other, sudden understanding in her eyes.

"Did you say bring some people in? These men...they're all your contacts? They're informants?"

Silent moments spun between them while Brognola turned the answer over in his mind.

"It's not for publication," he informed her stonily.

"I know that, dammit."

Bolan nipped the grin before it had a chance to spread, but Turrin wasn't quick enough, and he could see the longtime undercover man begin to relax a little.

"We've been working on this thing forever," Hal confided, holding Susan with his eyes. He gestured toward the photos with a listless hand. "These people are informants, and between them they've been steering us toward heavy busts for years. The very fact that they're on film could be the end of everything. Their lives, their families..."

At mention of families, Brognola lapsed into silence, brooding. Bolan had already briefed the lady on Hal's situation, with the Fed's permission, touching on the highlights from the disappearance of his family to the raid against DeVries. The four of them were in agreement that the move against Brognola's wife and children must be linked directly to the frame at work, the confiscation of his private files. Without those documents, it might be difficult to prove that Nino and the rest were business contacts, that they worked for him and he was not in their employ. Without those files to back him up, Brognola would be forced to pit his unsupported word against the damning evidence of photographs that showed him huddled with some of the most powerful thugs in the country.

And, while he fought his private battle in the courts, the men depicted in those photographs would start to disappear. They might already have begun to vanish, and their lives could certainly be counted down in hours now if Nicky Gianelli or his counterparts of La Commissióne had copies of the snapshots. There would be no need for lengthy trials with evidence like that against the Family's enemies.

"I've got some calls to make," Brognola said, and Bolan knew their minds were operating in a single channel. There might still be time to save some lives—save all their lives, with any luck.

He watched Brognola lumber from the room and turned to Leo, feeling Susan Landry's eyes upon him, watching, waiting.

"Okay, Sticker, what's the bottom line?"

Leo Turrin had been startled by the Executioner's suggestion that they bring the lady in, but Leo was accustomed to surprises, and he had recovered swiftly, going with the soldier's judgment that she might be useful somewhere down the line. She wasn't hard to look at, he could say that much for her already, and he hesitated for a heartbeat while he put his thoughts in order.

"You were right about DeVries," he told Bolan. "It was Family, for sure, but you can kiss off any solid trace to Gianelli."

"Never mind," the soldier answered. "Gianelli runs this town. If outside talent's coming in, they're coming in through him."

"I'd say that's true. We still don't have a goddamned thing—excuse me, ma'am . . ."

The lady graced him with a smile. "I've heard the word before," she said. "In fact, I've used the word on more than one occasion."

Already feeling foolish, Leo forged ahead. "We still don't have a thing connecting Erskine with the Families, but then again, we shouldn't hope for anything on paper. If they had him on the pad, we'd have to check his bank accounts, his safe-deposit boxes, all of that."

"We can assume he was a player," Bolan said, shrugging off the need for proof that Gianelli owned DeVries. "The Family wouldn't tag a Fed unless they had a way to cut their losses in the end."

"Exposure?"

Bolan nodded.

"I'd be looking for it somewhere down the road. Right now we need to figure out what made them punch his ticket."

Susan Landry raised a cautious hand, reminding Leo of a little girl in school, except that she was anything but little, anything but childish in her figure and her face. She was all woman, and she had a subtle way of never letting any man forget it for an instant.

"He might have been exceeding his authority."

Bolan frowned. "It's possible," he granted. "He was pushing it. He might have stepped on someone's schedule."

Susan was ahead of him.

"They might have wanted all the so-called evidence preserved for court appearances. If someone found out that DeVries was leaking it ahead of time..."

"They would have tried to plug the leak."

"Which means..."

"That they were out for all concerned, not just De-Vries."

The recognition hit her like a fist above the heart, and Leo watched her slump back on the sofa, going pale. The brush with sudden death had strung out her nerves already, but the acceptance of the fact that she had been a target of the gunners would be something else again. There was a world of difference between coincidental intervention in another's tragedy and having someone sentence you to death.

"You'd better keep out of sight until this all blows over," Bolan told her gently. "If the Family was planning on a double funeral, they'll be looking for you now."

"Where does it end?"

"With Gianelli," Bolan told her, "or whoever else is running down the frame on Hal. It ends when we've recovered everyone and everything that's missing."

"All right."

The lady seemed resolved to living under siege, but Leo thought he could still see signs of strain around her mouth, her eyes. And she had reason, certainly. If Gianelli had his hunters looking for her on the streets, she had a perfect right to worry. It was a threat that might have put some stony soldiers on the verge of tears, but she was holding like a champ, at least externally. And in the business she had chosen, it was the exteriors that counted. You could dazzle them with footwork, and if they didn't see you sweat, they might—just might—be duped into a serious miscalculation when they tried to take you out.

The no-sweat factor had been Turrin's own salvation on a number of occasions, but he couldn't bring himself to handle grim nostalgia at the moment. Here and now was bad enough, and if he wanted here and now to hang around awhile, it needed all of his attention.

Careless soldiers rarely lived to rake their pensions in, and Turrin had survived the hell of Southeast Asia, years of burrowing within the Mob, by taking care of details, trusting in his instincts and responding when they flashed a warning signal to his brain. Right now he knew that they were all in danger—not just Hal, his family, or the woman from the media. The net was closing fast, and if they couldn't find a loophole, couldn't cut themselves a new way out, they would be snared. Irrevocably. Irretrievably.

They would be dead unless they found a handle on the situation soon. Perhaps, if Bolan and Brognola were successful at their midnight meeting with the enemy...

A flicker on the edge of vision brought his head around, and Leo found Brognola standing in the doorway to the den. The guy had aged a decade since his family disappeared, but he was looking even older now, his shoulders slumped, dark rings beneath his melancholy eyes. A silent moment passed while everyone regarded him with curiosity, and when he spoke at last they had to strain to catch his words.

"Too late," he said, and for a moment Leo thought that he was going to drop it there. "Somebody rigged a charge to Nino's car this afternoon, between the time he reached his office and the time he started home for dinner. They tell me there was goop enough to take out half a city block. He's gone."

THE CAB RIDE BACK from Hal Brognola's to the condo parking lot where she had parked her Honda gave Susan Landry time to think. About her life, her work and the possibility of her own violent death by the hand of some Mob hit man. She was no stranger to the rough assignments: street crime, underworld investigations, brushfire wars. But in the past she had drawn solace from her status as a paid professional observer. She had been outside the action for the most part, looking in. On the occasions where it had been necessary for the Executioner to save her bacon, she had stumbled into situations where her life was jeopardized. In Cleveland. In the Farnsworth business. And, she had believed at first, in her encounter with DeVries.

The knowledge that she might have been deliberately selected as a target, that another man or group of men had casually decreed her death, was chilling. Susan wondered how professional combatants lived with that forbidding knowledge day to day—and in a sudden flash of understanding it became clear to her. Mack Bolan had been living with a contract on his head since he had first thrown down a gauntlet for the Mafia at Pittsfield, in the first days of his private war. He had been living in the cross hairs ever since.

It was the dedication of the man that gave her pause, and Susan wondered how she would perform now that she had been declared a moving target. Her immediate reaction was an overwhelming urge to run and hide. But she could not exist in darkness, could not ply her trade without some access to the streets.

And she had promised Bolan she would help. That was the worst of it. She was committed for the grim duration of his Washington campaign, and there was every likelihood that they would all be killed before the sun came up on Monday morning. It would be a miracle if they survived the weekend and despite her Catholic background, it had been some time since Susan Landry put her faith in miracles.

She owed the soldier her assistance in the search for Hal Brognola's wife and family. She knew that he had compromised himself, risked much to have the others take her in, accept her in their council. She was not their equal—she did not delude herself on that score for an instant—but there might be things that she could do. Her contacts with the CIA, for instance. And some leads at Justice that were temporarily closed to Hal.

It was the hint of Company involvement that disturbed her most. They had discussed it briefly, after Hal had poured a drink and downed it straight, when they were finished grieving for Nino Tattaglia, a man she had never known outside of glossy photographs. From the expressions on their faces Susan gathered that there had been more than business between them, but she had not dared to ask.

It had been Bolan who first broached the subject of the CIA's involvement—or its possible involvement—in abducting Hal Brognola's family. The smaller man, who had been simply introduced to her as Leo, had his reservations, opting to believe that Nicky Gianelli had sufficient troops and wherewithal to snatch three people on his own, without assistance from the federal government. It took Brognola to command Turrin's attention with his mention of "reliable reports" that some of Farnsworth's cronies might be working with the syndicate toward some end that was not as yet entirely clear.

Ignoring the sporadic stabs at conversation from her cabbie, Susan concentrated on her private thoughts, replaying portions of the conversation from Brognola's den.

"So, what's the hook up with the Company?"

"They've been hooked up for over twenty years."

"You're reaching. All that stuff about Fidel..."

"So, now it's not Fidel. Now it's Baby Doc, or the Sandinistas, or it's just some of the good old boys who need some reassurance that their tracks are covered."

"All of this for old times' sake?"

"Goddammit, I don't know. But if my source is right about Lee Farnsworth's crowd still hanging on at Langley, you can pick your motives by the dozen."

"*If* your source is right, okay. So, how reliable's this Mr. X? How highly is he placed?"

"He's at the top. They don't come any higher."

Hal Brognola's eyes had bored into her own, and something passed between them. Susan knew that he was handing her the story of a lifetime, and she knew that most—or all—of it would never see the light of day. She had already sworn herself to secrecy, the price of being granted entry to their huddle in the first place, and she would not break her word to Bolan. The man meant more to her than that, although her feelings were demonstrably irrational, perhaps insane.

She would attempt to use her contacts in the Company to learn if any of Lee Farnsworth's bosom friends were still around, still in position to conduct a covert operation of the sort that had embroiled Brognola's family. If she could unearth any solid evidence, then she could . . .

What?

Crank out a series that would cinch her for the Pulitzer?

Produce a book that would expose the inner workings of the secret government?

Susan Landry was committed to a course of action diametrically opposed to every instinct. Rather than exposing crime, corruption and the rest of it, she was collaborating with a wanted criminal—a murderer, no less—and helping to select his future targets. Rather than attempting to exonerate Brognola through the media, by showing up the shoddy frame for what it was, she was involved in dark guerrilla warfare with the Mob—and possibly with renegades inside the very government that both of them were seeking to protect.

The secret witness angle was a story in itself, but once again she knew that it was out of bounds. Already one of Hal's important contacts had been murdered, and before he reached the others on his list, they might be dead, as well. She could accomplish nothing positive by publishing their names while they survived. But as for those who had been sacrificed . . .

The germ of an idea had taken root in Susan's mind and it was growing rapidly. There just might be a story, after all, provided she could get the facts to back it up. A story of the men and women who had given everything they had to strike a blow against the savages, and who were paying for it now in blood. If she could write *that* story—from the viewpoint, say, of an informant who had been found out and executed by the mob—there was a chance that she could turn another spotlight on the syndicate, give Gianelli and his cohorts reason to remember her.

Before they killed her.

A chill had wormed its way beneath her scalp, but the woman kept herself from trembling with thoughts of Bolan. If the soldier's plans worked out, there would be no more Nicky Gianelli for her to expose, no renegades at Langley, no more threat to Hal Brognola's family.

If Bolan's plans worked out.

And if they didn't, then she would be honoring his last request for an obituary, dammit, putting heart and soul into the lines that summarized a valiant life. She couldn't do him justice on the printed page, but she would do her best, and Susan knew that Bolan would have counted that as fair enough.

But she was hoping that she would not have to write those lines. Not yet. Not here and now. Not while there was so damned much left to say.

17

They had removed her watch upon arrival at the safe house, but Helen Brognola knew that there was less than ninety minutes left. Her information had been gathered from the muffled conversation of their captors, from her internal clock that marked the passing hours faithfully, if imprecisely. It was past ten-thirty now.

The meeting had been scheduled for the stroke of midnight, Helen knew that much. She also knew that Hal would be on time, or early. He had not been late for anything in years, and he would not start now with so much at stake. But Helen wished that she could warn him, prevent him from appearing at the rendezvous. She could have saved him, given a chance, but there wouldn't be another opportunity.

She idly wondered how long they would live past midnight once the thing was done. Long enough, perhaps, to find a makeshift weapon, seek some measure of revenge against the animals who were already moving to destroy her world. If there was nothing she could do for Hal, there might be something that she could accomplish for the children, even with her death.

And death was coming.

Soon.

There had been little hope from the beginning. She had realized it when none of their abductors took precautions to disguise themselves. And having understood that she, Jeff and Eileen were not expected to survive and testify in court, the only question still remaining dealt with time. At first, she thought, it had been Hal who saved them, doggedly insisting that they each speak to him by telephone before he would consider the demands of their abductors. Later, once the snatch team got their orders from outside, their deaths had taken on the status of a planned event, the intervening hours finite.

If there was any doubt at all, the bits and pieces of a conversation gleaned by listening at the door had wiped all hope away.

"What are we waiting for? Let's get it over with."

"We're waiting 'cause we got our orders. I'll tell you when we go."

"We're wasting time."

"You're getting paid, man. Settle down."

"The cops—"

"Don't have a frigging idea where we are. Besides, another couple of hours, and they'll all be busy out at Arlington."

"The meet still set for twelve?"

"It's set. They're looking at a clean sweep."

"Then we can get this over with?"

"We're waiting for the call."

"Suppose they're late?"

"Suppose they are. You got a date or something?"

"Tell you what I wouldn't mind, and that's a piece of what we got in there."

"She's half your age, you horny bastard."

"So? I like 'em young."

"You like 'em any way that you can get 'em."

"True. So true."

"Well, you can keep it in your pants until we get that call."

"And then?"

"We'll see."

Helen kept the certain knowledge of annihilation to herself, and started looking for a weapon once again. They had already scoured the room, found nothing but the furniture itself, the chairs on which they sat, and those would stand small chance against the automatic weapons carried by their captors.

It was not the thought of death so much that frightened her. The startling concept of her own mortality had been uniquely driven home at thirty-three, when doctors had removed a pea-sized nodule from her breast. They had determined it to be benign, but in the interim she had prepared herself for painful, wasting death, and having faced her fears up close, she knew they had no power in themselves. You were alive until you died, and after that... well, she would have to wait and see.

It was the threat against her children, the apparent threat to Hal, that worried Helen now. Her husband was a man accustomed to the dark side, long conditioned to a world where murder was routine. He would protect himself as best he could, and given any opportunity at all, he would survive. It would be difficult, of course. The odds would be against him, but Helen knew what he could do. At home he seldom spoke about his job, and never brought the bloodshed with him when he left the office. But she knew that he had killed on more than one occasion, stopping men who meant to take his life, the lives of others. He was strong and as hard as nails when he was angry, though the family had seldom seen that side. She knew him as a man of grim determination, and she knew that given half a chance he would survive.

A lump formed itself in Helen's throat as, for seemingly no rhyme or reason, she remembered the skinny young law student whom she had fallen in love with. And after marriage, through births, tottering steps and painful puberty he had been at her side, her children's, wincing silently and feeling the pain as Jeff and Eileen resolutely bore the ravages of growing up. The strength they showed then was a testament to the Brognola blood.

Now someone wanted the Brognola blood....

Helen dismissed this grisly train of thought and concentrated on the here and now, her children. They were intelligent with the resilience of youth, but they were in a cage from which there might be no escape. Without their father's history of dealing with the savages, they were completely unprepared for what was happening around them.

Helen knew they would resist when it was time, but what could Jeff accomplish in the face of armed professionals?

She worried most about Eileen and what she might be forced to suffer once the signal for their execution had been given. Two of their abductors—the gorillas, Gino and Carmine—had been ogling her from the beginning. If they were unleashed with time to kill before they finished it ...

She closed her mind to the disgusting, painful images and concentrated on discovering a means of self-defense. A gun would be ideal, of course, but there was little chance—no chance—that she could get her hands on any of the hardware carried by their kidnappers. She would stay alert in case they dropped their guard, but in the meantime they were down to bare survival with the tools at hand. Provided they could find the necessary tools to start with.

Helen forced herself to study her surroundings carefully, alert for anything she might have missed. A simple bedroom with adjoining bath, the furniture comprised a queen-sized bed devoid of sheets and blankets, with a pair of mismatched wooden, straight-backed chairs. The empty closet had been stripped of hangers, anything that could have been converted to a weapon. In the tiny bathroom, drinking "glasses" made of Styrofoam were something less than lethal.

Still, there would be something. There was always something.

Bathrooms meant hot water. They could let it run till it was scalding, fill the little cups, and somehow lure one or both of the gorillas into range before the water cooled. A dash of liquid fire across the eyes, and if they weren't all shot to death immediately, there was just a chance that one of them could seize a weapon, turn it on their captors ...

She shook her head, disgusted with the fantasy that had attempted to seduce her. It was ludicrous, attacking armed professionals with little cups of water. They would all be killed at once unless the gunners were delayed by laughter, forced to catch their breath before they opened fire. It was a foolish plan. Worse yet, the thought of running water had awakened stirrings in her bladder, forcing Helen's full attention from the problem of the moment into confrontation with the routine problems of biology.

The plastic seat was cold, and Helen warmed it with herself, examining the stark surroundings for potential weapons, noting that the shower curtain had been left in place, its plastic curtain hooks completely useless to her now. Assuming she could get the curtain off its rod—

She froze, humiliated by the knowledge that the answer had been there before her all the time. The rod. A hollow shaft of lightweight metal held in place by tension, it could be dismantled by a child. It would not weigh enough to make a decent fighting staff, but if they flattened one end, mashed it down and twisted it somehow, they might produce a clumsy sort of lance. If it was driven into unsuspecting, unprotected flesh with adequate velocity and force...

There was another rod inside the closet, Helen realized, and that one was a hefty wooden cudgel mounted into brackets that facilitated its removal in the interests of space. No tools would be required, and in a few more moments they would have a staff, a spear—the makings of a mini-arsenal.

She flushed the toilet and tugged up her slacks—immediately conscious of another weapon close at hand. Before the tank refilled itself, she found the shutoff valve and closed it tight. She raised the heavy lid, aware that it could do some damage if the slab of porcelain was smashed against a human skull, and laid it carefully across the sink. She studied the assembly of tubes and floats and wires that had released mankind from midnight rambles to a reeking privy in the yard, and knew that it could serve her now in other ways.

She broke three fingernails and cut her fingers twice before she finished disassembling the mechanism, salvaging the slender float arm and an eight-inch metal slat that had been previously connected to the flush handle. Either one was stiff and sharp enough to savage unprotected eyes and throats at need, assuming she got close enough to try. Without a wrench to loosen pipes beneath the sink and give herself a bludgeon worthy of the name, it was the best she could do.

But she could not do everything alone.

They had four weapons now, albeit primitive and flimsy in 'the face of submachine guns. She would need the full cooperation of her children if they were to have a chance at all.

The risks were staggering, but there was finally no alternative. Inaction was a form of suicide, she realized, and once their deaths were finally decreed, the end would come in seconds for herself, for Jeff. But not, perhaps, for young Eileen. The leader might not have the interest or the energy to finally restrain Gino and Carmine once the killing started. When it came right down to it, the leader might enjoy a little stolen sex himself.

If there had been a chance, however slight, of their survival, Helen might have counseled Eileen to submit, to save herself by any means and confront the ordeal another day, when she was safe and sound and out of there. But they were doomed; she knew that much with numbing certainty. And knowing that, she saw no need to make it easy for their would-be murderers.

It went against the grain to simply watch her life, the lives of both her children slip away. A fighter as long as she could remember, the lady knew that she would go down fighting. Before she let the gunners take Eileen and foul her with their touch, she was prepared to die, prepared to kill.

Soon now. At midnight or a little after. When the gunners got their orders on the telephone.

She called the children and showed them what she had already done, and set about dismantling the shower rod. The closet would be next, and they would take it one thing at a time, while time remained.

A maximum of sixty minutes now, and Helen felt a tightness in her chest as she began to count her life, her children's lives, in measured heartbeats. They had one chance in a hundred thousand of surviving, but she could not let that single opportunity slip by without attempting to secure it. By midnight she would know if she was capable of killing physically; the mental qualms had long since disappeared.

And she would need the grim resolve that had already settled on her shoulders, worming deep into her heart and mind with tentacles of ice. She was relying on the threat against her children to provide her with the killer instinct she would need to do the job.

By midnight.

By the witching hour.

Sixty minutes minimum, and counting down.

A lifetime.

"TIME TO GO."

Brognola checked his watch and nodded, startled by the hour. Saturday was damn near gone, and Sunday morning promised little in the way of respite from the empty ache he felt inside.

"Okay."

He finished wiping down the Smith & Wesson .38 and stowed it in a holster riding on his hip. The Bulldog .44 from Charter Arms was snug beneath his arm in horizontal rigging that would shave a heartbeat off his draw, and both were loaded with the lethal Glaser "safety slugs" designed for heavy stopping power. Copper-jacketed projectiles filled with Number 12 shot suspended in liquid Teflon, the bullets were designed to exit from the muzzle at terrific speeds, exploding savagely on impact with a human target. And if impact from the Glasers failed to drop your man, there was the grim fringe benefit of creeping poison, Teflon working through the veins until it reached the heart, occluding vital passages and valves, arresting life.

More Glasers went into his pockets, rattling softly as he hoisted off the bar stool, following the others. Leo was already waiting for them by the door, one arm pressed tight against his side, securing the Uzi that he carried beneath his trench coat. He was tight-lipped, somber, but his hands were steady, and Brognola had no fear that he would fade when it was in the fan.

Mack Bolan wore his nightsuit underneath a bulky top-coat, weapons visible as bulges to Brognola's eye. A casual observer wouldn't notice, and in any case they would not be encountering a crowd at Arlington this time of night. The Unknown Soldier would be keeping any secrets to himself, and as for their intended contacts...well, they would be seeing Bolan's hardware right up close and personal. With any luck at all, it just might be the last thing that the bastards ever saw.

Provided that they kept the date, of course.

In spite of their precautions, there was a possibility that the contact team might smell a rat, take off without completing the connection. Hal would never know until it was too late, and he would have to live with his decision. But in the meantime he was banking on their plan, betting everything that they would keep the rendezvous.

No matter that it was a trap. That much was obvious from the beginning. Anyone possessed of the ability to follow him for months on end and photograph his meetings with a number of important undercover operatives had no need to negotiate for secret witness lists. The snapshots and phone logs were persuasive evidence that Justice had been penetrated weeks before the move against his family. If further evidence was needed, it would be found in the fact that Justice staffers hadn't yet identified the undercover agents. Someone on the other side was miles ahead of federal investigators when it came to cracking Hal Brognola's private orgcrime network.

From day one his work on SOG was strictly need-to-know. No more than half a dozen people in the government had access to his files, the true identities of agents in the field. Brognola had designed the system to be fool-proof...or as nearly so as he could make it, short of absolute—and unattainable—infallibility. The files that had been confiscated from his office would contribute little to the enemy, but from the photographic evidence, they needed little more in any case.

That left him with the question of a motive, and the man from Justice finally admitted to himself that he was getting nowhere in his effort to deduce the "why" behind his family's abduction. If the goal had been to simply put him on the spot, the shooters could have found a simpler way without resorting to assaults upon his wife and children. Privately convinced that he was meant to die this night, Hal still believed that there was more behind the plot than cut-and-dried assassination.

They had brainstormed through the evening, getting nowhere as they wrestled with the scattered pieces of the puzzle. Someone had been working through DeVries, and from the evidence of his elimination, Hal was betting that the someone had been Nicky Gianelli. Whether Gianelli had been in the set alone was something else entirely, and Brognola had no way of finding out the answer, not until his family was safe and sound, his full authority at Justice reconfirmed.

If he survived the meet at Arlington, there would be enough time to think about the job, about pursuing Gianelli to the corners of the earth. It might require a lifetime, but Brognola would not rest until the D.C. capo had been killed or locked away forever.

If he survived...

It was the top priority now. He would be useless to his family if it went sour at the meet, if he did not live long enough to pluck them from captivity with Bolan's help. Hal cherished no illusions that he might be able to complete the job alone. If not for Bolan's help, if not for Leo's selfless offer of assistance, he would have been walking into Arlington alone, condemned to die.

With two guns beneath his coat and two friends at his back, he had a chance to pull it off, salvage something from the rubble. They were looking at a double cross in Arlington; he knew that much before they ever left the house, but his opponents would not field an army in such close proximity to Washington. They would be waiting for a single man, convinced that he would follow orders and come alone. Three gunners, maybe four would be enough to do the job. He would be very much surprised if they were faced with greater numbers, and the hardware they were packing should be adequate to do the job.

Bolan had agreed that there was more than mere assassination in the wind, but he had kept his speculations to himself. Whatever happened, he would be on hand to stand with Hal against his enemies. As always.

Brognola sometimes wondered where he would have been, what course he would have taken, if the Executioner had never crossed his path. If Bolan's father had been wise enough to bypass dealings with the loan sharks up in Pittsfield, or if Striker's plane had gone down while en route from Vietnam to the United States and graveside ceremonies for his murdered family. What might have been, if there had been no holy war to suck Hal in and change his life forever, leading him to heights and depths that had been unimaginable in his other life?

It didn't matter now. Bolan's everlasting war was grim reality, and Hal had signed on voluntarily, his eyes wide open to the risks involved. From grudging admiration of the soldier's talents he had passed to something more like hero worship tempered with a veteran's knowledge that no single man is impervious to death. He sided with the Executioner because the guy was doing something, fighting in a world where action had been voted out of style, where wait-and-see was everything. He had enlisted in the soldier's fight because he finally had no choice, and Bolan's exit from the Phoenix Program had not dimmed Brognola's admiration for the man, nor his commitment to the everlasting war.

The war was coming home for Hal Brognola now, in ways that he had never seriously contemplated, but it did not change his mind. The move against his family might finally destroy him, but as long as he survived, he would continue striking back against the enemy with everything he had.

He understood Mack Bolan now as he had never understood the man before. He felt the pain that finally transcended human suffering, becoming simultaneously more and less than simple pain. If he should fail to rescue Helen and the kids, Brognola knew that wound would never heal while he survived. And at the same time, he was conscious of the fact that it would not impair his own ability to single out his enemies for retribution. Private suffering did wonders for a soldier's visual acuity. Brognola could see clearly now: his duty, the potential consequences—everything except the outcome of his rendezvous with death at Arlington.

For that he would be forced to wait, and if his luck ran out there would be Bolan, running on against the savages, a doomsday engine programmed for destruction of the enemy. It gave Brognola peace of mind to know that one man's death could not abort the holy war.

He needed peace of mind tonight and strength to see him through the early morning darkness. Whatever daylight might reveal—success or grim disaster—he would face it and move on. While life and strength remained he would continue fighting, from his post at Justice or outside the fold. If necessary he would wage his battle from a prison cell.

And when they finally brought him down, he would be braced to take as many of the bastards with him as he could. It was the only way Brognola knew to play the game, and he had learned it from a master.

Time to go, and death was waiting for him in a graveyard full of heroes. If the shadow overtook him there, he would be satisfied to rest among them for a while, secure in the knowledge that an Executioner remained to carry on the fight. It was the best that he could do in terms of hope, and it would have to do for now. For Arlington and his fate.

18

Darkness and the ranks of gravestones seemed to stretch away forever, lost in murky shadow. Hal Brognola felt almost as if the dead were watching him, awaiting his reaction to their presence, looking for a signal that he understood them. At once he shrugged the morbid thought away as he realized that they were not deliberately spying on his grief. The dead knew nothing of his problems and if they had known, they probably would not have cared.

Before he reached the cemetery gates, Brognola pulled his four-door to the curb beneath some overhanging trees and doused the lights. He did not kill the engine, for he wasn't stopping long. If anyone was watching, he was banking on the fact that he was early to assuage their fears. They would believe that he was killing time, or having second thoughts about his mission, dawdling before he was committed irretrievably. With any luck at all, they would not understand that he was dropping off a passenger.

Behind him on the curb side, Bolan was already EVA before the car had come to a stop. Brognola scarcely heard him opening the off-side door and closing it again. They had removed the dome light prior to setting out, eliminating any chance that Bolan's move would be betrayed to watchers in the shadows.

Finished sooner than he had anticipated, Hal remained in place and counted down the fifteen seconds that had been allowed for his delivery of Bolan to the jump-off point. It was excessive, granted, but a rolling stop would probably arouse suspicions if his enemies were staking out the rendezvous, and he was not about to gamble with the calculated odds. Not when the lives of his wife and children were at stake.

The Executioner had chosen fifteen seconds as the optimum delay. It gave him ample time to clear the vehicle and find shelter in the shadows ringing Arlington. It also granted Hal the extra time he needed to apparently examine his dilemma, making up his mind. Another moment, and he would have drawn attention to himself; a moment less, and there would have been no apparent purpose for his pulling to the curb.

One down.

The other—Leo Turrin—would be riding with him to the drop. He was sequestered in the trunk, as comfortable as Hal could make him with a blanket folded up beneath him to provide some insulation from the road. The trunk lid was open far enough to let him breathe, secured in place by taut rubber fasteners that could be easily released. There was a possibility Brognola's contacts might wish to look inside the car, to make sure he had come alone as ordered, but the chance of anyone checking the trunk was remote. If their precautions took them that far, they would find themselves confronted by an Uzi primed and ready to dismantle anyone within effective range, and they would have a second, maybe less, to flip the mental coin and cast their vote for life and death.

Whichever way it went tonight, Brognola hoped that some of them would opt for life. He had no interest in the welfare of his enemies beyond a wish to see them all eternally consumed by hellfire, but he would require at least one prisoner to provide him with the information he required. The whereabouts of Helen and the kids, for openers. And after that . . .

So many questions, dammit, and he wondered whether there was enough time to answer all of them before he bought the farm. He needed names and motives, evidence to make it stand in court if it should go that far—but most of all he needed those infernal names. If he could finally identify the men responsible for the abduction of his family, then justice could proceed at once. Tonight. This instant.

Gianelli was involved, of course. If Hal had nurtured any doubts about the mafioso, they had been erased by the annihilation of DeVries. And yet there was the possibility—the probability—of other hands behind the move against his family, the frame so clumsily designed that it could only be a cover for some larger plan. It was the owner of those other hands whom Hal was anxious to meet in person. Only one of them could walk away from that encounter, and if neither walked away... well, then it might be worth it anyway.

The flanking move was Bolan's brainchild, and Brognola had immediately seen its wisdom. Granted that the meet at Arlington would be an ambush rather than a swap of hostages, and assuming that the enemy would want the job done right, they would have snipers among the headstones, hidden in the trees, to catch him in a cross fire once he left the car. It would be Bolan's task to pick out the snipers and pick them off before they had a chance to do their job. In the alternative, he would be left to mop the place with their remains, exacting any vengeance that he could upon the stragglers in Brognola's name.

The gates were open—they were always open—and Brognola rolled on through, the ranks of silent dead surrounding him. He sought one special monument, the meeting place, and paid no mind to all the other fallen soldiers lying head-to-heel in midnight darkness. There was enough time to greet them later if he lost it, if his adversaries carried out their strike on schedule.

The Unknown Soldier had been waiting for him, patiently, secure within his stony anonymity. Brognola felt a kinship with the nameless dead, and wondered if his mind was slipping as he killed the headlights once again, allowed the car to coast the final twenty yards.

But no. The kinship did exist. He felt it in his gut, and wondered if the Executioner could feel it as he moved through the darkness, rigged out for doomsday and prepared for death. Lord knew that Bolan had much more in common with the unknown dead than Hal could ever have.

They were alike in many ways, these unacknowledged warriors. One had shed his life in open combat, stripped of his identity by hungry flames. The other lived, fought on, but he was relegated to a kind of limbo, publicly rejected by the nation he was serving with his blood and sweat.

And tears.

To hell with anyone who thought the guy was nothing more than some sophisticated death machine. Brognola knew the truth, had seen the soldier grieving for his dead— and for the living who were victimized from day to day. The warrior's sacrifice of self, of family and future was no accident. His choice had been deliberate, made with eyes wide open to the facts of life and sudden death. He knew precisely what was coming to him somewhere down the road, and yet the only fear he felt, the only fear he showed, was for the innocent who suffered at the hands of human savages.

Brognola killed the engine and spent a moment feeling for his weapons, making doubly certain that they would be there when he required them. Perspiration slicked his palms, and he wiped them on his trousers, leaving the keys in the ignition as he left the car.

You're too damned old for this, he told himself, and instantly he answered back; not yet.

Not while one man could make a difference in the world. Not while the lives of loved ones were at stake. The day a good man grew too old for fighting off the cannibals, he had grown too damned old to live.

Brognola circled toward the rear of the car, his knuckles trailing on the broad expanse of trunk lid, tapping lightly twice, not loud enough for any sound to carry past the shadows of surrounding trees. He spoke no word, received no answer from within the trunk, but knew he had been heard and understood.

Whatever happened next, it was a free-for-all. There was no way to finally anticipate the enemy, prepare for every conceivable move. He would be forced to play the cards as they were dealt, and if he drew the ace of spades, the death card, then he still had Leo and Bolan to secure a prisoner, extract the vital information, do the best they could for Helen and his children.

BOLAN WORE THE SHADOWS like a cloak, allowed them to envelop him, insulating him from contact with the dead. There were no hostile ghosts among the fallen here, all soldiers of a common side, but he could not afford the time required for a communion with them now. He had a job to do, and it required his total concentration.

The fifteen-second lag time had permitted him to scale the cemetery wall and strike off toward the meeting point, alert to any sign of sentries as he moved through darkness toward the killing ground. Whoever had arranged the meeting with Brognola had not invested in perimeter security, and it might cost them in the long run. If they were counting on Brognola to keep the rendezvous alone, then they were starting at a disadvantage.

But he went in expecting treachery, convinced that Hal's opponents had no serious desire to talk with him. They were setting up an ambush. He had been convinced of it from the beginning, and the only problem still remaining was the length to which Hal's enemies had gone. How much more logical it would have been to follow him as they had clearly done for months, and fix some semblance of a workaday routine. So simple to prepare an ambush on his way to work, the drive back home, or any one of countless other stops Brognola made repeatedly throughout an average week.

The very complication of the present scheme—abduction of his family, with its attendant risks, the hackneyed midnight meeting in a graveyard—spoke to Bolan now of some other goal. And in the final moments of their drive to Arlington, the soldier felt that he had grasped some semblance of the answer.

Hal's opponents urgently desired his death, that much was clear. But they had never counted on his going to the meet alone. The hunters had been hoping for a pair of targets on the firing line, two victims for the price of one.

They had anticipated Bolan's urge to help a friend. Helen and the kids were bait not only for Brognola, but for Bolan . . . and the suck had worked. So far.

The Executioner did not object to playing out the prearranged scenario as long as he could add a few embellishments along the way. It might work out to everyone's advantage in the end, but his concern for Brognola's family still claimed top priority. Until they were recovered safely, or confirmed among the dead, he would proceed with the discretion of a surgeon doing delicate exploratory surgery. Once precious flesh was safe again, or finally sacrificed, he would be free to move against the dark malignancy with cleansing fire and steel.

If he could just identify the cancer first.

Smart money went on Gianelli as the front man, but there would be someone else behind him. The hint about Lee Farnsworth's old connections back at CIA had set the soldier thinking, but there was no time at present to assess the information. Bolan needed more, and now, three minutes from zero hour, he found it.

Sentry number one was huddled in the shadow of an oak tree, shifting nervously from foot to foot, the silenced Ingram MAC-10 submachine gun scarcely visible on rigging underneath his arm. His hands were empty for the moment, and he checked his watch compulsively at fifteen-second intervals.

Two minutes, thirty seconds, and the guy quit dancing, glanced around him at the darkness, finally deciding he was safe from observation. Bolan heard the zipper whisper open, watched him struggle with reluctant underwear shorts and listened to the raindrop patter of his urine as it hit the tree trunk. The soldier waited until he zippered up before he moved like silent death and closed one hand across the gunner's mouth and nose.

He twisted, raised the slim stiletto, pressed its needle point against the juncture of the sentry's skull and spine. He found the opening that Chinese call "the wind gate," penetrated, stirring briskly as he reached the brain. The sentry stiffened, loafers drumming briefly on the turf, and then became a lifeless weight in Bolan's arms.

He eased the dead man to a prone position, riffled through his pockets briefly, but found them empty. It was the identifying mark of a professional, discarding any traces of ID before a stand. He knew that if he searched the body further, he would find the clothing free of labels. The fingerprints might even have been surgically removed.

No matter. Bolan's interest in the sentry was distinctly limited, and he was satisfied with having cut the hostile odds a fraction, evening the score. There would be other gunmen waiting in the darkness, more professionals prepared to kill on order, and it would be Bolan's task to find as many of them as he could before Brognola sprang the trap.

Two minutes left.

Already he could hear Hal's car approaching in the middle distance, closing on the designated meeting place. Already he could see the Unknown Soldier's tomb, illuminated in the darkness like a guiding beacon.

Two minutes, and the sentry's death had taught him something else about their enemies. The gunner was not Gianelli's, and he had not been recruited off the streets with promises of easy cash for half an hour's wet work. He was— had been—a trained professional, a killer, and he had not drawn his paycheck from the Mob. That left a single, grim alternative, and Bolan bore it with him as he left the recent dead behind, moved out in search of other targets.

He was hunting now, alert to any sign or sound of human prey, aware that every gunner taken out before the battle increased the odds in favor of survival. For the Executioner. For Hal Brognola and his family and for Leo.

They needed every edge available, for Bolan had miscalculated in his reckoning of the potential force arrayed against them. Now he realized their enemy was anything but short on triggermen and hardware. He could field an army on a moment's notice, with no questions asked, no explanations offered. He could murder with impunity—or at the very least, with little cause for apprehension that he would be brought to hook.

The risks were greater than he had anticipated, most especially for Hal Brognola, who had everything to lose. It might be physically impossible to bag a prisoner as Brognola had desired.

Indeed, they might be lucky if they got out of Arlington alive.

THE SMELL OF OIL AND RUBBER in the trunk assailed Leo Turrin's nostrils, but he didn't mind. The spare had been removed to give him room, and with the blanket that Brognola had provided as a sort of mattress, he was scarcely bruised at all. The Uzi reeked of cosmoline, but he drew comfort from the old familiar smell.

If Hal and Bolan were correct in their prediction of an ambush, Leo was a sitting duck inside the trunk. A single burst of automatic fire could turn his hiding place into a coffin; any spark produced by ricochets might set the fuel tank off beneath him, broiling him alive before he had a chance to pop the lid and make his break. It was a risk that had been weighed and analyzed before he had agreed to ride shotgun for Brognola—not that there had ever been the slightest doubt that he would come along. His closest friends were wagering their lives tonight, and he could no more take a sideline seat than he could voluntarily stop breathing.

Leo owed it to them both, for all the times Bolan or Brognola had been there to pull his fat out of the fire. But if his life had never been at risk, if he had never walked the razor's edge with only these two friends to steady him and keep him on track, he would have volunteered in any case. For friendship's sake.

And when you got right down to basics, there *was* nothing else.

The bond of fellow warriors in an endless, losing battle, holding out against the overwhelming enemy until their luck and life at last ran out. They struck against the savages wherever and whenever possible. In the meantime they looked out for one another, for the families that waited, never really safe, behind the lines.

Because the goddamned battle lines were everywhere these days, and it could just as easily be Angelina out there in the darkness—*had been* Angelina, back in Pittsfield—and Leo knew that he could count on Hal or Bolan, if the world rolled over on him one day soon. They wouldn't let the wife and kids go hungry, wouldn't let them want for anything or fall into the hands of enemies.

A soldier watched his buddy's back, and that was it. No need to ask for help or offer thanks to any of the living when the smoke had cleared. Tomorrow it could be someone else's world in jeopardy, and yesterday's potential victim would be riding with the cavalry again.

Inside the trunk he heard Brognola kill the engine. He felt Hal shifting in the driver's seat, imagined him as he went through the ritual of double-checking weapons, getting ready to go EVA against an unknown enemy. His door slammed, sent a tremor through the car and Leo felt himself begin to sweat.

Hal drummed his knuckles on the trunk, the sound reverberating hollowly, and Leo grimaced, feeling like a mouse inside a kettle drum. He heard Brognola's footsteps gradually receding on the pavement, finally lost, and Turrin wrapped one hand around the tight rubber bands that held down the trunk lid.

He had been told to wait for contact while Brognola scouted the territory, waiting for the enemy to show himself. If Hal and Bolan were mistaken, if the hostiles were sincere about exchanging Helen and the kids for information, it would go no farther; Hal had lists of phony names and numbers that would have the bastards chasing their tails for a month. But if the others were correct in their assumption of an ambush, if the gunners opened up on Hal from who knows where, it would be Leo's job to spring the trap and cover Hal's retreat, while Bolan flanked the enemy and hit them where they lived.

It had all sounded fine on paper in Brognola's living room. But it was dark outside, and there were God knew how many hiding places in the cemetery, any shadow adequate for lurking snipers who could drop Hal in his tracks. Snipers who could riddle Leo as he tried to scramble from the trunk, all knees and elbows in the crucial instant when surprise evaporated.

Leo was a goddamned sitting duck and didn't like the feeling, but at least he wasn't out there in the open with the cross hairs planted on his face already. He found the Uzi's safety catch and eased it off, prepared to come out firing and to make the most of his advantage while it lasted.

If they didn't kill him first.

If someone didn't stitch the car with armor-piercing rounds and leave him leaking like a bag of mangled groceries in the trunk, or light him up with tracers in a flash of detonating fuel.

Too many *ifs*.

And it was too damned late, in any case. He was committed now whichever way it played. There was time to think of Bolan, wonder if the soldier was all right, if he had run afoul of roving sentries in the darkness. Then the sound of voices drifted to him from the outer darkness.

He could recognize Brognola's voice, but could not make out any of the words. The other voice was unfamiliar, and he didn't have a prayer of understanding anything the stranger said. He was about to ease the trunk lid open wider when the voices were eclipsed by sudden gunfire, the staccato yapping of an automatic pistol, answered by the booming echo of Brognola's Bulldog .44.

He ripped the taut elastic free and kicked the lid back, rolling clear before the enemy could swing around and bring him under fire. Already homing on the sound of gunshots, moving in a combat crouch, he held the Uzi primed and ready, eager for a target to present itself.

The shit was in the fan, and there was no safe way around it now that battle had been joined. As other weapons chimed in from the darkness, muzzle-flashes winking from the shadows, Turrin drew small consolation from the fact that they were fighting in a graveyard. If they lost it here, at least he would not have to travel far. With any luck, there might be room for one more soldier in the hallowed ground of Arlington.

19

Brognola had been waiting for the voice, but when it came to him from out of the gloom he was startled all the same. He lurched around, embarrassed, hoping that the darkness had concealed his momentary fear. He concentrated on the voice and willed his hands to cease their trembling.

"You're alone?"

"As ordered."

Hardmen liked that tone of deference. He kept his fingers crossed that it might lead the contact to relax his guard.

"I ought to check the car."

"Feel free."

The shadow had a human shape now, drifting nearer, pausing less than fifty feet away. His contact hesitated, thinking on it, and Brognola flexed the fingers of his gun hand. Waiting.

The shadow had made up its mind.

"Forget it. Hell, we trust each other, right?"

Brognola did not answer. He was working on the voice, trying to remember where and when he might have heard it in the past. It was familiar and yet...

"You brought the list?"

Brognola slipped his left hand in the pocket of his trench coat, and the shadow tensed, prepared for treachery. He tried to gauge the man's reaction time, encumbered by a greatcoat as he was, his hands apparently encased in gloves. If he was a professional the extra layers of clothing might not count for anything, but then again...

He had the empty sheets of paper in his hand and now he held them up, allowed the shadow just a glimpse before his arm fell back against his side.

"All right. I told them you were good for it. Some of them had their doubts, but I was on your side."

"I'm touched."

"Hey, don't go bitter on me, friend. We're in this thing together."

"No quite."

"Well, damn, I'm sorry you feel that way."

The shadow was advancing slowly, one hand edging toward his open coat, a movement so relaxed, so casual that Hal might easily have missed it if he had not been on edge, expecting the betrayal to begin at any moment. He saw the cross-hand draw before his enemy was even close, his own reaction taking him away and low, outside the first instinctive line of fire. The Bulldog .44 was in his hand before his belly hit the pavement, teeth clenched tight to keep the precious air from being driven from his lungs on impact.

And it was the shadow's turn to jump this time. The guy was dragging out an automatic from beneath his arm, side-stepping in a last-ditch bid to save himself. But he was far too late. Brognola braced the Bulldog in both hands, squeezing off in double-action as his human target tried to bring the automatic into rough alignment with his face. A blind man could have made the shot at something under forty feet, and in the instant that he fired, Brognola's night eyes were performing perfectly.

Round one punched through the target's primly buttoned vest and rocked him on his heels, the automatic booming in reflexive fire. He was already going over backward when Brognola's second round ripped through his armpit, flattening to mutilate one lung before it came to rest behind a shoulder blade.

Hal was scrambling to his feet when the surrounding darkness exploded in his face. Converging streams of automatic fire erupted from the shadows, tracking, searching for him, driving him to the ground again. Aware that Bolan had been right, deriving little in the way of consolation

from that knowledge now, he scuttled crablike on his belly
for the cover of the Unknown Soldier's monument. Around
him bullets screamed and whined on impact with the pavement, snapping overhead as hidden gunners tried to find the
range and elevation.

An enemy round traced liquid fire across his buttocks and
another whispered past his head. Scrambling for his life,
Brognola felt like some enormous lizard struggling to cross
the highway, caught by traffic in the middle of the noonday
rush. Another moment and the whispering death would
overtake him.

But he had taken one of them, and he wasn't finished yet.
He was alive and fighting.

The monument was looming over him, and Hal was
braced to make a final rush for cover when the gunner
showed himself, a slender shape detaching from the deeper
shadow of the Unknown Soldier's tomb, an errant shaft of
moonlight glinting off the silenced Ingram in his fist. Brognola fired instinctively, the Bulldog rising as he cranked off
three in rapid-fire, the big rounds ripping in from groin to
solar plexus, their explosive impact devastating at a range
of less than fifteen feet.

The gunner sat down hard, his back against the smooth
face of the monument, and Hal was scrambling past him
even as the shadow gunners realized that he was still alive,
that it had been their comrade slouched in death against the
tomb. He snatched the Ingram from lifeless fingers and slid
into cover as reactive fire began to eat the night around him,
seeking flesh and finding only darkness.

They would try to flank him now. It was inevitable. They
could not afford to let him live, and they did not have time
to wait him out. Already, someone might have heard the
gunfire, though he wondered who would be abroad in Arlington at midnight.

From the direction of the car he heard a burst of submachine gun fire ripping like a buzz saw through the smoky
darkness. Turrin had arrived, and he would give the hidden
gunners something else to think about before they made
their move. The odds were shifting, balancing upon a ra-

zor's edge, and any sudden jolt might skew them in Brognola's favor.

A jolt from Bolan, if the soldier was alive.

If he had not been ambushed in the darkness by a wary lookout. It happened to the best, but as he hunkered in the shadows with both hands locked around the captured Ingram, Hal was praying that it had not happened here tonight. They needed Bolan desperately if they were going to survive.

They needed Bolan now.

BOLAN FOLLOWED THE REPORTS of gunfire from the point where he had stalked and killed the second sentry, instinctively homing on the sounds of combat. The second guard had delayed him, struggling briskly, giving up his life reluctantly to Bolan's blade. If the lookout had been a fraction swifter, Bolan might have been the one stretched out beneath the willow's trailing fronds, his lifeblood soaking into grass that had already seen enough of death.

But Bolan's nameless enemy had not been swift or alert enough to save himself, and now the Executioner was closing on the sounds of battle, one fist wrapped around the silver AutoMag. He offered up a silent supplication to the universe, aware that he might be too late already. Hal and Leo might be dead or dying, riddled where they stood by snipers Bolan hadn't had the time to neutralize.

Bolan shrugged the morbid thought away before it had a chance to claim his full attention. Someone still was firing beyond a gentle rise in front of him. He recognized the booming voice of Hal's off-duty Bulldog, followed shortly by the chatter of Leo's Uzi, answering the muffled weapons of the enemy.

He topped the rise and melted into shadow, sweeping down upon the hostiles from their flank. He counted half a dozen muzzle-flashes, automatic weapons all, and he was closing on the nearest of them when the line began to break from cover, closing in on Hal and Leo in a pincer movement.

It took a moment, but he spotted Turrin lying behind a gravestone, waiting for a target to present itself before he wasted any more ammunition. Hal was harder to detect, and Bolan was about to let it go when a precision burst erupted from the shadow of the Unknown Soldier's monument, the nearest hostile gunner dead before his face impacted on the pavement.

Everyone was firing now, the hostiles rushing helter-skelter over thirty yards of open no-man's-land with automatic weapons blazing. Two of them immediately pinned Brognola down with probing fire. The other pair was veering off toward Leo, splitting up to flank him in a pincer of their own, assuring that there would be one survivor left to pin him down no matter what transpired.

But they had not included Bolan in their reckoning.

The soldier dropped to one knee, sighting down the barrel of the AutoMag and making target acquisition on the farthest mark first. He sucked a deep breath in, released a portion of it, held the rest to steady up his aim, already tightening his finger on the trigger, bracing for the heavy recoil.

Boom!

And downrange, closing on the Unknown soldier's monument, a gunner stumbled, sprawled, a fist-sized portion of his skull evaporating as 240 grains of screaming death punched in behind one ear, exploding through the ruins of his face to find the night again. His body wriggled briefly on the pavement as it undulated toward the curb and finally came to rest within a dozen strides of Hal Brognola's hiding place.

The second gunner had been taken by surprise, his own momentum broken by the disintegration of his comrade, and the momentary stall was all Brognola needed. Rising from the shadows of his sanctuary, tracking with his captured stutter gun, he cut the shooter's legs from under him and nailed him to the pavement with a fiery figure eight.

Big Thunder swept along the battle line and chose another target as the two surviving hitters tried to close the net on Leo Turrin. Bolan rode the recoil out and saw his target

stagger, gutted by the heavy Magnum round before he had
a chance to open up on Leo's blind side. Sagging to his
knees, he swiveled toward the lethal darkness, bringing up
his weapon, dying for a chance to take his killer with him.

Bolan let him see Big Thunder's muzzle-flash, the second round impacting on his scalp as the hollow man collapsed backward.

Turrin had already taken out the final gunner, stitching
him across the chest point-blank and following him down,
the Uzi emptying its magazine before he let the trigger go.
The guy was as dead as hell, and as the silence settled in
around them, ringing in the soldier's ears, he knew that they
had failed.

They had no prisoners.

A nagging dread enveloped Bolan as he started down the
grassy slope. Survival had been paramount, he told himself; the moment had not granted any leeway for selective
fire. When all the chips were down the instinct for self-
preservation took control. As he had killed to save his
friends, so Hal and Leo killed to save themselves.

He knew the arguments by heart and recognized their
truth, but there was precious little consolation in the fact
that they were still alive. By their survival, they had sen-
tenced Helen and Brognola's children to an almost certain
death. By slaughtering the opposition gunners, they had
wasted any chance of learning where the hostages were kept.

There would have been provisions for a callback to let the
hit team know Brognola had been taken down. They would
be waiting for instructions, where to take the wife and kiddies, how to handle the disposal...and there would be
backup plans in case of an emergency. If everything went
sour and no one called, they would have made provisions for
a scrub, elimination of the witnesses and evidence, a way to
cut their losses while they had a chance. He might have
coaxed the necessary information from a prisoner, per-
suaded him to talk as if his life depended on it, but they had
already blown their one and only chance.

Before he reached the pavement, Bolan saw Brognola
moving down the line of bodies, pausing over each in turn

and reaching down to check for vital signs. It was a futile effort, but the soldier left him to it, seeking Leo.

And finding him where he had fallen, propped up with his back against a tombstone, grinning through the rictus of his pain. Both hands were pressed against the inside of his thigh, and Bolan spied the pant leg, slick with blood from knee to ankle.

"He clipped me," Leo grated through his pain. "The bastard shot me after he was dead."

"You're lucky." Bolan crouched beside his friend and stripped off Leo's belt to make a tourniquet. "He might have *really* nailed you if he was alive."

"That's funny," Leo told him, but he didn't laugh. "So, how'd we do?"

"We got them all."

And Turrin recognized their failure instantly. "Well, shit."

"You need a doctor."

"Doctor, hell, I need a frigging keeper. If I could've winged that bird—"

"He would have blown your head off," Bolan finished for him. "Let it go."

"That's easily said."

"We didn't walk in here to make a human sacrifice. If that was it, you could have shot yourself before we left the house."

"Don't rub it in."

"Can you stand up on that?"

"I'd damn well better."

Bolan had the wounded warrior halfway to his feet when Hal Brognola's voice arrested both of them.

"Goddammit! Here! I know this guy!"

The others were beside him in a moment, Bolan serving as a crutch for Leo, who favored his belted, bloodied leg. Brognola grimaced at the sight.

"Are you okay?"

Leo's smile was forced. "I'm canceling my polka lesson for tonight. You make this dude?"

The question brought him back to the immediate priority.

"It's been a year or so," he told them both. "The name was Smith or Jones or some such throwaway. He worked for Milo Grymdyke."

"Ah."

The sound escaped from Turrin almost as a whisper, and Brognola couldn't tell if it had been inspired by pain or recognition.

"So, who's Grymdyke?" Bolan asked.

Brognola fielded it. "He's CIA. Clandestine Ops. I don't know what he's doing now, but he was handling the foreign wet work back when Farnsworth was around."

"I'd say he's gone domestic," Bolan offered, tight-lipped.

"Yeah."

"Where do I find him?"

"This one's mine," Brognola snapped. "I'll handle Grymdyke."

"Leo needs a doctor. Now."

"All right. I'll drop you at your car and you can run him by emergency receiving."

"Put it on the other foot. If Grymdyke gives his sponsors up, there won't be any time to waste."

"Time's all I've got," Brognola answered bitterly. "We blew it."

"Did we?"

"Look around you, dammit! Do you notice any walking wounded here? Somebody's waiting for a callback, and the frigging telephone is never going to ring." He felt the tears beginning in his voice and bit them back. "It's over, all except for mopping up."

"And if it's not? If there's a chance, however slim?" The soldier didn't waste his breath on phony reassurances. "I'll step aside if you say you can handle it alone."

The tears were in his eyes now, blinding him.

"God *damn* it."

"Let's get Leo in the car."

Brognola took his wounded comrade's other arm around his shoulders, helped him back to the sedan. When he was safely stowed in back, Hal slid behind the wheel with Bolan riding shotgun on his right.

"You handle it," he said when they were rolling, and the taste of shame was bitter on his tongue. "I'm out."

"The hell you are. I've never seen you quit before."

"You've never seen me throw it all away before."

"So is this where you write them off?"

"You're acting like I have an option." They were rolling toward a stoplight and he punched on through the red, ignoring horns and screeching brakes on either side. "I fucked it up, or else we all did. Either way, it's done."

"You're wrong. There's still a chance, and if we blew it, then the play's not over till you make things right."

Brognola made a sour face. He knew that things would never be quite right again.

And Bolan would not let him rest.

"Where can I get in touch with Grymdyke?"

"Last I heard he had a place in Alexandria, not far from Langley."

He was startled to recall the address with crystal clarity, the sort of trivia a tortured mind can vomit up in times of desperation. Hal repeated it for Bolan, listened as the soldier played it back.

"That's him. Assuming that he hasn't moved."

Assuming that the front man he had wasted back at Arlington had not been working on his own.

Assuming any one of half a dozen different scenarios that might make chasing Milo Grymdyke a colossal waste of time.

But they had time now, he remembered. There was no more need for haste. They had already crossed the deadline, fumbled in the end zone, trashed the play beyond repair. It didn't matter if he had to follow Grymdyke to Afghanistan and back. Brognola had the kind of time that men alone possess, free time in such abundance that it gradually crushes them beneath its weight.

He could not make himself believe that there was any hope. It would accomplish nothing, holding on to phantoms while the living still required assistance. Leo's blood was soaking through the seat, and Hal could not ignore the sacrifice his friend had made in the attempt to win his wife and children back.

He concentrated on the next light, and the next one after that, intent on dropping Bolan at his car before proceeding on with Leo to emergency. There would be police and questions to be answered, once the doctors got a look at Leo's leg, but that was fine. Hal had the time for questions now and there might even be some answers waiting for him.

God knew there was nothing else ahead of him but empty nights and hollow days, beset with memories of faces he would never see and voices he would never hear again except in dreams.

In nightmares.

He could hear them now, and they were whispering embittered accusations, carping on his failure. They had every right and he did nothing to evade them, taking all of it inside and nurturing his shame.

He had a single reason left to live, and that lay in the hope that Bolan might allow some stragglers to survive. There was a chance that one or two of Hal's tormentors might escape the cleansing fire, and he would have a reason to continue living while *they* lived, committed to extermination of the animals who had already torn his world apart.

When they were finished he would have to find another motive for survival, or surrender to the darkness that surrounded him already. For now, it was enough to concentrate on traffic, on the winking lights and on his pain.

He had sufficient time for any tasks that still remained unfinished, and there would be pain enough, he knew, to see him through his days.

20

Cameron Cartwright set the telephone receiver in its cradle, swallowing an urge to rip it free and fling it through the nearest open window. Years of playing cloak-and-dagger had prepared him to control his own emotions, and no hint of strain showed through the passive poker face. For all the outward evidence he might have just received a bulletin about the next week's weather. An astute observer might have marked the concentration lines that formed between the salt-and-pepper eyebrows, indicating that the man from the CIA was lost in thought. But none would have surmised the sharp anxiety, the brooding anger that was building inside of him.

When Cartwright lost control—say, once a decade—he was careful to surround himself with solitude before the fact. It was incongruous, this preparation for a tantrum with meticulous attention to detail, but perfectionism was his trademark, and he could not let it go this late in life. Routine was part and parcel of his life, although clandestine warriors theoretically abhorred the semblance of a pattern in their daily lives. It had been years since Cartwright worked the field, and if he seemed to have gone soft with age, with his advancement up the ladder of the Agency's command, there was a frame of steel still hidden underneath the middle-aged upholstery.

He was adept at dealing with disaster, fielding crises that might break a lesser man, but there were limits even so. His shoulders might be broad, but he was growing tired of carrying the world upon them, bearing burdens that should rightfully have fallen onto others.

Nicky Gianelli was a constant thorn in Cartwright's side, the more so since he had conceived his master stratagem for dropping Bolan and Brognola with a single stroke. No matter that the two of them were strictly Nicky's problem, he had asked for help—demanded help—and there had been no graceful way for Cameron to disengage. As long as Gianelli had those files he would be in the driver's seat, and Cartwright's only hope was to survive the bumpy ride with life and limb intact.

He blamed Lee Farnsworth for the problem. It had been Farnsworth who recruited Gianelli's predecessors for the war against Fidel, who had continued the assassination efforts—in defiance of repeated White House orders—after the Bay of Pigs disaster. When spokesmen for the Mafia's *Commissióne* had bitched about the federal drive against their brothers of the blood, it had been Farnsworth who conceived the series of scenarios that culminated on an autumn afternoon in Dallas. And before the smoke had cleared, it had been Farnsworth—with some help from Cartwright, granted—who had agitated for a special panel to investigate the murder of the President; a panel that would close the door on ugly rumors permanently, and prevent the furious attorney general from initiating an investigation of his own.

It would be thirty years before you knew it, but the Mob had never tired of dropping little reminders into Farnsworth's ear. When aircraft was required to haul the fruit of countless poppies stateside, the CIA had volunteered to fly the covert "rescue missions," braving hostile fire and customs agents to supply a growing army of addicted zombies in the streets of Everytown. When Momo Giancana thought his mistress had been looking for a little action on the side, the Agency provided wire men to investigate the "boyfriend," finally absolving him and thereby, doubtless, lengthening the poor schmuck's life. When the IRS expressed a passing interest in foreign bank accounts, the cry of "national security" was sounded to repel investigators.

It had worked to everyone's advantage through the years. The Company, for its part, had been granted access to the eyes and ears of underworld associates from Brooklyn to Marseilles, Los Angeles to Bangkok and Taiwan. The eyes saw many things, those ears heard many whispers that might otherwise have been ignored. The godless enemy was only human, after all, and when he paid for pleasure in some foreign port of call, he spent his ruples with a good friend of the Agency.

When there were problems, when attrition claimed the principals—Roselli, Giancana, Lansky—there were always others standing by to take their place. As for directors of Clandestine Ops, a few had voiced their outrage at the Agency's peculiar bargain with the devil, but they changed their tune the moment something interesting surfaced in the cesspool. None had finally possessed the nerve—the guts— to terminate Lee Farnsworth's monster. None so far.

Cartwright thought he might decide to do that little job himself.

But it would be no little job, and Cartwright recognized the problems he would face if he attempted to disrupt the status quo. For openers, he was already ass-deep in the most horrendous foul-up since the Watergate fiasco. Worse, since this particular disaster had been foisted on him by outsiders, in defiance of his own expressed concerns. It had been Gianelli's baby from day one, and now that it was starting to unravel, Cartwright knew that he would be expected to be brilliant and save the day.

Except, he knew, it might already be too late.

The move against Brognola's family was a calculated risk, but he had finally agreed with Gianelli that a threat to innocents would be the quickest draw for Bolan. It had worked, and now that Bolan was in town, the question of disposal still remained unanswered while the precious moments ticked away.

The contract on DeVries had been another calculated risk, and it had backfired in their faces. Gianelli's face, to be precise, since it had been his show. The shooters had been his—all four of them, stretched out in cold drawers at the morgue beside DeVries—and there would doubtless be some questions for the capo when detectives got around to tracing those IDs. The gunners had been sanitized to some extent, but they were traceable—hell, anyone was traceable—assuming Justice chose to go the whole nine yards. And with a ranking staff investigator dead, the whole nine yards would only be for openers.

As if the fumble with DeVries had not been bad enough, there were another eight men dead at Arlington, and they were his men this time, dammit. Trained professionals, selected for their expertise in handling the damper side of covert operations. Every one of them had been a skilled assassin with kills on foreign—and domestic—soil to prove his worth. They should have taken Hal Brognola easily, exterminated Bolan almost as an afterthought . . . but something had gone horribly, irrevocably wrong.

The body count was bad enough, but the placement had been even worse. When morning papers hit the stands, their headlines would be shrieking crap like MASSACRE AT ARLINGTON and SLAUGHTER AT THE UNKNOWN SOLDIER'S TOMB. They should have staged the meeting in a junkyard, on the river, any fucking place but Arlington. He had been showing off, and it hadn't worked for shit.

From all appearances the guests of honor had escaped unharmed. If either one had suffered injuries no evidence remained behind. A homicide detective serving double duty as another pair of Cartwright's eyes reported evidence of blood around a gravestone where no body had been found, and they were checking on the local ER logs, but Cartwright would have bet his life that they were pissing in the wind. With eight men shot to hell they could be typing blood for months and leave a tubful unaccounted for. From personal experience he knew that wounded men could travel awesome distances before they finally died.

The worst of it was Hunter Smith. He would be traceable directly back to Grymdyke's office, and from there . . .

Goddamn it!

More loose ends that would need looking after tonight, before the mess got any worse. Grymdyke was tough enough, a veteran of the Nixon purges, but if he should smell indictments in the wind, he might decide to cut a deal and save himself from prosecution. Copping out was almost SOP in Washington, and Cartwright was continually disgusted by the way bureaucrats betrayed each other.

That didn't matter now. He had to keep his wits about him. They were already running desperately short of time, and Gianelli stood no closer to the prize—Mack Bolan's head—than he had been six months ago. They might have missed their only chance already, Cartwright knew. The way the bastard had been tearing up the town, the way he handled eight of Grymdyke's best, the man from CIA had little hope of trapping him in Washington. They had already played their strongest hand, and he had walked away.

Not quite.

He hadn't walked away with any hostages, and while he was intent on rescuing Brognola's family, the bastard had an Achilles' heel. It just might be possible to stake the wife and kiddies out, trick Bolan into coming for the bait . . . and his death. He would be skittish after Arlington—he might be making tracks already—but he had the reputation of a gung-ho soldier unaccustomed to retreat. Brognola's family had drawn him here, and they would hold him here until he set them free . . . or died in the attempt.

It would be tricky, but . . .

Suppose he muffed it, fumbled one more time? Reluctant to accept the notion of defeat, he had presided over or participated in enough snafus to realize that true survivors always made contingency arrangements in advance. Before you ever fired a shot in battle, you examined ways of cutting losses, covering your ass in case of failure. If Cartwright planned to walk away from this one free and clear, without a target painted on his back and handcuffs on his wrists, he would be wise to leave his options open, cover all the bases going in.

Brognola's wife and kids would have to die, that much was obvious from the beginning. Whether they survived the night would logically depend upon their usefulness, as balanced out by any risks that their survival might entail. Alive they were the kind of witnesses that juries loved, and they could send his pickup crew away for life. Once that had been accomplished, Cartwright lost his hold upon subordinates who would be looking for an easy ride. Alive, Brognola's family was a lethal time bomb waiting to explode, and it was only logical that they should be defused as soon as possible.

He briefly weighed the options of permitting them to live for, say, six hours, giving Bolan one more opportunity to risk himself on their behalf. All things considered, though, the man from the CIA did not believe that live bait would be necessary to his plan. As long as Bolan *thought* they were alive, he would feel honor bound to make the futile, ultimately fatal, gesture. Logic cast its overwhelming vote for death, and Cartwright seconded the motion with a scowl.

The order should have gone through Grymdyke, but his second-in-command was now a problem in his own right. If the Bureau hadn't tumbled to him yet, his hours were numbered all the same, and while he lived he was a threat to everyone around him. Typhoid Grymdyke, bet your ass. Except that his disease was many times more lethal than a virus of the flesh. Exposure. Public condemnation. Loss of power in official circles. Death was infinitely preferable to embarrassment in the clandestine service—most especially if the death was someone else's.

Someone, say, like Grymdyke's.

Cameron Cartwright harbored nothing in the way of animosity against his second-in-command. Eliminating Grymdyke was a way of making up for damage that the man himself had caused through negligence. If he should disappear without a trace, the Justice probe would languish at his doorstep, starved for information that would never be forthcoming from above.

The odd man out was Nicky Gianelli, and the very thought of him made Cartwright clench his fists in anger. Twenty-seven years of honorable service—more or less—was hanging in the balance for him now, because of Gianelli's wild vendetta. While the capo possessed the crucial files containing Cartwright's name, the evidence against him, he would never be entirely free.

While Gianelli lived . . .

Of course there were a thousand ways to take him out, but it must be accomplished with discretion. Nothing that would smack of CIA involvement, certainly. Perhaps a word to other, rival mafiosi, urging them to carve a slice of Washington from Nicky's pie. It would be simple, once the reigning capo was removed.

That left the files, and Cartwright knew that he could never trust a rival mafioso to deliver them intact. A bargain might be made, but once another capo took the throne, once he deciphered the importance of the files, then Cartwright would be right back at square one. He might waste weeks or months and millions of illicit dollars, winding up with someone who was worse than Gianelli.

A replacement would never be the problem. Any time a ruling capo went to jail or bit the bullet, there were half a dozen heirs apparent standing by to take his place. The key was simply dumping Gianelli, and recovering the files that would be always close at hand. It was the kind of job the CIA was made for, and there were professionals on staff to handle every phase of the procedure, from assassinating Gianelli to location and removal of the documents. No sweat, provided Cartwright picked the team himself, avoiding stumble bums like those who left their carcasses at Arlington.

Eliminating Gianelli had its risks, of course. If Cartwright should blow it, if the greasy bastard tumbled to his plan and then survived, there would be hell to pay. It was unlikely that a contract would be let upon a ranking officer of the CIA, but nothing was impossible. More probably, selective information would be circulated to the media—the goddamned *Post*, the frigging networks—and before you knew it there would be another round of hearings, blue-nosed senators forgetting where their campaign contributions came from, looking for a little mileage at the Agency's expense.

It had been bad enough when Hoover's files had surfaced some years back; at least the old man had been dead and gone before they started dumping on him. But Hoover's antics at their worst would look like Halloween amusements next to Dallas and Los Angeles. Before the snoops had finished with him, Cartwright would be lucky if they let him bite the bullet—and he knew that no such mercy would occur to the inquisitors.

He could almost hear Lee Farnsworth's voice, a dusty whisper in his memory. *The moral of the story is: don't miss!* When he was ready for the move on Gianelli he would have to make it stick the first time out. There would not be a second chance, and Cartwright could not tolerate the obvious alternatives to victory.

He didn't count on any problem with the syndicate, provided his initial move on Gianelli was successful. Nicky's "brothers" in the outfit were a bunch of cutthroat bastards who would sell their mothers if the price was right, and if his sources were correct, they cherished no enduring love for Gianelli. There would be some confusion at the outset, capo blaming capo for the hit, the old dogs watching one another warily before they fell on Gianelli's rackets like a pack of jackals, but their petty palace politics held no significance for Cartwright. If he needed any cover for his move, it had already been provided, courtesy of Nicky's private little war.

The Executioner would handle Gianelli for him, and if evidence was needed, the technicians in Clandestine Ops could muddle through the details. It was known that Bolan had a certain style, a preference for certain hardware, which amounted to a signature of sorts. It shouldn't be too difficult to sell the media or Nicky's fellow goombahs on the notion that the Executioner had struck again, perhaps in grim retaliation for the murder of DeVries. As for Brognola's family, the wild-assed warrior had abducted them upon exposure of his one-time friend's connection to the syndicate. It was regrettable that they could not be saved, but if their sacrifice illuminated Bolan's state of mind, his swift degeneration into madness, then perhaps their deaths were not in vain.

It was a neat scenario, and it covered all the bases. He could even pass off the Arlington disaster as an attempt to trap the Executioner, a valiant effort that had cost the lives of eight outstanding agents in the field. The media would buy it, grudgingly at first, but with renewed enthusiasm once the Agency produced some solid "evidence." He knew the Mob would buy it, after all the grief that Bolan had bestowed upon them through the years. And with a bit of luck the boys at Justice just might buy it, too.

Except for Hal Brognola.

He would never buy it in a million years, no matter how they recreated history or tried to sugarcoat the bitter pill. With the elimination of his family, the man had nothing left to lose, and he would blow the whistle loud enough to wake the dead at Arlington.

Through no fault of his own Brognola had become a liability to Cameron Cartwright, and the man from the CIA decided instantly that there would have to be another corpse. Another victim of the Executioner, perhaps: a civil servant linked to underworld corruption, and who had paid the price of his divided loyalties in blood.

It was poetic justice, when you thought about it long enough.

But Cartwright did not have the time for poetry tonight. His heart and mind were on the firing line, intent on salvaging a victory from disaster.

One more chance to do it right.

And if he blew it, Cartwright knew, he would be a long time dead.

21

It was a fifteen-minute drive to Alexandria, and Bolan used the time to sort out the pieces of the puzzle that he had already managed to acquire. The gunners who had taken out DeVries were Mafia, most likely part of Gianelli's private stock, while those who bought the farm at Arlington were past or present CIA. He didn't like the implications, the malignant odor that his nostrils had detected early on, but in the last analysis he had no choice. If he was going to retrieve Brognola's family intact, he would be forced to hold his nose and forge ahead.

Brognola's hunch on Milo Grymdyke might be all he needed to complete the picture . . . or it might turn out to be another damned dead end. There was no way of judging in advance, and so he made the drive from Arlington, aware that if Brognola's hunch was wrong, the wasted quarter hour could mean life or death for the big Fed's family. If Grymdyke had no part in the arrangements, or if some other faceless spook was phoning in an order to scrub the hostages, then it was too damned late already.

He might arrive too late to help the innocent, but he would still have time to hunt down the guilty and let them have a taste of hell on earth before he offered them the sweet release of death. Above all else, a taste of hell for Nicky Gianelli—something in the nature of a preview for the afterlife. If there was any lasting justice in the universe, if life was not a string of futile gestures climaxed by oblivion, then Gianelli and his kind had hell and worse in store for them. But first, it was Mack Bolan's turn to stoke the fire.

He found the address that Brognola had recalled from memory, and circled once around the block. The house was modest in comparison with others in the neighborhood, set back behind a broad expanse of manicured lawn, almost secluded by surrounding trees and hedges. From all appearances Milo Grymdyke liked his privacy, a carryover from his years in the clandestine service. That was fine with Bolan; he preferred their little interview to be conducted quietly, without arousing the anxiety of Grymdyke's neighbors. Failing that he would rely on speed, the hour and reaction times delayed by sleep to see him safely off before some busybody raised an alarm.

Discretion meant avoiding the appearance of unorthodox activity, and Bolan knew that he could not afford to park in front of Grymdyke's house. Although it was not late, comparatively, lights had been extinguished in the homes on either side of Grymdyke and across the street. A sweep of headlights, slamming doors, might be enough to rouse the neighbors and suspicions.

On his second driveby, Bolan marked the narrow alley that meandered behind the houses fronting Grymdyke's street. The residents deposited their rubbish here, in preference to planting cans and bags along the sidewalk out in front, a further bid to maintain the beauty of the neighborhood. He killed the headlights going in, aware that he might well be driving over nails or broken glass, preferring darkness to the relative security his high beams would provide. By counting rooftops that were visible above the fences, Bolan knew when he had reached the rear of Milo Grymdyke's property. He parked the rental car, shed the overcoat that covered his blacksuit and was EVA within another moment.

Grymdyke's wall was six feet high, constructed of cinder blocks with broken bottles set into concrete along the top. There were assorted ways around the obstacles, but Bolan didn't have to look that far. A wrought-iron gate was set into the wall, allowing Grymdyke to deposit garbage in the four bright cans that lined his fence outside, and once he had determined that the gate was free of booby traps, the soldier scrambled nimbly over, crouching as he touched down on the lawn.

No dogs. No sign of any sensors, though he wouldn't know for sure until the hidden floodlights pinned him in their glare. The soldier hesitated for a moment, conscious of his vulnerability, relaxing slightly when there was no call to arms, no sudden blaze of artificial daylight in the yard.

There was a light, however, burning in an upstairs window that he took to be a bedroom, or perhaps a study. Grymdyke might be sitting up and waiting for a call from Arlington, assuming that the shooters had been his. Assuming that Brognola's information was not sadly out of date and useless. Grymdyke might be reaching for the telephone right now, to order disposition of the hostages.

An ivy trellis climbed the wall in back of Grymdyke's house, ascending to the balcony outside that lighted window. Bolan thought it over for a moment, weighing odds and angles, banking on the spook's inherent paranoia to insist upon some sort of burglar alarm inside the house. The Executioner might be able to gain entry through the door that seemed to open on a modern kitchen, might have seconds left to bypass any circuitry connected to the door.

It had to be the trellis. For the sake of time, surprise, he could not try the door or downstairs windows. Standing silently in darkness, Bolan tried the trellis with his weight. When he was satisfied that it would hold, the soldier scrambled upward with a smooth agility. He reached the balcony in seconds, pausing there and listening before he eased one leg across the railing, followed slowly by the other.

From beyond the sliding windowpane that stood open, the night breeze ruffling drapes inside, he heard voices. He recognized a woman's although the words were breathless, indistinct. A man responded urgently in monosyllables.

He edged the curtains back with his Beretta, sighting down the slide into a woman's face, her head thrown back, red hair cascading over naked shoulders. The rest of her was naked, too, and Bolan had an unobstructed view of luscious breasts in motion, hips rotating as she rode a man stretched out beneath her. He saw the man in profile—hawk nose and receding hairline, bushy eyebrows, cheeks and forehead slick with perspiration.

"So good," she crooned. "Oh, Milo..."

"Do it, baby. Work it out."

He almost hated to disturb them. Almost. But his mission took priority above their pleasures. He swept the curtains back with one arm, kept his pistol leveled aimlessly between them as he stepped into the room. The woman's eyes snapped open at the unexpected sound, the color draining from her face, and she scrambled backward, leaving Grymdyke high and dry.

"Hey, what the hell—"

The spook was on his elbows, rising, when the muzzle of the 93-R's silencer made contact with his temple.

"Easy, Milo. Don't go off half-cocked."

"I hear you. Just take it easy with that thing, okay?"

Ignoring Grymdyke for the moment, Bolan pinned the woman with his eyes and nodded toward a closet that was standing open on the far side of the master bedroom.

"Get in there and close the door."

He didn't have to tell her twice, and she was poetry in motion as she raced across the room, all fluid lines and luscious curves. He thought about securing the closet door when she was inside, then put it out of mind. The woman wasn't going anywhere, and every second counted now. He turned to Grymdyke, backing off a pace and letting Milo stare into the Beretta's unblinking eye.

"So, what's the story, man?" There was bravado in the voice, a tremor underneath it that the naked man could not successfully suppress. "I haven't got much cash on hand, but what I've got is yours."

The soldier let him see a frosty smile.

"I met a couple of your friends at Arlington tonight," he said by way of introduction.

There was a flicker of surprise behind the narrow eyes...and something else. His manhood had already started to wilt, and it folded up like last week's roses.

"That right?"

"They didn't have a lot of time to talk, but they referred me on to you. I'm looking for some information."

"Try the Yellow Pages."

"Fine."

He leveled the Beretta, finger tightening around the trigger, totally committed in that instant to the image of his target's brains upon the satin pillow case, his grim determination telegraphed to Grymdyke through the weapon's muzzle.

"Hey! Hold on a second."

"Why?"

"You wanted information, right?"

"So, talk."

"You haven't told me what you're after, man."

"Wrong answer."

"Wait!"

The voice was edged with panic, and Bolan knew that he believed. The spook had seen his death in Bolan's eyes and didn't like the view.

"You don't give anything away," he muttered, when his voice had reached a semblance of normality. "I'd guess you're looking for a matched set, am I right?"

"Go on."

"Three pieces, very fragile. While they last."

"You'd better *hope* they last."

"Don't worry. I'm waiting for a call."

"Stop waiting."

"Yeah, okay. I read you. If you wouldn't mind my asking..."

"No survivors," Bolan told him flatly. "Yet."

It took a moment for the spook to swallow something that was threatening to choke him, but when his voice returned it was strong and firm, with just the bare suggestion of a tremor underneath the velvet-coated steel.

"You've got some balls."

The sleek Beretta's muzzle dipped six inches off target.

"So do you."

The color faded from Grymdyke's cheeks, but he was not surrendering. Not yet.

"I'm not just waiting for a call, you know. I've got to make one, if you get my drift."

The soldier read him loud and clear. And if the agent wasn't lying to save his skin, it meant that there was still a chance that Bolan had arrived in time.

"How long?"

"One-thirty."

Bolan didn't have to check his watch. If Grymdyke spoke the truth, Brognola's family had a short half hour left to live. Beyond the deadline, if he didn't call, the cleanup crew on site would automatically dispose of any hostages.

"How far?"

The agent thought about it long enough to know his life depended on the answer, its sincerity.

"We've got a safe house just outside of Sleepy Hollow. Maybe twenty minutes north, with traffic." Grymdyke rattled off an address, which the soldier memorized.

It was more like twenty-five without, but Bolan didn't quibble.

"One more question."

"Let me guess. You're looking for the sponsor, right?"

The soldier's eyes responded with a mute affirmative.

"It's Family business, guy. You're biting off a mouthful here."

"I'm interested in Gianelli's hot line to the Company."

He saw the agent flinch, was satisfied with the reaction.

"Hey, you know that much, you know I can't go into it."

"All right."

He was a microsecond from the final squeeze when Grymdyke raised both hands, palms outward, as if flesh could turn the parabellum round aside.

"Goddammit, wait!" His chest was heaving like a man experiencing cardiac arrest. "The bastard's not worth dying for."

"I'm listening."

"The sponsor's Cameron Cartwright, get it? He's the honcho at Clandestine Ops."

"What's his connection with the Family?"

"Who knows? Directions to the crapper in that place are need-to-know. I didn't ask, he didn't offer, get it?"

"Yeah."

It added up in Bolan's mind. If Cartwright had been managing the move against Brognola, he would not enlighten his subordinates beyond the bare essentials necessary for completion of their individual assignments. They would not be privy to his motives, his associations, the potential payoffs of his scheme. In retrospect, it was unusual for Grymdyke to be conscious of the Mafia connection, but his background with Clandestine Operations, his propensity for wet work had undoubtedly familiarized the man with CIA connections to the syndicate.

But time was running out, and Bolan had to disengage. He might be able to prevent the worst, but only if he moved without delay. The problem lay in leaving Grymdyke, knowing that the man could not be trusted under any circumstances. He would call ahead, alert the gunners, ruin everything. If Bolan ripped the phones out, wasting precious time, he only had to run next door or cross the street.

If he was able.

All of this flashed through Mack Bolan's mind, and in that instant he observed the sidelong glance that Grymdyke cast in the direction of a nightstand on his left. The single glance told Bolan everything he had to know, and he could not afford to let the opportunity escape.

He drifted toward the open window, lowering the Beretta carelessly, aware that Grymdyke would be waiting for an opening. The guy would read his move as overconfidence, the kind of error that could get a soldier killed at times like this. He saw the muscles bunch in Grymdyke's shoulders, in his thighs, as he prepared to make his move.

And when it came, the spook was quicker, more adept than Bolan had expected. He had been rehearsing, planning for a moment such as this when he would have an opportunity to test himself. He reached the drawer and ripped it open in a single fluid motion, dipped inside and drew the long-slide .45, already tracking into target acquisition in perhaps a second and a half.

It very nearly saved his life.

The 93-R whispered once, and Bolan knew immediately that it was not a mortal wound. The parabellum round ripped into Grymdyke's rib cage, spun him sideways and the .45 exploded in his fist. Somewhere behind him Bolan heard the slug hit plaster, and a little yelping scream escaped the confines of the closet.

Bolan fired again, impacting on a pallid cheek and boring through to find the brain. His target folded, lifeless fingers loosening around the .45, lifeblood already forming pools among the folds of shiny satin underneath.

A backward glance informed him that the woman was safe and sound. The single round from Grymdyke's .45 had missed her closet sanctuary by at least a yard, and she was snuffling now, awaiting further gunplay in the sheltered darkness of her cubicle.

He left her to it, picking up the beside telephone and dialing information for the number of the hospital where Hal had taken Leo. When he raised the nurse on duty in emergency he had Brognola paged and waited, cursing to himself, while several moments passed in wasted silence. Finally he recognized the big Fed's voice and let him have the Sleepy Hollow address, waiting while Brognola gave it back verbatim.

"Twenty minutes," Bolan told him, glancing at his watch. "We're on a deadline."

"Dammit, that's not long enough."

"You're wasting time."

He cradled the receiver, going out the same way he had come, descending swiftly, pushing off the trellis halfway down and sprinting back in the direction of the gate and his rental car. He had precisely eighteen minutes left when he slid in behind the wheel.

And Hal was right: it wasn't long enough. He didn't have a hope in hell of reaching Sleepy Hollow, tracking down the address and attempting any sort of rescue by a half-past one. It was a washout, doomed to failure from the outset—but if Bolan had no hope, he also had no viable alternative. But he had to *try*, and only when he saw the mortal evidence of failure lying at his feet would he be free to seek revenge.

Against the Gianelli family for openers. Against the honcho at Clandestine Ops who put the ball in play and caused so much unbridled havoc in the lives of decent folk. The bastard would be sorry he had started with Brognola, sorry he was ever born, before the Executioner was finished with him. He would plead for death, accept it as a blessing when it came.

Mack Bolan was surprised by the intensity of hate that welled up inside him. How long since he had braced himself to kill from righteous anger? Had it been Detroit? Miami? Pittsfield? Had it been so long since he allowed himself to feel? The question nagged at him taunting, and for an instant he wondered whether he had grown inured to suffering, immune to pain.

And in that instant, he immediately knew the answer.

He had not forgotten how to feel. Pain had been a part of Bolan's war from the beginning, from the moment when he stood before a row of graves in Massachusetts, saying his farewells to home and family. He had survived the pain and learned to cope when lesser men might easily have sought escape through drunkenness or death. He had survived to turn that pain around and forge from it a weapon to destroy his enemies. With each new wound he suffered, each new loss, the soldier braced himself to wreak vengeance on the savages arrayed against him. In a world of dog-eat-dog, it was the swiftest, most ferocious hound who led the pack.

It might already be too late to salvage anything from Sleepy Hollow. Bolan would not write Brognola's wife and children off, but neither would he count on miracles. If they were dead before he reached them, if the nightmare become reality, there still might be a chance for him to overtake the cleanup crew. From there, he had a date with Nicky Gianelli, and another with the honcho from Clandestine Ops.

There would be nothing he could say to Hal. The man from Justice had not asked for any promises, aware that they were impossible to keep. His sorrow would be boundless, and eradication of the animals responsible would not assuage his grief.

But it would help the Executioner.

His private pain was forged from equal parts of loss and anger now, with anger grappling for the upper hand. And it would help him to watch a bullet rip through Nicky Gianelli's face. To lock his fingers tight around the throat of Cameron Cartwright, squeezing out the breath of life until the man's tongue protruded and his eyes rolled blindly back into his head. It would be good to kill again.

Relax, Bolan told himself. The anger, he knew, could get him killed if he allowed it to control his actions. If he reached the safe house before the occupants departed, he would be outmanned, outgunned, and he would need his wits about him if he hoped to see another sunrise.

Relax, he told himself again.

Forget about the intervening miles and concentrate on distance covered, time remaining. Bolan knew the folly of defeatist thinking, realized the fatal error of giving up before the battle had been joined. If anger ruled his mind, he would be little better than a bullet fired at random, free to ricochet around the battlefield until it spent its force and fell to earth in vain. He needed something more along the order of a guided missile now, a death machine complete with built-in homing instinct that would let him find the necessary targets, root them out and burn them down with surgical precision. Forget about an old friend's family on the line, he counseled himself, and concentrate on picking off the savages. Make it count. And if the final sacrifice was necessary, take as many of the bastards with you as you could.

It was the only way to wage a war, and Bolan knew enough of living on the edge to realize that death was never far away. If this was all the time remaining to him here tonight, then he would use that time to best advantage, running up a score against the enemy before they took him down.

And he would teach them all a thing or two about the costs of everlasting war while he was at it. Offer them a lesson in the grim reality of suffering.

He stood on the accelerator, felt the car grudgingly respond, its engine laboring. Another fifteen minutes, and he wondered if Brognola had the slightest chance of showing up before the roof fell in. For once, he almost hoped that Hal would be late.

The man should not be forced to watch his family die.

There would be ample opportunity for him to witness death before the sun rose over Washington again. This one time, though, if there was any mercy in the universe, the soldier hoped Brognola might be spared.

But it was not a night for mercy.

It was a night for blood.

22

"He's late!"

"Take it easy. We've got time."

"He should've called by now."

"I'll give him ten more minutes."

"Dammit, Blake, the man said half-past one."

"And I said give him ten, so just relax."

The quarreling voices were distinct enough that Helen had been able to identify the speakers. Blake would be the blond one, the leader of the team, and he was standing firm against his two accomplices—for the moment. Their contact—someone calling with instructions? orders?—had already overrun his deadline, and the two gorillas were becoming restive, anxious to be on about their business.

Helen knew only too well what that business was, and she kept the dark suspicion to herself. The only call their captors might anticipate would deal with their release . . . or execution. She cherished no illusions of eleventh-hour stays, no last reprieve. The call, when it was finally made, would seal their fates, and any small delay could only provide an inkling of hope.

Whatever came they were prepared to fight and die with something close to dignity. Her Catholic background had prepared her to believe in miracles, but Helen recognized the odds against success. They would be facing automatic weapons in the hands of trained professionals, their only armament consisting of a wooden staff, a shower rod-cum-javelin, and the internal hardware from a toilet tank. No point in calculating odds; the melancholy end result would only weaken her resolve, and at the moment Helen needed every ounce of strength that she possessed.

She was determined to resist, if not in hopes of breaking free, then merely for resistance as an end unto itself. She would not let herself or her children be methodically eliminated like a string of brainless sheep marched off to slaughter. If they could strike one blow, or kill one of their enemies, they would have left some mark behind, a sign of their humanity, their will to live. Surrender at the final instant was unthinkable, a crime against Hal's memory and their life together.

No sounds came from the other room, and Helen stood back from the door, her children's eyes upon her as she turned to face them. They were waiting, tense, expectant, and the tears in Eileen's eyes were tears of anger mixed with fear. Jeff's face had aged impossibly, and Helen cursed their captors for the theft of innocence from both her children.

Were they innocent? Was anybody innocent today? In a society conditioned to accept a toll of sixty murders each and every day, six violent rapes per hour, was there even such a thing as innocence? Could children weaned on television news and splatter movies ever grasp the concept of a life immune to fear? It did not matter in the end. They were *her* children. And as far as she was concerned, they would always be innocent.

For bringing fear and grief into their lives, she owed the gunners any pain that she would finally be able to inflict. For snuffing out their lives, she owed the bastards more—and knew that she would never have the strength, the opportunity, to pay her debt in full.

If Hal was with her now...

God, no.

If Hal was with her, then the bastards would have all of it, her family and life itself wrapped up in one large bundle, ready for disposal. While he lived, while he was able to pursue their captors and make them scurry for their lives, then justice was a living breathing possibility.

And Hal was still alive. She sensed it, knew instinctively that his survival was the reason for her captors' agitation, the delay in their receipt of final orders. A meeting had been set for Arlington at midnight; Helen knew that much from listening to one-sided conversations on the telephone. Whatever had transpired, her man had walked away from it intact. If he was dead the gunners would have heard the news by now. The three of them would have been dead by now.

Which meant they still had time.

The leader, Blake, had said ten minutes. Gino and the one called Carmine were reluctant, but they both had gone along... from fear, uncertainty, whatever.

It was incredible, this measuring of life in minutes, knowing that you would be dead by, say, 1:45. Unless Blake stalled his comrades one more time. Unless a call came through.

"Be ready," Helen told her children in a whisper. "We take the first one through the door."

"Right on." Jeff's knuckles whitened where he gripped the wooden closet rod, converted to a makeshift fighting staff.

"I'm ready." Armed with metal slats extracted from the toilet tank, Eileen looked very soft and frail, a princess dressed in blue jeans and a checkered flannel shirt.

"All right."

The shower rod was cool and slick in Helen's hands, its tip already bent and flattened into something like a clumsy spear point. She would not be winning any prizes for originality or manual dexterity, but it would have to do. If she could reach soft flesh, perhaps a vital spot...

It was enough to fight. The killing, if she got that far, would be a bonus. No, a miracle.

And while her background had prepared her to believe in miracles, tonight Helen Brognola knew that she was on her own.

"THEY'RE STILL INSIDE?"

Brognola's voice was strained, almost inaudible, and he was winded from the final sprint that had delivered him to

Bolan's side. They looked away, his eyes returning to the lighted windows of the safe house.

"Could be they're waiting for a call."

"From Grymdyke?"

Bolan shrugged. "Don't look a gift horse in the mouth."

"If they're alive . . ."

"Not now."

Brognola got the message and nodded solemnly. "How do we play it?"

"You stake out the front. I'll take the rear approach."

"All right." He had begun to move when Hal reached out to place a warm hand on his shoulder. "Hey...and thanks, you know?"

He knew, damn right, and he could read the questions, the accumulated pain engraved across Brognola's face. He knew precisely what the Fed was going through, and with that knowledge came the certainty that there was nothing he could do to make it any easier.

If Hal's wife and children were still alive, against all odds, they had a chance. If someone in the crew had gotten antsy and snuffed them in the safe house in defiance of established rules, then there was still the matter of exacting vengeance. Either way it all boiled down to chance and opportunity, the factors that no soldier on the firing line could possibly control.

The drive from Alexandria had taken twenty-seven minutes, and he had been on the scene another three before Brognola showed. He would have moved without the Fed, but there were angles of attack to be computed, odds against survival to be weighed and finally discarded. Anyone who blundered blind and ignorant into an established hardset was asking to be killed, and while the Executioner had long abandoned any lasting fear of death, he did not plan to throw his life away on futile gestures, either.

If he could not readily identify the enemy or count the hostile guns inside, at least he could attempt to chart the layout of the safe house: doors and windows, rooms accessible from the exterior, the likely fields of fire inside and out.

If he could not protect the hostages, he could try at least to minimize their risks. Provided they were still alive, of course. Provided that the gunners were not primed to wipe them out at the first sign of interference. If the hostages were covered or if the safe house had been wired to self-destruct, then they were beaten going in.

Which did not abrogate the Executioner's responsibility. No way.

He had a job to do, for his closest friend and his family...and for himself. The savages inside that safe house needed to be taught that there was no place safe on earth for animals who violated families. They needed a reminder that the abstract justice they had learned about in school was still alive and well, if not precisely obvious in day-to-day existence on the streets. There was a price to pay for every crime, a consequence for every violation of the laws men had erected to preserve a civilized society. And if the courts had fallen on hard times, if judges and DAs appeared unable to enforce those laws across the board, the job might fall to others.

To an Executioner.

He slid through the darkness like a living shadow, circling the house, keeping to the trees and hedges, using up a precious minute on his circuit of the killing ground. The house was small, a single-story number with apparent bedroom windows boarded over in the rear. The hostages would be sequestered there, but Bolan dared not go for them directly. He would have to take the gunners first, eliminate the threat before he turned to scan the house for survivors. When the savages were taken care of, when their lesson had been learned, there would be time for toting up the gains and losses.

He found a door that opened on the little combination kitchen-dining room and risked a glance through windows that had not been washed in years. There was no sign of life inside the darkened room, but he caught a hint of shadowed movement through a doorway leading to the living room beyond. If they were concentrated there, he had an opportunity to take them unaware and nail them down before they could react against the hostages.

He worked a thin stiletto along the doorjamb, raised the screen door's latch and held his breath against the possibility of rusty, squeaking hinges. When the door swung back without a sound, he used one knee to hold it open, concentrating on the dead bolt that secured the kitchen door in place. It took a moment, but his pick eventually overcame the tumblers and he eased the door ajar, prepared for any challenge from the darkness, any sound that might betray an enemy within.

He stood inside the kitchen with the silver Lawgleg in his hand, the smell of dust and ancient Pinesol in his nostrils. It was time for thunder, and he left the sleek Beretta in its armpit sheath as backup to the heavy .44 AutoMag in his fist. The soldier had already milked surprise for all that it was worth; when he emerged to face the enemy, he wanted them to hear his thunder, smell the gun smoke that accompanied cleansing flames.

And it was down to seconds now, a span of heartbeats, waiting for Brognola to complete his move and find a suitable position in the front. He heard the doomsday numbers falling in his head and knew that soon he would be forced to move, regardless of Brognola's readiness. Before the gunners panicked and decided to proceed without a call. Before one of them started getting hungry and emerged to fix himself a snack.

Before it was too late for all concerned.

OUTSIDE, BROGNOLA PRESSED himself against the wall surrounded by the thorny hedges that had sheltered his approach. Thick drapes were drawn across the picture window to his left, preventing any glimpses inside the safe house or learning anything of Helen and the kids. They must be still inside, he guessed; the cleanup crew would not be here unless they still had work to do.

But were the hostages alive?

It violated every regulation in the nonexistent book for gunners to eliminate their marks inside a safe house. Still, things happened in the field that could not be anticipated in an office. Not in Langley, not in Washington, not even in the White House. Circumstances altered cases, and he knew the gunners must be itchy now, aware that they were running overtime. They would be anxious to evacuate the premises, and carrying a body would be easier than shepherding a hostage any day.

The man from Justice made his mind a blank, deliberately expunging visions of his wife and children stretched out on the floor inside, already zippered into body bags or wrapped in plastic shower curtains for the ride to an incinerator or construction site where they would simply disappear. The Company was good at working disappearances, although its paid magicians usually practiced out of country. So there was all the more incentive to see the job behind them before somebody dropped a wrench into the works. If they were taken in the midst of pulling down domestic violence, if the slightest hint should find its way to Senate oversight committees, all concerned were in the soup. They didn't need that kind of heat at Langley, and Clandestine Ops would move the earth to keep it quiet.

Brognola's mission, failing to secure Helen and the children, would be simply to ensure that all involved—survivors, anyway—were treated to a dose of grand publicity. He thought of Susan Landry, other contacts he had cultivated in the media, in Congress, and he knew that he could pull it off.

Unless he bought the farm right now.

Survival was the first priority, at least until he was convinced that he had come too late for his family. If he came too late to save them, then survival paled beside the grim priority of personal revenge.

But he could not be sure until he was inside. Until he saw them for himself.

For now his target was the door, ten feet away. It was secured with double locks and opened on the living room—or so he had surmised without an opportunity to case the floor plans. The gunners would be concentrated there, and he would stand a sixty-forty chance of being riddled on the threshold if he moved too soon. It all came down to Bolan now, and while he waited, Hal prepared himself to do or die.

The Bulldog .44 had been reloaded after Arlington, and now its weight was reassuring in his fist, a tangible extension of his rage. The snubby .38 was in his other hand, a lighter weapon, every bit as deadly with its load of Glaser Safety Slugs. He would be forced to kick the door—the Glasers wouldn't penetrate—but with the anger and frustration churning in his stomach, Hal was certain that it wouldn't be a problem.

Getting in was easy. Getting out alive was something else again.

The animals inside were not the authors of his pain. They were performing under orders like attack dogs on the leash, and he would not be satisfied until he found their trainer, looked the bastard squarely in the eye and pushed a bullet through his guts. A Glaser, if he still had any left when he was finished here. If not . . . well, he would have to improvise.

Fifteen seconds later he had worked his way along the wall until he reached the porch, ignoring thorns that snagged his trench coat, plowing bloody furrows on his hands and wrists. The pain was nothing. His mind was on the mission . . . and what lay beyond.

Ten seconds, and he stood before the silent door with guns in hand, his pulse a numbing drumbeat in his ears. If Bolan was on schedule, he would be inside by now. If he had been delayed...then what? Then nothing, dammit. Hal was going in regardless, holding to the schedule that they had agreed upon.

He had not come this far, endured this much, to stall and blow the only fleeting chance that he might ever have. If there was any chance at all it lay within, and Hal was grabbing for it, reaching out to catch the lifeline that could save him yet—or, failing contact, that could pitch him into outer darkness, save him from the burning ache that had resided in his stomach since he walked into the empty cabin . . . how long ago?

It seemed like forever.

Whatever life was left for him lay inside, and he was only seconds away from a close encounter with his destiny.

TEN MINUTES COME AND GONE without a call. Blake Lindsay checked his watch once more and muttered something unintelligible as he retrieved his mini-Uzi from the couch beside him.

Grymdyke must be fucking crazy to ignore the schedule as he had. It was unheard of, leaving agents in the field without their orders, hanging on with hostages in tow and no idea of what was happening outside. Blake didn't give a damn about the drop at Arlington, whichever way it went, but he had been assured by Grymdyke—his control—that there would be a call no later than 1:30. It was now 1:43, and he could think of no excuse for stalling Gino and Carmine any longer. They were itching to be out of there, and he could not restrain them any longer. It was time to leave.

Another minute wouldn't hurt, he thought, and then decided against it. If Grymdyke had intended to make contact, he would certainly have called by now. His negligence was inexcusable, and Lindsay meant to take it up with his superiors unless he had a change of heart and dealt with Milo on his own.

It would be satisfying, but there were the realities of life within the Company to be considered. Protocol and channels, all that kind of bureaucratic bullshit. He had Grymdyke dead to rights, but there were ways and means of dealing with a drone who couldn't pull his weight. It wasn't like the old days when you took some bastard on an outing to the Everglades and left him there. Perhaps in Third World fields of operation, if you covered up your tracks, but these domestic jobs required a different level of finesse.

They weren't supposed to handle any jobs *inside* the United States, of course, but there was worlds of room between "supposed to" and reality. No bunch of Senate snoopers could prevent the Company from doing what it was designed to do: protecting the security of the United States. If they believed that all the enemies were on the outside, that the boys from Justice had domestic radicals in hand, well, they could think again. These days the FBI was busting more subversives in its own damned locker room than in the streets, and Lindsay was acquainted with the dangers that had long been overlooked, deliberately ignored.

He didn't know the rationale behind this thing with Hal Brognola—didn't need or want to know the motivation. It was adequate for him that someone up the ladder had identified a threat and chosen him to deal with it. The bastard must be dirty, or the Company would never have selected him for termination. As for rubbing out the wife and kiddies, well, like some renowned American had said, nits make lice. A traitor's brats would grow up pissing on America, bet your ass, and you could never nip the problem soon enough. If you could solve your problem with a swift preemptive strike, you never had to fret about the bastards sneaking up behind you later on.

Whatever Grymdyke might be up to, he had blown it, and it would be Lindsay's job to save the play. If Milo couldn't do his job, that didn't mean the operation had to fall apart. The Company was full of men who pulled their weight, and there was still room for advancement.

The thought of seeing Grymdyke busted—even terminated—for his failure to perform was satisfying. The idea of moving up to take his place beside the honchos at Clandestine Ops was something else entirely, something Lindsay had been playing with for longer than he could remember. Power came with rank, and if he played his cards right, starting now...

That was the problem. Starting now.

Disposal of the hostages had top priority. They had to go, and Lindsay didn't want to waste another minute with them at the safe house. They had been here too long already, and his scalp was tingling the way it did when danger was approaching, as it had before the ambush in Angola, or before the roof fell in around him in Nicaragua.

Time to move before the tingling got any worse. A few more moments, and it wouldn't matter; anyone who traced them could surround an empty house and blast away until the cows came home for all he cared.

He stood up, knee joints popping like two muffled pistol shots, and he suppressed a smile as his two accomplices jumped. They had been advertised as top professionals, but that was a mafiosi for you. Stick a gun in some pathetic bastard's hand and let him drop some bozo on the street, they started calling him a soldier, like he'd been through Benning or the CIA academy. The average button man was long on muscle, short on brains, and these two most emphatically were no exceptions to the rule.

"It's time," he told them, reading the relief on both their faces. "Gino, bring them out."

"Awright."

A few more minutes and they would all be in the car and tooling out of there, en route to an abandoned auto graveyard that the Company maintained for such emergencies. The place had not done active business in a dozen years, but it maintained a working crusher and a furnace more than adequate to finish off the job. Brognola's wife and children would not simply disappear; they would have ceased, quite literally, to exist.

A few more minutes, and he had it made.

The only problem, if it was a problem, would be taking out the two torpedoes while their backs were turned. That made five bodies for the crusher, and Lindsay knew that he could do it standing on his head.

It was the kind of job he relished, after all.

23

"Gino, bring them out."

She heard the shuffling footsteps, recognized the sound of death, and pressed a finger to her lips before she took her place behind the door. The children nodded understanding—Jeff with something very much like eagerness, Eileen with trepidation written on her face.

They had no chance at all, but if they surrendered meekly, they would only be cooperating in their own destruction. Better to make a stand right here, inflict whatever injuries they could, and by their deaths create a further inconvenience for their captors.

Someone would be forced to clean up afterward, remove all signs of violence. The house was meant to be a prison, not an execution chamber, and it pleased her now to think that by seizing the initiative she might destroy the careful plans of men who meant to harm her family. The longer she delayed them, forced them to remain behind scrubbing bloodstains and patching bullet holes, the better chance there was that Hal would find them. And justice would be done.

She stopped herself.

Not justice.

Justice would have seen her children safely out of there, alive, unharmed. If there was any justice in the world, Eileen and Jeff would never have been taken hostage in the first place.

No justice, then...but there was retribution. And revenge could be the next best thing, especially if it was the only course of action still available.

The footsteps paused outside their door, no more than eighteen inches from her now, and Helen realized that she was trembling. She bit her lip and clutched the makeshift spear against her chest, prepared to strike the moment the gunman showed himself. As planned, Eileen was standing to the left, her weapon clutched behind her back, and Jeff was seated on the bed, the staff concealed beneath the bed frame at his feet. It would require precision timing if they hoped to pull it off, but . . .

Helen stopped herself before the thought could form. They didn't have a hope in hell of pulling anything off, and she knew it. At best they were engaged in a delaying action that was certain to spell their end. Any victory would lie in taking one of their abductors with them.

But if they could take him fast enough, if she could seize his gun, then what? Then kill the others, dammit. Or at least attempt to kill them. Anything was better than waiting to be snuffed out like some pesky insect.

She heard the doorknob turn, and braced herself. The bedroom door swung inward, and she *felt* her enemy as he surveyed the room, a heartbeat's hesitation on the threshold.

"It's time to go," he growled. "Where's Momma?"

"In the bathroom," Eileen told him meekly.

"Get her off the pot, sweet thing. We got a schedule here."

Just one more step.

He cleared the doorway, visible to Helen now, and she was moving, pushing off from her position in the corner, knowing he would hear her, *feel* her coming at him from behind, not caring anymore. She held the makeshift lance in both hands, leveled from the waist, her target area the roll of flesh above his belt, right side.

There was a kidney there, the stomach, liver, small intestines. Could she skewer him? Or would the homemade spear glance off, producing no more than a bruise?

The gunman sensed his danger and swiveled to meet her as she charged, his movement altering the target area an instant short of impact. He was bringing up his submachine gun, but she did not flinch. Peripherally, she saw her children closing for the kill as she made contact below the rib cage. She felt her metal shaft punch through the fabric, flesh, and then it kept on going, in and in.

His scream was punctuated by the rapid-fire explosions in her face. The muzzle-flash of Gino's weapon seared her cheek, and Helen caught a whiff of burning hair before the the weapon's recoil drove it up and backward, riddling the ceiling. Traveling on sheer momentum, she collided with the gunman, knocking him off balance. She recoiled and went down on one knee. He kept falling and spastic fingers released the submachine gun as he hit the floor.

She heard something whistle past her face, and Helen saw the wooden closet rod strike home against the gunner's nose, flattening on impact, bright blood jetting from his nostrils. And again, across the eyes, with enough force that something fractured audibly—the pole? his skull? From nowhere, Eileen fell upon him, slashing at his face and throat with jagged steel until her hands and shirt were slick with blood.

Helen realized she had no time to watch him die. She scrambled for the submachine gun, metal warm and deadly in her hands, wondering if it would respond. There must be more to it than simply pulling on the trigger. But she had no opportunity for study now. Already there were pounding footsteps in the corridor outside and startled voices clamoring for Gino.

She rose to meet them, tasting death and knowing that no matter what should happen next, she had already left a mark upon her enemies.

FROM HIS POSITION in the darkened kitchen, Bolan watched the gunner amble past in the direction of the bedrooms. The Executioner began to move, prepared to take his target from behind when further movement from the living room delayed him. The other guns were stirring, and he still had no idea of their numbers or their capabilities.

Two voices, he figured, by the sound of it, though there might be others who refrained from speaking. If the crew was small enough, the risks were lessened, but it only took a single bullet to drop a woman or a child. One lucky round could stop a hellfire warrior in his tracks and bring his everlasting war to an immediate conclusion if he took foolhardy chances.

They wouldn't kill the hostages inside. Too messy in a safe house they had obviously used before and would want to use again. Discretion would compel them to remove the prisoners to another site where blood and noise would cause no inconvenience. Someplace where the bodies could be made to disappear forever.

He was in the doorway when he heard the ragged scream, a man's voice, tattered on the razor's edge of unexpected pain. A burst of automatic fire eclipsed the scream and was itself immediately silenced. Sounds of struggle came to him through the open doorway, and he glimpsed a slender woman kneeling on the gunner's chest, her hands descending, wrapped around a makeshift dagger, stabbing at his throat, his eyes.

The door swung wide, and Bolan recognized Brognola's wife from photographs that he had seen years before. She was moving toward him, cradling an Ingram she had captured from the fallen hardman, locking eyes with Bolan for a startled instant. There was nothing close to recognition in her face, and as he heard the enemy approaching on his blind side, the soldier knew that he could run or stand and die.

He spun in the direction of the open kitchen doorway, hit a flying shoulder roll as Helen fired. The parabellums buzzsawed into plaster, woodwork, gnawed a twisting track along the wall where Bolan had been standing seconds earlier. A second stutter gun responded from the living room, and Helen kept on firing, fighting to control the unfamiliar weapon as the magazine ran dry. The enemy was answering with short, precision bursts that drove her back and under cover.

"Goddammit, Gino, answer up!"

But Gino's comrades weren't expecting an answer from him now. They were already sealing off the corridor, preparing to attack, aware that Helen or whoever must be running low on ammunition now, perhaps already out. If they could just be sure...

"Get in there, Carmine."

"Fuck you!"

"I said *get in there*!"

Lying prone in darkness, pressed against the bullet-punctured wall, the Executioner could imagine Carmine staring at the muzzle of an automatic weapon, ticking off his options in the fractured second that remained. No options, really, when you thought about it that way.

"Shit."

Bolan heard him coming, braced the AutoMag in both hands, sighting down the slide at empty space before the crouching figure showed itself. He was no more than fifteen feet away when Bolan stroked the trigger, sent 240 grains of screaming death across the intervening space at 1,500 feet per second.

Impact lifted Carmine off his feet and slammed him against the wall. He hung there for an instant, crucified, then gravity tugged at him, leaving traces of himself behind as he began the dead-end slide.

"Carmine!"

Number three was all alone in there; the soldier would have bet his life on that. In fact, he *had* already bet his life, for now he had to cross the narrow no-man's-land of empty corridor, past Carmine's body, in the face of pinpoint automatic fire, to tag his final enemy. As long as number three remained in place, alive and capable of fighting back, the soldier's only other move was a withdrawal from the kitchen, leaving Helen and the kids pinned down, alone.

No options, right. Like always. And the flow of combat, the relentless give-and-take of battle was determining his moves. It was the price of taking on an unknown enemy on strange terrain. One on one, he had a chance: no more, no less.

The way to take it would be low and fast, assuming that his enemy would fire instinctively at waist level. Bolan would have seconds to spot the bastard's muzzle-flash and pin him down before he could correct his aim.

Unless the shooter was professional enough to know that he would come in beneath the normal line of fire.

The AutoMag's report would be enough to tell him that he wasn't facing down Brognola's woman now. He would be conscious of an armed intruder in the house, aware that he was on his own against a nameless, faceless enemy.

That made them even. And anything that shook the bastard's confidence from here on in would be a point in Bolan's favor.

But he was out of time, and stalling put the ball in his opponent's court. He could not afford to lose his slim advantage. He had to move right now, and once the move was made, he knew there could be no turning back.

BROGNOLA HEARD A MUFFLED SCREAM and recognized the voice as male. It might be Jeff, and yet . . .

A burst of automatic-weapon fire ripped through the house as Hal kicked savagely against the door twice. If there was anyone inside the living room, they had to hear him now. They would be waiting for him if and when he crashed the door, their weapons swiveling to cut him down before he crossed the threshold.

More staccato firing came from inside, and Brognola threw his shoulder against the door, grunting with the impact, startled as the door gave way and sent him sprawling onto slick linoleum.

Somehow he retained his grip on both revolvers, and now he crawled across the entry hall on knees and elbows, keeping low, expecting to be shot at any moment. From somewhere to his front, the roar of stutter guns was etching out a heavy-metal harmony. Two weapons answering a third, their bursts precise and economical in contrast to the other's angry rattling.

A firefight, then, and he was closing on their flank, apparently unnoticed. It was too damned good . . .

He froze as ringing silence suddenly descended on the firing line. Then he heard someone calling for Gino.

There was no answer, and Brognola prayed that Gino was among the dead. The silence seemed to stretch for hours, though it must have only been a moment.

The same voice called out again, this time for Carmine.

From his hidden vantage point, Brognola risked a glance and spied two gunmen crouched on either side of what appeared to be a darkened hallway. At the far end light was spilling from an open doorway. The leader, blond and muscular, was leveling a mini-Uzi at one of them. Brognola realized this guy must be Carmine.

Carmine hesitated for another instant, finally took it in a rush, hunched over, fading into darkness. Hal was braced to make his move when he was stricken by a thunderclap that seemed to shake the very walls around him. Carmine's silhouette obscured the muzzle-flash, but there was no mistaking the report of Bolan's AutoMag. The single round eliminated Carmine as a threat and left the blonde alone.

With Hal.

Whatever waited for him down that darkened corridor now demanded action. Hal was scrambling to his feet before the thought took conscious form, already firing as he rose, half-blinded by the fury that consumed him in the presence of his enemies.

The first two rounds were wide, the Glasers gouging plaster, detonating harmlessly on either side of his intended target. Now the blonde was pivoting, the Israeli-made SMG tracking onto target, yellow flame erupting from the muzzle as he fought back skillfully. He was firing high, and the vest Hal wore would not have saved him if it weren't for Bolan, bursting from the kitchen, blazing with Big Thunder as he came.

The hardman hesitated, torn between two targets, and the delay was all Hal needed. Firing for effect, he unloaded with the Bulldog and the snubby .38 until the hammers fell on empty chambers, clicking like metallic pincers. In all the blonde had taken seven of the Glasers, two of them directly in the face. The bastard was already dead before he toppled backward to the carpet, leaking like a human sieve.

But Hal could not stop squeezing off, the dry-fire clatter of his weapons coming to him from a distance, through the mist that fogged his mind. He kept on squeezing until the Executioner stood before him, reaching out to twist the empty guns from his hands, which had already started trembling.

"It's over."

Bolan's voice seemed distant, hollow in Brognola's ears. How could the soldier be so far away and still reach out to touch him? Hal's mind was grappling with the problem when a hint of movement on the edge of vision brought him right around to face the hallway, with its lighted doorway standing open at the end.

And he was dreaming, had to be. His mind had snapped. How else could he be seeing Helen and the children when he knew that they were dead before he crashed the door? How could they be alive and calling to him now?

Bolan slapped him on the shoulder, but Brognola was already running, sweeping Helen up in one arm, reaching for his children with the other, and he couldn't see them clearly now, goddammit. There was something in his eyes.

But he could hold them, touch them, hear their voices. And he knew, incredibly, that he was not too late.

It was enough. For now.

"We need to move."

Mack Bolan didn't want to break Brognola's mood, but there had been too damned much shooting even for a sparsely settled neighborhood. Unless the other residents were deaf or comatose, police would be arriving soon. The family reunion would have to be postponed.

Four faces, wreathed in smiles that contradicted teary eyes, were beaming at him now. Brognola nodded, herding Helen and the children past the riddled corpses toward the door. Outside, they found a sprinkling of porch lights burning in the neighborhood, illuminating former darkness, adding urgency to Bolan's own demand for haste.

"I'll follow you," he told Brognola. "When you've got them safe, we need to talk."

Brognola's smile had disappeared.

"It isn't finished."

"No."

Not while the brains behind Brognola's grief were still at large. Not while a crony of Lee Farnsworth still held power in the CIA. Not while Nicky Gianelli walked the streets of Washington as free and clear as any decent citizen.

They owed a blood debt to Brognola, to the Executioner. Before the final curtain fell on Bolan's hellfire tour of Wonderland, the cannibals would have to pay. In full.

"I'll follow you," he said again, already moving toward his car half a block away. There was whispering behind him as Hal conducted his family toward his own sedan.

The drive would give him time to think, collect the final scattered pieces of the puzzle. Motive still eluded Bolan, but he had enough to surmise that Gianelli was the guiding force behind the move against Brognola's family. Elimination of a ranking enemy at Justice had been tantalizing, obviously, but it took a back seat to the ambush laid for Bolan. Gianelli had been banking on the Executioner's assistance to a friend in need, and he had very nearly pulled it off. As for the CIA involvement, underworld connections with Clandestine Ops ran deep at Langley. Bolan had no reason to believe they had been terminated during the investigations of the seventies, any more than they had been eliminated by the dictates of a president in the early sixties. Indeed, there were suspicions—some still nurtured within official circles—that the gangland-CIA connection had been linked somehow to the removal by assassination of that President. Some even whispered that his brother, running for the presidency in 1968, had been taken out by agents of the same unholy coalition.

Bolan had no hard and fast opinion on the deaths of presidents and candidates. He knew enough about clandestine Washington to realize that Gianelli might have had a dozen different handles on the Company—from Asian heroin through all the machinations aimed at Castro in the days before detente. If Cartwright was a carbon copy of his mentor, Farnsworth, he was rotten to the core.

If not, then he was dirty all the same. The Executioner had never shrunk from the concept of guilt by association. Public figures who aligned themselves with public enemies were worse than savages in Bolan's mind. They consciously abandoned sacred oaths of office, violated public trusts in the pursuit of private gain, and Bolan didn't buy their hollow protestations of indignant innocence. When you lay down with jackals, you got up with fleas . . . or worse.

It wasn't finished while the architects of Hal Brognola's private hell were still alive. So long as any vestige of the Farnsworth clique survived at the CIA, the Executioner himself had debts to collect. For April Rose, Andrzej Konzaki, Aaron Kurtzman—all the others who had suffered through the treachery of men presumably committed to protection of their country and its people.

It would not be finished until that debt was paid.

And then?

He shrugged the question off and knew that *then* would take care of itself. His debt was here and now. Before another dawn broke over Washington, the soldier meant to close that overdue account and wipe the ledger clean.

With blood.

24

"I'm telling you they blew it, Nicky. Are you reading me? A frigging homicide detective took the call!"

"Relax."

The mobster's voice was oily, self-assured, but his apparent confidence did nothing for Cameron Cartwright. It was over. They were caught up inside the worst scenario he could have possibly imagined. Somehow, local officers had found the safe house. Not just officers, but homicide detectives. That meant death, and any way you sliced it there was trouble on the way.

Brognola's family was alive. Cartwright's crew would never willingly have compromised the safe house with an on-site execution. And if forced to kill a hostage on the premises, they would have cleaned it up without involving the authorities. Police meant phone calls from the neighbors— worse, from one of the surviving captives—and a call to the police meant someone had surprised his team.

The implications of that were too frightening to consider, even for a survivor like Cartwright. It meant surviving witnesses, embarrassment and nagging questions from detectives and investigative journalists.

Even with the precautions he had taken with the safe house, there were ways to trace his men. In death, they posed a threat that none of them had ever constituted while alive. Their faces, fingerprints, surviving records that had somehow missed the shredder when they joined Clandestine Ops... There were a million ways to blow a cover, dammit, and if Grymdyke had already been exposed...

"I'm leaving," he informed his host, abruptly turning from the window to confront the man whose personal vendetta had rebounded to destroy them all. "I'm getting out."

"*We*'re getting out," Gianelli corrected. "I could use some sun, and God knows you've been looking pale these past few weeks. You like the Virgin Islands, Cam?"

He thought about it, shrugged.

"It doesn't matter what I like," he said at last, resigned to exile. "It's as sure as hell I can't stay here. Not now."

"You're getting all worked up for nothing," Gianelli told him, smiling like a hungry shark. "We aren't hung yet, not by a long shot. Just because a couple of your boys got bumped..."

"A dozen, counting Grymdyke. And the four you wasted on DeVries."

"Forget them," Gianelli answered, waving pudgy fingers in a gesture of dismissal. "Buttons are a dime a dozen. So, tonight you lost a dime. Big deal. You catch some sun, let all the badges chase themselves around in circles for a month or so, and by the time they're finished, nobody remembers who they wanted in the first place."

Cartwright didn't buy it for an instant, but he kept his mouth shut, watching Gianelli as he rose and punched the button on a desktop intercom. The houseman's voice came back like talking gravel.

"Yes, sir?"

"Pack up some bags, Vinnie. Sunshine stuff, enough for three, four weeks. And have them bring the car around."

"Yes, sir, Mr. Gianelli."

Straightening, the little mobster killed the squawk box, turned to face his guest.

"You'll get a chance to pick up something when we land. Who knows? You might go native on me once you meet those local broads." His laughter sounded like bones rattling inside a burlap bag.

The man from the CIA was not concerned with luggage or the shopping opportunities wherever he might find himself a day or week from now. He was concerned about survival, preservation of his liberty, the heat that would inevitably follow an investigation of the shootings at the safe house.

Even if the homicide detectives couldn't trace its ownership, the very fact that they were asking questions would alert his own superiors within the Company. It was impossible to keep them in the dark, and once they started asking questions, he was finished. Dead. When they found out that he had launched domestic operations on his own authority, joined forces with the syndicate to target government employees and civilians, they would not be reckoning in terms of prosecution.

Hit-on-sight with no questions asked would be more like it. And never mind the capo's fairy-tale scenario about returning home with all forgotten in a month or two.

The honcho from Clandestine Ops knew he was never going home again. No way in hell. They wouldn't let him. Worse, they would be hunting him, alert to every movement in his old accustomed haunts, and branching out when Cartwright failed to show himself within a reasonable time. He was a man condemned without a country now, and there would be no sanctuary for him in the Virgin Islands. Maybe in Fiji or Nepal if they didn't smell his spoor and put the hunters on his track again.

He could defect, of course. The Soviets would welcome him, with certain reservations. At the very least they would protect him from his former comrades in the Company, and after he had proved himself reliable, there would perhaps be certain luxuries permitted.

While his information lasted, anyway.

He was a walking gold mine to them now, but in six months, a year...

How quickly would the Company replace him in Clandestine Ops? Tomorrow? The next day? Certainly, they would not wait until next week. And from the moment of arrival, his successor would be busy changing codes, recalling agents in the field, and generally scrambling to save CO from any damage or embarrassment. It was astonishing how many operations could be scuttled or diverted in a single day, as Cartwright knew from grim experience.

But he would still be valuable to the Soviets. Or to their ranking competition, the Chinese. So many options left before him yet, he had been premature in giving up, preparing for disaster. He could still save something from the ruin of his life...and he could still repay the man who engineered his personal catastrophe.

Before he struck his bargain with the Soviets, Chinese, whoever, Cartwright meant to settle his account with Gianelli. It was Nicky's fault, the whole damned mess, and Cartwright meant to pay him back before he faded from the scene forever.

Nicky liked the Virgin Islands. Fine. They would be beautiful this time of year, festooned with foliage, creeping vines and flowers. More than adequate, he thought, for one small wreath.

CIGAR SMOKE WREATHED his head as Gianelli watched the limo being loaded. An hour more would see them at the airport, trundling aboard his private jet and southbound, homing on the sun, deserted beaches where a man could rest in peace.

He chuckled to himself and quickly glanced around to see if Cartwright might have grown suspicious of his sudden merriment.

The guy was fading fast, no doubt about it. He had never been a ramrod, not like Farnsworth, but at least he had maintained a kind of dignity before this whole Brognola business blew up in his face. If he had handled it correctly, following advice from Gianelli rather than relying on his cloak-and-dagger bullshit, they would both be in the clover now, instead of going on the lam. Brognola would be worm food, with his family and Mack the Bastard right there in the hole beside him. Nicky Gianelli would have been the freaking Boss of Bosses, and Cartwright could have asked for anything...within reason, of course.

But he had blown it, fucked the whole thing up so badly that they were preparing for a predawn flight to nowhere. That was Cartwright's fault, and never mind the fumble with DeVries. If Gianelli had been guilty of miscalculation there, his error should have granted Cartwright all the warning that he needed to prepare a decent trap at Arlington. And failing that, he could at least have scrubbed the hostages instead of letting them escape and sing for every goddamned federal agency in town.

The guy was all washed up, and just in case he didn't know it, Gianelli meant to break the news, up close and personal. It was the least that he could do for someone who had scuttled all plans and left him in the middle of a shit-storm.

But tomorrow would be soon enough. The white deserted beaches of the Virgin Islands were ideal for such a conversation . . . or perhaps the boss of Washington would rent a car, go driving in the forest with his friend and confidant. Whichever way he played it, only one of them was coming home from the enforced vacation, and it wasn't Cameron Cartwright.

He would have liked to plug the bastard here and now, but there were still amenities to be preserved. Besides, his piece was safely packed away in the luggage.

It could wait. Anticipation only made the execution that much sweeter. In the meantime, he could put a few refinements on the basic plan, some personal embellishments to make the job his own, a memory to cherish in the coming years. He might decide to make the bastard crawl awhile before he—

"Ready, Boss."

"Okay."

He turned to find the man from the CIA staring at him intently, dark suspicion in his eyes. He wondered for a moment if the bastard might be psychic, finally decided he was simply shell-shocked from the beating he had taken in the past six hours. If he had an inkling that his flight would be one-way, well, what the hell? So much the better. Let him stew a little, sweat it out while Nicky put the final touches on his plan. It served the bastard right.

"Let's go."

The guy was edgy, and look at how he almost jumped when Gianelli spoke to him. The capo fought an urge to laugh out loud. It wouldn't do to make him bolt before they reached the airport. Better to pretend that everything was hunky-dory until just before he sprang the trap.

Cartwright scrambled in before him, Nicky bringing up the rear and settling back into the Lincoln's rich upholstery. Up front, his driver had the wheel, with Vinnie riding shotgun, armed and always itching for a fight. If anybody tried to stop them on the road, the dirty bastards would regret it . . . for about a second and a half before they died.

"C'mon, already. Move this thing."

The edginess was catching, dammit, and he forced a laugh to let his loyal subordinates know that he was cool. From where he sat, the boss of Washington could almost smell the fear that radiated off of Cartwright in offensive waves.

The engine growled to life and high beams speared the darkness of the curving driveway. They were leaving fear and danger behind for a little hunting trip, with Cameron Cartwright in the role of pheasant.

"Hey, what the hell—"

The exclamation had erupted from his driver's lips, and Nicky was already craning forward, peering through the windshield as a black-clad figure seemed to rise from nowhere in the middle of the drive, his face all painted like a minstrel and the biggest silver cannon in the world protruding from his fist, the muzzle pointed square at Gianelli's nose.

The mafioso felt his bowels begin to loosen, clenched his knees against the shameful legacy of childhood, biting back the sudden fear that wrapped around his heart.

"Goddammit, Eddie, punch it! Run the bastard down!"

BOLAN HEARD THE TANK before he saw it coming, dinosaur V-8 announcing its arrival with a roar. A heartbeat later, the headlights burned around a corner of the driveway, pinning him at center stage. He raised the silver AutoMag and braced it in a two-handed shooter's grip, sighting down the slide, aiming square between the dragon's glowing eyes.

Fifty yards, and Bolan waited, knowing that the limo would be armored fore and aft, perhaps impregnable. And yet he had to try. If they missed Gianelli now, if Cartwright was allowed to slip away, it might be months or years before they reestablished contact. Too much could happen in the intervening time, and Bolan would not tolerate a debt so long unpaid.

At forty yards he squeezed the trigger, riding out the Magnum's recoil, squinting in the lights and watching as his bullet etched a harmless smudge across the windshield, inches from the driver's scowling face. He dropped his sights and triggered three more rounds in rapid-fire, aware that there would almost certainly be armor plating on the grille and praying for a chink, a weak spot, anything at all.

The whining ricochets were drowned by growling engine sounds, the throb of Bolan's pulse inside his ears. At twenty yards he knew that it was hopeless. He threw himself aside before the tank could plow him under like some disoriented chipmunk caught out on the center stripe by rolling death.

He landed painfully and rolled, aware of screeching rubber as the wheelman swerved to take him, missing him by inches, almost losing it before he straightened out again and pushed it to the limit. Bolan twisted, gnashing teeth against the sudden, stabbing pain as he unloaded with the AutoMag, one bullet spanging off a hubcap, two more flaking paint from armored fenders as the crew wagon rolled on.

The AutoMag was empty, its slide locked open on the smoking chamber, and he didn't have the time to slam a fresh clip home, assuming it would make the slightest difference. He might as well have peppered Gianelli's wagon with a BB gun, for all the good that he had done.

And the man who tore Brognola's world apart, who tried to set up Bolan for a fall, was escaping.

BROGNOLA STRUGGLED FREE of the clinging hedges, muddy to his knees and reeking of the dusty juniper that had already gouged his face and hands unmercifully. His complete attention was focused on the winking taillights of the Lincoln, on the bulky weapon in his hands.

The tube was made of fiberglass, designed to telescope for storage but extended full-length now and primed to fire. The LAW—light antitank weapon—was, in essence, a disposable bazooka with a one-shot capability and an effective range of some four hundred meters.

More than twice the distance to the armored limousine, if he was quick and sure enough to do it right.

Brognola stumbled, cursing bitterly before he found his footing in the middle of the driveway, feet braced wide, the LAW across his shoulder. One hand was wrapped around the firing lever, mounted topside like a clothespin. He was watching as the man in black bailed out, his Magnum rounds deflected by the Lincoln's armor plating.

Gianelli had them beaten if Brognola missed his one and only shot. There would not be a second chance if he muffed it now.

And he was counting down from five, aware that flankers could be closing on him from behind, a backup car with gunners meant to convoy Gianelli out of town.

He squeezed the firing lever and felt the back-flash scorching empty air behind him, blinded for an instant as his stinger sped away downrange. He held his breath and waited through an instant that extended to eternity, prepared to run them down on foot if necessary.

The rocket bored directly in between those cherry taillights, an explosive missile striking home between the dragon's backward-looking eyes. It detonated in the trunk, an oily ball of fire enveloping the tank's hindquarters, rolling forward through the passenger compartment, greedily devouring flesh and fabric, leather upholstery and carpeting.

The Lincoln had become a rolling crematorium, decelerating as it reached the wrought-iron gates, already standing open, and continued to the street beyond. It stalled there, blocking lanes in both directions, settling on melted tires, and Hal imagined that he heard a single, childlike scream before a secondary detonation ripped the night apart and spilled a rippling lake of fire across the road.

The empty launcher clattered to the ground, and he could see the man in black scrambling to his feet and favoring one shoulder, working at it with his other hand. The firelight on his painted face made Bolan look mysterious and savage, like some hunter from primeval times, transported to the present day in search of mythic dragons.

They had killed two dragons here tonight, and the leaping flames beyond those open gates were rapidly devouring the hurt, the bitter memories. In time, perhaps, he would be able to ignore the scars. In time. But for tonight, the fire itself was victory enough.

EPILOGUE

"So, DeVries was being paid by Cartwright?"

"Or by Gianelli. Either way, it cuts the same."

"I see."

The President was frowning deeply, glaring through the windows of his limousine past Bolan and Brognola, toward the glistening Potomac.

"And the so-called evidence on Hal?"

Brognola shrugged.

"It was accurate...as far as it went. Surveillance caught me talking to or meeting with a number of our key informants on the orgcrime strike force. They were seriously compromised."

"How many have we lost?"

"One verified so far—Tattaglia in Baltimore. And we've lost contact with two others. Bruno in Atlantic City and Morelli in New York. The rest have been reshuffled. Given half a chance, they should be free and clear."

"All right." The presidential scowl was lightening slowly. "So you could say we're status quo?"

"As near as possible." Brognola cleared his throat. "I feel responsible for any damage suffered by the strike force of the witness program, sir. If I had been less negligent—"

"We've been through all of that." He made a gesture of dismissal. "And the plain fact is, we can't afford to lose you at the present time. I'll hear no more about this resignation nonsense. Clear?"

"Yes, sir."

Relief was mingled with the sadness in Brognola's voice.

"And as for you—" he turned toward Bolan, hesitating momentarily before he spoke again "—I hope you'll reconsider your position."

Bolan had already reconsidered the proposal from the White House—a renewal of his pardon, yet another new identity, immediate resumption of his role within the Phoenix Program based at Stony Man—and he was smiling as he shook his head in an emphatic negative.

"I'm sorry, sir. It isn't possible."

"Of course, it's possible. I'll *make* it possible. One signature from me, and you'll be right back where you started."

"That's the problem," Bolan answered softly. "I'd be losing ground."

"Goddammit, you'd be losing all those Wanted flyers, and the bounty on your head. You'd have protection from the government—"

"Like last time?"

There was sudden bitterness in Bolan's voice. The President looked pained, but did not flinch from Bolan's stare.

"You know what happened there as well as I do. It was unforeseeable, an aberration."

Bolan nodded.

"Like the move against Hal's family. Like Cartwright's team surviving Farnsworth and continuing to run Clandestine Operations for the Company."

"I'm looking into that right now. It's top priority. If any of the bastards made it through last night, I'll personally supervise their prosecution."

"Fine. And next time?"

"What? Why should there be a next time?"

Bolan smiled.

"There's always been a next time, sir. And always will be. Humans being what they are, you can't expect to operate without corruption and betrayal."

"Hell, if everyone was perfect, we'd be out of work," the President replied. "All three of us. But since they're not, God knows we need a man like you on our side."

"I've been on it all along."

"And your objection is?"

"Too many strings," the soldier told him flatly. "When you buy the license, you accept its limitations. I can't work that way. Not anymore."

"And how long do you think you can last alone?"

"I never gamble on tomorrow," Bolan answered.

"Dammit!" But the chief executive could see that he was beaten. "If you ever change your mind—"

"You'll be the first to know," the Executioner assured him, reaching for the door handle as the armored limo coasted to a stop beside his waiting rental car.

"God keep."

"And you, sir."

Bolan closed the door upon Brognola and his boss, already moving out before the driver dropped it into gear and pulled away. For half a second he was tempted to run after them, to call them back, and then the moment passed. He was alone. Again.

It was the price of everlasting war, this solitary vigil on the fringes of society. Before the day was out they would be hunting him again, on orders of the President, with Hal Brognola theoretically in charge of the pursuit. It mattered literally that the huntsmen had no spirit for the game; their gunners in the field would not be conscious of the reticence in Washington, nor would they falter if they found an opportunity to bag their prey.

Survival day-to-day had always been the name of Bolan's game. He had already sampled government security and found it lacking. Worse yet, he knew that once beneath the federal umbrella he would be constrained in choice of targets, limited in his ability to strike at will, against the cannibals who mattered most.

The enemy was constantly in flux yet never-changing. At the heart of it, where Bolan lived and fought, his opposition was the same as it had been in Vietnam, in Pittsfield, from the early days of his impossible crusade against the Mafia. The enemy was evil man, the cannibal who preyed upon his gentle neighbors day by everlasting day.

And Bolan's answer to the human predators today, tomorrow and forever—was the cleansing fire, strategically applied, without a host of bureaucrats to second-guess his moves.

It was the only way to fight a war. The only way to final victory, if any such existed in the universe.

"And how long do you think you can last alone?"

Not long, perhaps. Until this afternoon, perhaps tomorrow.

Long enough to strike another blow against the cannibals.

But not in Washington.

He could feel the heat already, and the soldier didn't plan to be around when it intensified. Safe passage had been guaranteed, provided that he took advantage of it now.

The Executioner was finished with his work in Wonderland. His enemies were waiting for him elsewhere, everywhere, and he did not intend to keep them waiting long.

4 FREE BOOKS
1 FREE GIFT
NO RISK
NO OBLIGATION
NO KIDDING

TAKE 'EM NOW

FOLDING SUNGLASSES
FROM GOLD EAGLE

Mean up your act with these tough, street-smart shades. Practical, too, because they fold 3 times into a handy, zip-up polyurethane pouch that fits neatly into your pocket. Rugged metal frame. Scratch-resistant acrylic lenses. Best of all, they can be yours for only $6.99. MAIL ORDER TODAY.

Send your name, address, and zip code, along with a check or money order for just $6.99 + .75¢ for postage and handling (for a total of $7.74) payable to Gold Eagle Reader Service, a division of Worldwide Library. New York and Arizona residents please add applicable sales tax.

Remove from pouch...

unfold once...

Gold Eagle Reader Service
901 Fuhrmann Blvd.
P.O. Box 1325
Buffalo, N.Y. 14240-1325

unfold twice...

and they're ready to wear.

GES1–RRR

Offer not available in Canada.

TO GET YOUR FREE SOUVENIR POSTER...

Simply collect four coupons and return to Gold Eagle (and a
check or money order for $1.00 for postage and handling) OR
send two coupons plus a check or money order for $6.50
(includes postage and handling) made payable to GOLD EAGLE
READER SERVICE, and we'll rush you this fabulous 30" x 24"
souvenir of Bolan's most high-voltage action. (New York State
residents add applicable sales tax.)

ACT NOW!

Coupons are available in every action-packed Gold Eagle
series—MACK BOLAN, ABLE TEAM, PHOENIX FORCE, SOBs,
VIETNAM: GROUND ZERO— during the months of April and
May. Offer expires August 31, 1987, so rush your order today
and receive your poster that captures the greatest moments in
Bolan's enemy-destroying career!

--✂

Mail to GOLD EAGLE READER SERVICE:

901 Fuhrmann Blvd.
P.O. Box 9033
Buffalo, NY
14240-9033

RUSH ME THE BOLAN #100 POSTER RIGHT NOW!

Enclosed are four Gold Eagle coupons
plus $1.00 for postage and handling   _____

Enclosed are two Gold Eagle coupons   _____
plus $6.50 (includes postage and handling)

Name _____
                          PLEASE PRINT

Address _____

City _____ State _____ Zip Code _____

Offer limited while quantities last or until August 31, 1987
Allow 6 to 8 weeks for delivery.